COLDWATER

COLDWATER

JEFFROVIN

ADAPTIVE BOOKS

AN IMPRINT OF ADAPTIVE STUDIOS | CULVER CITY, CA

Copyright © 2015 Adaptive Studios

Visit us on the web at www.adaptivestudios.com

Library of Congress Cataloging-in-Publication Data: 2015943525

ISBN 978-0-9960666-7-9
Ebook ISBN 978-0-9864484-6-1

Printed in the USA.
Designed by Neuwirth & Associates, Inc.

Adaptive Books
3578 Hayden Avenue, Suite 6
Culver City, CA 90232

10 9 8 7 6 5 4 3 2 1

COLDWATER

PROLOGUE

Exciting.

That was the one word Rick Samuels thought he'd be using, a lot, when he took this job.

On the home stretch of his senior year, at the annual job fair in the halls of Clareton High, Samuels felt it was amazing that he was seriously being scouted by what he thought was the high-prestige Nuclear Regulatory Commission. Scouted for a ridiculously high-paying job, and right here in town.

He was wrong. The job was anything but exciting. But the two most important things he'd sought—the serious scouting and the high-salaried job—were on the money, a joke he beat to death when he told his parents, his girlfriend, and everyone else in his circle.

Big deal, he told himself about the rest of the job: a little truth-fudging caused no harm and no foul.

Okay, so his employers turned out not to be the NRC, but he was still able to give his girlfriend the NRC pamphlet they had given him: *Nuclear Power Plant Licensing Basis for Seismic Hazards*, which was seriously impressive and backed up his contention that he was making the world a safer, better place to live. That excited her to no end.

As for his parents, no amount of hindsight could shake them from their core understanding: that their unfocused, unambitious, video-game-junkie son, who they were worried wouldn't even get into a community college, was going to collect twenty bucks an hour, get health coverage to boot, *and* would no longer be living at home. Once that truth sank in, they didn't care if those perks were for running Viagra over the Canadian border.

Thankfully, the other "facts" weren't *too* far off. He wasn't working for the NRC, but he was working for their good friends, the Consolidated Power Corporation. He even got to wear a nifty CPC shirt. And no, he wasn't exactly working in town, which was another white lie. He was assigned to a small but pleasant, fairly well-equipped blockhouse nestled in a valley stuck between the Yakima River and the Horn Rapids east of West Richland, Washington. Close enough to visit, which was all that really mattered.

He did get to visit the impressive CPC Corporate Headquarters in Benton City to sign his employment papers, however, and there he was informed that his partner and immediate superior would detail his job when he came into work the following Monday.

The following Monday, Rick was dazzled by the modern-seeming equipment in the plain but plush blockhouse, and also seduced by the bucolic setting that surrounded it. His folks, giddy with relief, had cosigned a lease on a new Toyota Corolla for his commute, and he was a little giddy himself to see it parked in the second of two spaces outside the "office." The space had the name "Richard Samuels" stenciled emphatically in black on the concrete wedge between the asphalt and the blockhouse's gray wall.

Rick wore his CPC shirt that first day. His superior—lately of the Jet Propulsion Laboratory in La Cañada Flintridge, California—did not. Professor Bernard Dumas looked like what Rick's parents would have labeled a hippie. He had longish, unkempt but thankfully clean hair; thick, wire-rim glasses; a full beard, and remarkable, piercing eyes that seemed to glow like coals. He wore a plain black shirt, slacks, and shoes, as well as a lab coat. He gave the sudden, striking first impression of a loose cannon, but his smile was so genuine and disarming that Rick felt remarkably at ease. Even Dumas's sardonic explanation of the job didn't faze him, despite the man's many muttered, muted editorial comments.

"The geniuses at Consolidated Power—apt name, that—decided in their wisdom to open their new power plant surprisingly close to a major geological fault line," Dumas told Samuels as he walked him slowly around the blockhouse's just-finished interior.

"I'm sure they know what they're doing," Rick said loyally.

To which Dumas replied with one of his barely audible mutterings while he gestured lackadaisically at their surroundings. There was a bathroom, a kitchenette, a surprising number of vending machines for just two people, and a work space dotted with consoles, seismographs, and desktop computer towers.

"When that sort of foolishness occurs," Dumas continued thoughtfully, in his normal voice, "the company feels duty-bound to open up a seismographic office to constantly monitor the comings and goings of the ground beneath our feet . . . and to appease the funding gods."

The two had arrived at Samuels's station, fronted by a constantly active screen that looked like a cross between a heart monitor and an air traffic controller's display. It was flanked by both a digital and an old-fashioned seismic data acquisition system that looked like a lie detector test. Dumas smiled upon the latter and gave it a loving pat.

"They didn't want to include 'Old Yeller' here," he said wistfully. "But she's always done right by me." Dumas shifted his disarming, trustworthy smile from the machine to Samuels's face. "So, there we are. My job is to analyze the data. Your job is to collect it."

And from that point forward, collect it is what Rick did.

For the first few months, maybe even the first year, he took the work very seriously. Every blip, every slight change, every unusual manifestation was spotted as if stuck with a rapier. Rick wasn't only collecting twenty bucks an hour; he had the safety of his parents, girlfriend, and—hell, all humankind on his shoulders.

But each blip, change, and manifestation resulted in just a shrug and a nod from Dumas, and the inspection visits from headquarters grew increasingly rare. Rick soon realized that the comings and goings of the ground beneath them were like a Rorschach test: the content seemed to change depending on the day and the viewer, but the overall design actually stayed the same.

Within two years, Rick came to find their other responsibility, compiling a newsletter for the company and its shareholders, to be a welcome change in the monotony. Its grand title amused Professor Dumas no end: *The Yakima Horn Seismic Detection Office Report on Geological Change and Its Effect on Public Safety.*

But even that minor diversion kept being pulled away from Rick. As the days, weeks, months, and years droned on with only the slightest of superficial changes, the demand for the report became less and less urgent. It started as a weekly pamphlet, then became monthly, then bimonthly, then quarterly, then biannually, and finally yearly.

"Why don't they just e-mail it at this point?" Rick wondered aloud.

"Like most officious material of an ultra-low level," Dumas informed him sagely, "it is the last to be recognized and the first to be downsized."

Rick looked around him and had to agree. It was more than just the newsletter. His Corolla, the computer towers, and even Old Yeller were simply seven years longer in the tooth. Nothing had changed but his waistline. Those vending machines were insidious. Where had the time gone? How had the hoped-for opportunities simply stagnated?

But every time he thought about chucking it all, he couldn't figure out anything else he really wanted to do, and the raises, smaller and smaller though they might be, just kept coming. He had long ago rationalized the entire thing as a ridiculously slow-moving video game that he kept at in the vain hope of someday winning.

Even the collection of material for the dying newsletter held no interest for him anymore. He used to find it fascinating. Now it was just tedious data. He could tell depression was setting in when he offered to stay put while Bernie brought this year's pamphlets to the post office in Richland. Rick used to jump at the chance to get out of the blockhouse. Now he just wanted to wallow in it, like a lukewarm bath you're just too lazy to get out of.

"Are you sure you don't want to go?" Dumas had asked solicitously, holding the box of pamphlets in the open door.

"Yeah," said Samuels, hardly glancing at him. "It's okay, I'm good."

It was a shame they both couldn't go, but someone had to be on the machines during working hours. That rule, like so many others, really didn't make sense, but those high-school scouts had chosen Rick well. There was something about him that said "I follow orders."

Dumas shrugged, but his smile stayed constant. "I'll get you one of those coffee thingies you like," he said, and left without waiting for a response.

Rick hardly noticed his departure. The door had barely closed after the man when Rick pulled out a drawing pad from his briefcase. In the last few months, the constantly shifting but never really changing screens had inspired him to start drawing. He was further inspired by his father's collection of old books, whose covers had some really wild and interesting paintings on them. Rick wouldn't know a Pollock from a Picasso, but he knew what he liked, and he liked colorful stripes and dots.

Even if Dumas had pointed out the similarities between what was on the screens in front of him and what was on the paper beneath Rick's fingers, he might not have seen it. But he was so intent on his new hobby, he didn't notice much of anything.

Not even when the monitors stayed the same but Old Yeller's previously steady arm started swinging wildly back and forth.

It took a few seconds for Rick to notice anything out of the ordinary. At first he thought the strange scratching sound was coming from his own pencils, but then he realized the sound was a lot faster than his hands were moving.

He stopped drawing. He glanced at the monitor inches from his face. No change. But the scratching sound continued just as quickly.

Rick straightened up and looked to his right. The vending machines glowed in their wasted-calorie way, with no sign of any breakdown.

Rick frowned. He shrugged, then glanced to his left as he started to return to his drawing. He noticed Old Yeller's arm.

It was as if Old Yeller leaped directly into his face, although it never moved. Reflexively, his fingers grabbed the lip of the console as if clamping onto a life preserver. His face snapped back toward the monitors and digital seismic machines. Nothing, nothing, nothing. But Old Yeller was yelling, and its arm would brook no denial.

Rick's smartphone jumped into his hand seemingly of its own accord, and his thumb was punching the numbers almost before he thought of them. As he did, all the screens started moving, and not in blips or slight changes, either. It was as if the entire block-house had become a maniacally moving abstract painting.

Thirty miles away, in Richland's quaint, near-empty, old-fashioned post office, Dumas's smartphone played the Grateful Dead's "Trucking," Dumas placed the box of pamphlets down on the worn wooden counter and glanced at the postmaster, who had probably been there from the beginning of the Pony Express. Only now he was dodging downsizing rather than desperadoes.

"Can I put this here a second, Frank?" Dumas asked politely.

"Take all the seconds you need," said the old man, and went back to quickly and expertly sorting the day's mail into the dozens of boxes on the far wall. People might prefer e-mail, but junk mail never rested.

Dumas smiled at the man's dedication, and brought up his phone. When he saw who was calling him, his smile faded for the first time in years.

Professor Bernard Nigel Dumas was not a credulous man. He knew there was only one reason why Richard Samuels would be calling him, and it was not to change the order of his coffee thingy.

Dumas pressed the green button on the glass face and stuck his smartphone tightly against his ear as if he had been waiting for this call for years. Because he had.

"Yes, Rick?"

"Bernie, Bernie! It's the Ring of Fire! Oh my god, this is it! It's the Ring of Fire!"

Even Frank heard what Rick was barking like a guard dog. The old postmaster turned with a look of concern. Dumas opened his mouth to calm his associate down, but then a strange fluttering distracted him. Frank didn't want to turn away from the galvanizing words either, but suddenly it felt like butterflies and birds were pelting him on the head and shoulders.

The two men turned toward the post office wall to see every single envelope slithering, bouncing, and jerking out of the boxes as if they were coming alive.

Then the roof fell in.

■ ■ ■

Hannah Lonnegin knew what it was as soon as her vinyl records shifted from leaning right in their stacked milk crates to leaning left. The first time it happened, she had been totally perplexed, then totally freaked out, but after three years in LA, it had become part of the scene.

Even her cat, Zanzibar, was beginning to take the tremors in stride. She used to react as if a row of fight dogs was lining up before her. She would turn into a screeching, snarling Halloween caricature. This time, she merely meowed and shot under the bed.

But Hannah's boyfriend, just back from college on the East Coast, was more shaken, literally.

"What's going on?" he bleated. "What is that?"

Hannah smiled benignly and uncurled from the trembling bed in her T-shirt and gym shorts. "Just an earthquake, Josh," she informed him lightly. "You'll get used to them."

She gazed benevolently upon the handsome young man from the rich Idaho family in his T-shirt and jeans, and motioned for him to join her in the doorway. As he approached, she wrapped her arms around his waist and smiled up at him as only a freckled, green-eyed redhead could.

"You might even get to enjoy them," she said warmly, going up on her tippy toes to give him a reassuring kiss.

But then, unlike the last few times, the shaking didn't stop. They found themselves holding each other even tighter.

"It's okay," she said in anything but certain terms. "It happens a lot. It'll pass."

But it didn't. Hannah remembered what her mother had told her when she was about to move out to California—her mother, who had never lived in a seismically active zone.

"If there's an earthquake, stay under a door frame. That's the strongest, safest place in a building."

What if that was an old wives' tale? Wouldn't the strongest place be an interior wall with weight-bearing studs? No—not if the roof caved in. *Crap*. Why hadn't she checked before this?

Hannah flattened her hands on Josh's strong back, determined to be reassuring. She looked up into his eyes, but when she saw the anxiety, even fear there, all thought left her. Her hands sprang to his chest, and her mouth opened, but nothing came out.

He opened his mouth in return and started to speak, but then the shaking slowed. The couple froze, hoping that it would continue to slow, but it did not. Instead, they both felt like they were standing on a wide, thick rubber band that was being stretched. And both intuitively knew what would happen once that rubber band snapped.

"Josh, I—!" she managed to get out before she heard a screech. Her head turned in the direction of an animal cry. Zanzibar bolted from under the bed as if shot from a cannon. The cat went right by Hannah's face and disappeared out the window.

Then the doorway cracked in two, half of it slamming down and crushing Josh like a watermelon under a sledgehammer.

1

REGION IX

General J.C. Passarelles's words had come back to haunt all of them.

As Wes Harding looked down through the helicopter windshield on the devastation that had once been Los Angeles, he could clearly remember every word of the speech the General had given only six months before, in the nation's capital.

"When a grade-five earthquake finally hits," Passarelles had solemnly told the FEMA Incident Workforce Academy graduates, "—and make no mistake, it will—the destruction will be beyond the imagination of each and every one of you."

The General was a squat, wide bulldozer of a man with a head like an Easter Island statue. From icy eyes within that stony brow, he glanced at the graduates' nurturing, understanding mentor, teacher, and boss, Doctor Thomas Malloy. Then he scanned the eager, determined young men and women sitting in the plain, square conference room in the monolithic headquarters of the Federal Emergency Management Agency in Washington, DC.

Wes thought that the General looked particularly hard and particularly long at his own blue eyes, but he might have been mistaken.

"You all know what earthquakes are," the General went on. "Hell, it is right there in the name, is it not? But how many of you know, truly know, the damage an earthquake can wreak?"

Each of the grads looked from Passarelles to Malloy and then at one another. They'd all had briefings, but they were unsure whether to respond or if it was a rhetorical question.

Thankfully, the General took the decision out of their hands. Turning sharply, the military man nodded at the blank screen that took up most of the wall behind him.

"Although earthquakes can occur anywhere on earth," he reminded them, "the majority of them occur at plate boundaries. These are known as interplate earthquakes."

As if the wall itself both respected and feared the man, the image of a map instantly appeared via PowerPoint magic. The image was an area they all knew well—a thick red line that traced the east coast of Australia, up the various Asian coastlines, across the Pacific Ocean, and down the west side of the Americas. The General identified it out loud at the same time all the young officers were thinking it.

"The Ring of Fire," he intoned. "Twenty-five thousand horseshoe-shaped miles of nearly continuous oceanic trenches, volcanic belts, and seismic plates. Home to more than seventy-five percent of the world's volcanoes and ninety percent of the world's earthquakes. That is *nine-zero*, people. When 'the big one' happens, it will happen here."

The General's tone became even more serious. "But what is 'it'? You," he said to a grad to his immediate right. "What will happen in the Philippines?" The young man stammered for only a moment before Passarelles snapped at him. "What happens when earthquake intensities are particularly strong?"

"L-l-liquefaction can occur," the grad finally stammered.

"Yes." Passarelles smiled like a shark. "Soft sediments can actually undergo liquefaction, a phenomenon that occurs when wet sediments amplify seismic waves. The ground literally behaves like water, and the string of islands known as the Philippines could disappear as if they had never existed."

Wes gave the faces of his fellow grads a quick survey. He could see that they were imagining the same thing he was: frightened Filipinos, already paralyzed by the awful shaking, trapped by suddenly rising waters, unable to do anything or go anywhere as the sea swallowed them.

Passarelles's head snapped to the grad closest to him on the left. "Japan!" he barked.

"There are more than eighty-five active volcanoes in Japan," the grad responded, suitably shaken, given the subject. "A powerful earthquake could cause a chain reaction."

"As well as?" the General prompted, his eyes veiled, his lips in a mirthless grin.

"As well as tsunamis," said another grad. "The 2011 Fukushima earthquake was six point six magnitude. If 'it' were even more powerful . . . ?"

"Landslides, mudslides, rocks raining down like missiles," the General told them flatly. "Japan would cave in on itself. The folks who were rendered unconscious or dead before being buried would be the lucky ones." He took a moment to gaze upward. "Let me put this in a context that some of our slower personnel will understand." The eyes narrowed and came down like twin turrets firing. "It would make Godzilla seem like a summer shower."

He ignored the uncomfortable rustling that rippled through the room.

"Iceland," he said, giving a little wave as if wiping the air. "Most sparsely populated country in Europe. Who cares what happens there?"

The grads couldn't tell if he was being sarcastic or not.

"Let us get a little closer to home, shall we?" He turned on the farthest grad to the right who, like the others, was rankling against the General's dismissal of an entire country. "Alaska," Passarelles demanded.

"Alaska," the young woman repeated stiffly. "One of the largest volcano chains in the world. There would be floods, tidal waves, lava, landslides . . . everything you said before."

"And?" Passarelles pressed.

"And?" the grad echoed, wide-eyed and helpless.

"And?" the General repeated before looking at each of them again, his expression disappointed. "I told you. Beyond your imaginations." He stared accusingly at Doc Malloy. "Quite possibly beyond your education."

Malloy held Passarelles's stare, but he also came to the rescue of his students. "What do we think of when we think Alaska, people?" he asked.

The rankling turned to disappointed fidgeting as the grads searched their already addled brains for the answer.

"Dog races?" one offered weakly.

"Moose?" said another softly.

That's when Wes got it. "Oil," he said. "We get almost ten percent of our oil from Alaska."

The smile Passarelles pinned Wes with was more accusing than congratulatory.

"Yes," he said. "And what are the limits of *your* imagination, young man? Go on."

Wes did not cower. He was the son of a college football coach. He felt that, in this case, the signal calling had been left up to him.

"Not only would we lose precious fuel, the recovery process would be extremely challenging," he stated matter-of-factly. "The effect of the leaked toxins on the environment would be equally catastrophic. There would be aftershocks. Mountainous terrain would be compromised in ways not immediately discernable."

He noted Malloy's encouraging, thankful look before Passarelles's grim delight reclaimed his attention. The bond between the young man and the scientist had been strong from the moment they met: Wes was the son Malloy didn't have, and Malloy was the kind of laid-back adult Wes had never known.

"Good," the General said, stepping from behind the podium in Wes's direction. Passarelles saw what everyone did: a short, fit, tousle-haired, blond, blue-eyed country boy who might look more at home by a haystack than a hovercraft. One who, like the barnstormers of a bygone age, wanted to swap ground for sky, clouds of wheat for real clouds.

Passarelles looked like he was going to shred him.

"Very good," the General continued smoothly. "Seems we have someone who can think outside the pipelines." No one dared chuckle at the General's play on words. "Let us continue with you for the best part, shall we?" He stared intently at Wes. "Region Nine," he said with bleak relish, naming one of the bureau's ten regional centers. "What will happen in Region Nine?"

Wes came from Ventura County, which was well within the borders of FEMA's Region IX. Their headquarters in Oakland, California, was responsible for the rest of the state, as well as Arizona, Nevada, Hawaii, Guam, American Samoa, the Commonwealth of Northern Mariana Islands, the Republic of the Marshall Islands, the Federated States of Micronesia, and more than a hundred and fifty sovereign tribal entities.

Wes felt his throat threaten to close up. He straightened his neck with a tiny click and inhaled, preparing. They weren't talking about theories and strangers now. Wes was about to describe the devastation that would hit not only the region but his home, his family, his friends.

"Roads would buckle," he said. "Buildings would crack. Electric lines would snap. Gas mains would rupture. Dams would break. Everything you mentioned before, sir—landslides, mudslides, tidal waves—all of that would happen, and then combine."

"Combine?" The General's voice was both urgent and empty.

"Electric lines would set off gas leaks. Explosions and fires would be endemic. Cars and trucks would slam into buildings and pedestrians. Buildings would smash other buildings like dominoes. Homes would disintegrate like matchbox models. Entire canyons would roll like tidal waves. Valleys would twist like they were in blenders. Seas of sewage would cover everything. Those not killed in the natural disasters could die of disease. LA would look like the far side of the moon."

Wes's statement hung in the air like a noose.

The voice of Doc Malloy came in with stentorian tones. "And the seventh plague would be the rain of our decadence: window-placed air conditioners, satellite dishes, and roof-top chaises *avec* sunbathers."

Their superior's interruption, blackly humorous as it was, managed to break the doomsday mood. But then something happened that Wes would never forget. Passarelles, seemingly angered by Malloy's desolate levity, placed his fists on the podium and hunched his shoulders, lancing each of them again with his granite gaze.

"Mark it well, people. The Ring of Fire. And its bastard step-child, the San Andreas Fault. Along these lines will come *your* personal trials by fire."

The statement jolted Wes, as intended, but it also annoyed him. The General was underestimating all of them.

"Everyone's aware that there will be blood in the streets," he spoke up. "Sir."

He was expecting a backlash. Somehow the dead, dismissive glance the General gave him was worse. Then Passarelles simply looked away.

"And it might be yours," he stated to the group. "But no one is suggesting you waste your valuable time or psychological resources visualizing that."

Abruptly, the General changed topic and tone and began droning on about lithospheric plates and tectonics, but every graduate was busy thinking about where they might land in the thick red line from Alaska's Attu Island, far west in the Bering Sea, to the tip of Los Cabos in Baja California Sur.

Afterward, they had all tried to laugh it off during a celebratory beer, but the image of that red horseshoe, and the General's warning, took up residence in their minds like a squatter. But not for long.

L ess than six months later, it happened, seemingly all at once. Antarctica, New Zealand, Indonesia, the Philippines, Japan, Russia, Canada, Alaska, California, Chile, Bolivia, Costa Rica . . . as if the Ring of Fire had snapped like a bullwhip.

"Einstein said that God doesn't play dice with the world." The voice of the pilot, Charlie Dewey, interrupted Wes's gaze over Los Angeles. "Looking at that down there, I wonder if he would change his mind about that."

The young Navy man's wisecrack slipped into Wes's ears through noise-canceling headphones. Given the rush of the wind and the hushed growl of the S-99 utility helicopter's twin turboshaft engines and four-bladed rotors, it would have been the only way Wes could hear him.

Wes couldn't disagree with the wiry African American pilot's description. They were staring at the grim wreckage of hundreds of thousands of buildings below them. Some structures of Los Angeles were still vaguely recognizable, but they were universally tumbled and torn.

"More like Satan stepped on it, Charlie," Wes replied.

"Some truth in that," the pilot answered.

Wes scanned the distance, the sea looking as it always had, untouched by the disaster on land, the surrounding bowl of California almost green in places. But he knew part of that image was only through the lens of memory. Most of the actually visible panorama was filled with a veil of rising toxic steam. Some of it was from pipes no one could close, some of it from vents rooted deep inside the earth. All of it blended into a yellowish miasma worse than the smog of the "old" LA.

Despite the fact that they had been trained in two different places by two different organizations, Wes and Charlie Dewey had both been taught not to get too emotional—to be sympathetic but not empathetic—to be like the lifeguard who saves the drowning without getting pulled down. But Wes wondered whether the job of literally staying in the air made it easier for Charlie to remember his training. His own job demanded internal role-playing, imagining himself into people's lives on the ground so he could find ways to improve them.

As Wes surveyed the scene, he acknowledged that everything Passarelles had predicted less than a year ago in that DC meeting room had come to pass. The Los Angeles basin had collapsed like a Lego set dropped into the La Brea tar pits. Wes focused on the Culver City clock that was now leaning over Washington Boulevard, its once-proud face covered in slime and mold, its hands frozen forever on the time everything ended.

How long has it been? Wes recalled. *Only forty-three days.*

The scope of the devastation was impossible to imagine, even for people acclimatized by media-touted disasters like Hurricanes Katrina and Sandy and the Fukushima nuclear meltdown. Dozens of countries had been affected; over a million people had died.

"I keep thinking it's a movie set," Charlie muttered, scanning the rubble half-submerged in fetid water. "If only, right? Get in your car and drive on out."

"Considering what we're up against," Wes absently replied, "we're doing okay."

"Yeah, I'm feeling real successful about now," Dewey said, bluffing with cynicism. "The Navy had me jumping through hoops, shooting hoops, and shooting *at* hoops, but they didn't get me ready for this."

"There was no way they could," Wes said to him. "There could never be enough earthquake and terror drills to prep for a real disaster. You just have to live it."

The pilot nodded once and pursed his lips.

Wes studied the weed-covered ruptures marked with neon circles, numbers, and crosses that his fellow assessors had made.

"We're doing better than the poor bastards down there, anyway," Wes observed—not with detachment but with sadness.

The Ring of Fire had left an ugly scar on the face of the earth, not just physically but emotionally. The coasts of Western Canada, Chile, New Zealand suffered; the inlands sympathized. The United Nations, the Red Cross, and FEMA had banded together with an uncommon spirit of cooperation to help the survivors. The rest of the world seemed to give silent thanks it wasn't them and went about their business, while donating every spare dollar, euro, peso, ruble, rupiah, yen, colon, and boliviano they could.

"Good thing we've got a strong hand on the stick," Charlie remarked. "If we were still running ops under 'ole, heckuva job Brownie,' we'd be up the proverbial creek without the proverbial paddle."

Wes rolled his eyes at the thought of the unit's previous leader, who was legendary for all the wrong reasons: he was the kind of inertia-bound bureaucrat who gave run-of-the-mill bureaucrats a bad name. Forty-eight hours after the Ring of Fire blew up, he was moved from the field to Washington, DC., where he now appeared in photos beside cargo planes that were coming and going as part of global relief efforts. General Passarelles had taken his place in Region IX.

Charlie peered through the clouds of still-swirling ash to spot any sign of the landing pad. Maneuvering through the dust of concrete, steel, glass, gypsum, lead, mercury, dioxins, and even asbestos was worse than navigating an Afghan sandstorm.

"What sort of name is Passarelles, anyway?" the pilot wondered absently, eyes intent below him.

Wes vaguely heard him while concentrating on his clipboard. *Initial back-check*, he read his notes to himself. *May 24. Grid 213, line 4. Baldwin Avenue as marked. 249 Baldwin, two fatalities, survivor reports husband missing, last name McGuinness. 251 Baldwin, six fatalities. Survivor reports father missing, last name Calloway. 253 Baldwin . . .*

"Sounds French," Wes answered.

Charlie snorted. "Sounds like a cheap trophy. Doesn't matter. He's the president's golden boy now. Had the fastest promotion track in military history, and not even West Point. What's the J.C. stand for?"

Wes looked up, his expression slightly troubled. "I don't know," he realized. "I don't think anyone does—"

"Bada bing," Charlie jumped in. "There it is."

Wes looked where the pilot was pointing, and brightened as the clouds of carcinogens opened up to reveal East 101—the camp where the top FEMA and Ring of Fire military personnel had set up their base. It was fenced on three sides to keep looters out and the registered populace in, so that bored or desperate camp dwellers wouldn't wander into the treacherous landscape. The fourth side of the camp was the sagging retaining wall of Route East 101, which held hundreds of dead flowers, pictures, flags, and flyers. As always, a long line of survivors shuffled along it, being checked, evaluated, categorized, and assigned to either a Combat Support Hospital, rest barrack, or evac chopper. The people in the line coughed as dust rose and spun toward the helicopter, but no one looked up. Choppers had replaced cars as the background of LA.

"Sorry, folks," Wes murmured. "One of these days we'll get you surgical masks."

Their landing pattern also revealed Route 101's west wall, and Wes shook his head as he gazed at it. This wall was also a giant memorial, but it was much more stark and macabre. There was no color anywhere along it, just black paint covering it with names of the dead, dates of the dead, and the symbols of their gods. It stretched as far as Wes could see.

The survivors called it Wall X. The X stood for "exhumed."

The sight of it caused the long day to settle squarely on his shoulders. So much death. So much destruction.

Charlie took a sec away from his landing protocol to note his friend's expression. He understood immediately. "Could be worse," he said encouragingly. "Could have been aftershocks. Looks like we dodged a bullet on that one."

"So far," Wes replied.

The chopper settled to the ground. As always, Wes marveled at Charlie's ability to thread the needle between so many other copters. All the pilots seemed to treat their whirlybirds like tractor-trailers at interstate rest stops after midnight—lining them up unscratched in almost impossibly small spaces.

The two young men descended from the relative peace and quiet of the air and headphones to barely controlled, noisy chaos on the ground. Before Wes could thank Charlie, the pilot vaulted out of the cockpit like a horizontal bar gymnast. His modus operandi had always been to appear only when it was flying time, then make himself scarce.

"Learned that the hard way," he had told Wes forty days ago. "You're standing around, people treat you like you're a greeter or a gofer."

Wes, on the other hand, missed not only Charlie's attitude, but also his solid presence. Everyone else seemed to be reenacting Pamplona's running of the bulls. As Wes searched through the crowd for his boss, his pace hastened to match the urgency of the crowd. Navy pilots were scurrying around their copters. Shell-shocked survivors were shuffling in quickstep like workers marching on a chain gang. Local police and firemen circled the area like cowboys looking for stragglers on a cattle drive.

Then there was Passarelles and his posse. He stood by the open door of a Sea Stallion rescue chopper, looking much the same as he had during the graduation ceremony, only now there were many more shiny things on his shoulders, sleeves, and chest. At FEMA, he had carried himself like a vulture looking for a victim. Now he looked like a lion leading his pride, or Patton about to have Rommel for lunch.

There were many more people around him as well. Since he was given the assignment of heading the Region IX recovery on a silver platter, Passarelles had created his own personal team of highly trained, highly motivated, highly loyal men.

"No women in his posse," Charlie had mentioned to Wes weeks ago. "I heard every guy on the team washed out of the SEALs, Delta, or Special Forces. And now they've got all kinds of need to prove themselves. Chips on their shoulders the size of trees."

It would be tough to tell who was who since they all wore visored headgear and special black uniforms at all times, complete with Passarelles's personally designed Ring of Fire patch on their upper arms. It pictured a literal ring of fire inside a "No" symbol—a circle with a diagonal line through it.

"These guys look like an army of *übermensches* to me.," Charlie had commented. "Nietzsche would be proud."

Leave it to the college-educated Dewey—the son of a pair of UCLA language professors—to invoke the name of a philosophical poster child to describe Passarelles's posse. Somehow the pilot had wrung a double major and a minor out of his NROTC scholarship at Cornell.

But Wes couldn't disagree with Dewey as he looked at the black suits now, hovering on each of the General's words, their ubiquitous MP7 submachine guns at the ready. *What do they have high powered assault rifles for anyway?* Wes wondered, and not for the first time. The only things to shoot out here were survivors and one another.

As he had with so many other nonessential questions that had sprung to mind since the disaster, Wes pushed it to the backburner, to be pondered in the wee hours. He wanted to report to Malloy while the information was still fresh in his brain, and inevitably wherever Passarelles was, Malloy wouldn't be far away.

Sure enough, as Wes turned his head to the right, his FEMA boss appeared in his vision.

Malloy looked older than his fifty years. He was standing beside another Sea Stallion, clipboard in hand. Rather than instructing his own select cadre of agents, Malloy was helping to evacuate a section of the survivor line. As Wes neared him, he noticed that, as usual, Malloy was dressed for a fishing trip or photographic safari in a khaki bush shirt, pants, vest, boots, and Tilley hat.

"Is that an 'e' or 'o,' ma'am?" Wes heard Malloy say hoarsely to the woman nearest the chopper's hatch.

"E."

"Very good," Malloy continued, checking his clipboard. "You're being evacked, Mrs. Jensen—"

"I'm being what?"

Malloy shook his head in self-deprecation and put a reassuring hand on the woman's arm. "Sorry. Evacuated, to Edwards Air Force Base. From there you'll be relocated according to where you have family or a preferred city or state to start your new life. It gets better from here, I promise."

At that moment Malloy spied Wes, waved him over with relief, and handed his clipboard to an Air Force man beside him.

As Malloy stepped forward and took Harding's elbow, Wes heard Mrs. Jensen cry, "But what about my husband?" The words were lost in the general din and were all but forgotten once Malloy navigated Wes into a mess tent. Malloy hastily grabbed a bowl of oatmeal and a cup of coffee amid the standard hustle and bustle, before plopping down at a picnic table. Once Wes sat down opposite him, he could see how truly haggard and mottled his superior looked.

"Are you okay, sir?" he asked.

Malloy rolled his eyes. "Oh sure, Wes, I'm fine. Forty-three days dealing with the worst disaster in Los Angeles history and I'm absolutely chipper!"

Wes tried to keep his mouth from turning down, but he couldn't quite keep all the concern out of his eyebrows.

Malloy chuckled tiredly, but he did chuckle, then feebly waved away the out-of-character outburst. "I'm fine, Wes, I'm fine . . . considering." He took a sip of coffee. "Not bad."

Wes wasn't sure whether he was talking about himself or the coffee.

"Anyway, it's not important how I am," he continued, all business. "I'll need you at evac to keep people calm and orderly."

Wes's eyebrows rose. Evac was Malloy's pride, if not joy. It was largely regarded as the most efficient unit in the whole processing chain, and Wes knew that seeing hope and relief dawn in the eyes of the survivors was fueling Malloy far more than coffee and chow. Having Wes sub for him there was high praise.

"Yes, sir!"

Malloy laughed, and seeing some weight lifted off his superior's shoulders made Wes feel better than he had for days.

"I know you'll do me proud," Malloy said. "Unfortunately, it's just for tonight. There's an important meeting at Griffith that I have to—"

"Griffith!" The interrupting voice was strident and female. Wes and Malloy looked up to see a frenetic woman beside them. "Griffith Park? What about Coldwater Canyon? My children were on a sleepover at the school there. The soldiers wouldn't let me through. They wouldn't tell me anything!"

Malloy was standing up to comfort her before three words were out of her mouth. "Ma'am, I'm sure they only had your safety as their main priority. I can assure you, we're all doing the best we can. All survivor updates are immediately forwarded to Edwards Air Force Base. But you must understand that the sheer magnitude of this ongoing rescue mission—"

A man at the next table whirled on them. "That's a standard military FU," he accused. "I lost my son up there. Coldwater Canyon is five miles away. Five! How does that not fit in your 'magnitude'? But I hear it's a forbidden zone. No one in, no one out."

Wes tried to be as helpful as his boss. "Sir, giving in to rumors is the worse thing we can do right now. We're all working as hard as we—"

"Drinking coffee?" the woman retorted. "Having a nice bowl of food while my kids . . ." She started to cry. "What are you doing? What are you *really* doing? My children are up there. My *children*!"

The woman collapsed back into a seat, sobbing. Thankfully, the man went over to comfort her, but not before stabbing Wes and Malloy with an accusing look.

Malloy exhaled slowly, and sadly motioned for Wes to follow him out of the mess tent. They emerged from their temporary respite back into the standard operating chaos.

Malloy frowned sourly at the activity before muttering, "So uplifting, how catastrophe brings out the best in people." He looked over at Wes. "I said at the beginning that I didn't want this thing to degenerate to Katrina levels of the authorities versus the citizens, didn't I?"

Wes chewed on the inside of his cheek while watching Passarelles board his Sea Stallion, emblazoned with an RoF symbol on its side. His posse disbanded in all directions to God knows where.

"Well," Wes answered, nodding at them. "I'm not sure how much jackbooted military 'contractors' help—"

Suddenly Wes was yanked in between the mess and CSH tents. He found himself staring into Malloy's angry and worried eyes.

"Keep your voice down!" Malloy hissed. "Have you been talking like this all along?"

"No," Wes said immediately and defensively, rubbing his arm where Malloy had grabbed him. "It just occurred to me—"

"Well, don't let it occur to you again," Malloy instructed. "Things are bad enough without you—"

"Hey, everything okay in there?"

Wes and Malloy looked over to see one of those "jackbooted military contractors" standing at the mouth of the canvas alley. His eyes were obscured by the RoF uniform's visor, and the barrel of his assault rifle was hovering between the ground and the tents.

"Yes, of course," Malloy said with assurance and annoyance. "Just going over the protocol for tonight while I'm attending General Passarelles's briefing."

The jackbooted military contractor straightened. "You're going to the briefing?" he blurted.

"Invited by the General himself," Malloy said.

Wes noted a little thickness in Malloy's voice, a watery aspect to his eyes. The man was probably working too hard, coming down with something.

The RoF man acknowledged that with a nod, then left. With bewildered expressions, Malloy and Harding emerged from their private talk. Although they peered intently through the crowd, at survivors, soldiers, police, doctors, nurses, and FEMA aides, the RoF guard was nowhere to be seen.

"Did we imagine him?" Wes wondered aloud. "Are we that tired?"

"Tired?" Malloy echoed sourly. He rubbed his eyes with his thumb and a forefinger. "We're effin' worn out. So—Wes." The fatherly tone that was now in Malloy's voice made Harding turn toward him with a new attitude. "General Passarelles is powerful here, but he is in full command up in Griffith and Coldwater. He keeps invoking the buzzwords 'national' and 'security,' which, as you know, stirs purpose and patriotism . . . instills loyalty and locks up his enclave better than a bank vault. If you rattle his cage—if any of us do—I don't know what will happen, Wes, but I feel certain something will. Something not good."

Wes felt that Malloy was speaking to him now not as a superior, but as his mentor and friend for years. "Thom—" Wes started, wanting to assure him that he had no intention of doing anything but his job.

But Malloy had already changed his tack. "I've always wanted to tell you how much Shirley and I enjoyed your visit at our lake cabin last summer."

"Oh, I did too—"

"My wife took quite a liking to you, Wes. She wanted to see if you could come back next summer. After all this." Malloy waved halfheartedly at their hellhole. "The cabin was virtually untouched, you know."

"Sure. I'd be honored."

"Maybe you can even stay awhile. I believe there's the daughter of one of her friends Shirley wants to set you up with. She said you two would be perfect."

"That's great, Thom—"

Malloy gripped his arm again, even tighter this time.

"But none of that will happen if you mess with the General."

"I'm not *trying* to mess with him, Thom!"

Malloy released his arm but leaned in close to Harding's face and spoke, staring directly into his eyes. "If you even *seem* to be questioning the General. *Capisce?*"

"*Capisce, capisce,*" Wes retorted, shaking his arm out. "Jeez, what is eating you?"

"You mean apart from everything?" Malloy asked, gesturing around him.

"Yeah, apart from that."

Malloy took a step back and softened into the Thomas Malloy Wes had come to know and love.

"Wes, I'm just watching out for my most promising student," he said affably, backing up toward the evac Sea Stallion. "You understand that, right?"

"Of course," Wes replied, his own expression still full of concern.

Malloy kept moving backward, as more and more people crossed his path. "You've got the evac covered tonight, right? Starting at twenty hundred?"

"Right," Wes called after him as more and more people crossed between them.

"Good, good," he heard Malloy call, almost swallowed up by East 101 standard operating chaos. "Stay out of trouble until then. Hear?"

"Hear!" Wes called, not at all sure Malloy heard him. The only thing he could be sure of was that Malloy was no longer in his sight.

Wes Harding stood in the middle of the camp as it seemed to whirl around him, trying to fully comprehend what had just happened. As terrible as the disaster was, the reaction and recovery had been going as well as could possibly be expected. So why had paranoia and politics suddenly reared their ugly heads?

Wes tightened his lips and made fists of his fingers. *Not going to let this nonsense distract me*, he thought. The long hours and mental toll were just getting to them all. Perhaps anything related to Passarelles did need to be handled with caution, but Malloy seemed to be turning the General into a bogeyman. Wes didn't have to swing to such an extreme, and anyway, after a good night's sleep, things would look better in the gray dust of morning. Hopefully, Malloy would get enough sleep to restore his perspective too.

Wes turned around and nearly tripped over a wet, scraggly cat that streaked right in front of him.

He stared after it in amazement, wondering whether it too was an apparition.

"Grab him!" he heard.

He turned again and nearly collided with a freckled, redheaded young woman in boots, jeans, and a hoodie.

"You could have helped, damn it!" she shouted at him. "He was right there!" And then she was past Wes, chasing full-speed after the cat.

"Hey!" Wes blurted. "It's dangerous to run in the—!"

A booming voice seemed to explode right behind him. "Stop her! Stop that looter!"

Wes almost cringed as three RoF guards barreled by him, their assault rifles swinging. He watched as they charged after the woman and the cat, oblivious to everything around them.

Wes stood there, stunned, wondering whether Charlie or Thom had slipped LSD in his water. But the feline, female, and fighters didn't fade away. They just kept running through the dust, dirt, and pedestrians, heading for the razor-wire barrier fences. Wes was in the process of turning away when the full import of the incident sank in.

They hadn't called her "intruder," "trespasser," or even "spy." They had called her "looter." Which was either a horrible mistake, since stray cats in the camp were definitely not valuable loot, or a deliberate misinterpretation. Worse yet, in this time of disaster, the word "looter" meant the men could shoot to kill.

Wes stayed motionless for only one more millisecond. He had a deep, sure feeling that he was watching three guys with something to prove—chips on their shoulders the size of trees—who had finally snapped and *picked* something to prove, no matter how wrong they were about it. And a civilian could pay for it with her life for it.

Wes sprinted after them, Malloy's words—"stay out of trouble"—still ringing in his ears. But Malloy also wanted the authorities and civilians to stay on the same side, which meant Wes needed to exert his authority, what little of it he might have, against the jackbooted military contractors.

2

HOLLYWOOD SPLIT

As Wes raced after the Ring of Fire team, the redhead, and the cat, he tried to call out to all of them, to any of them. But between the rapid pace they were all keeping and the ubiquitous dust, he couldn't get the breath. Instead, he had to watch as they all drew nearer and nearer to the razor wire.

Wes already knew it was twelve feet high and designed in the quick and standard way for easy installation and security. Every six feet, an iron pole was stuck deep in the ground. Across its skeleton was a chain-link fence. Coiled horizontally across the fence like a killer Slinky was what had become known as Razor Ribbon: a central core of high-tensile wire reinforced with a steel coil, around which were crimped laser-sharp barbs, designed to both grip and pierce.

If anyone hit the barricade, even if they weren't running, their flesh would be ripped to bloody confetti—and these people weren't just running, they were pouring it on.

Wes watched helplessly, following as fast as he could. The fleet, dodging cat seemed certain to be the first victim. He was at least twelve feet ahead of his nearest pursuer, but the animal would be trapped or destroyed unless he changed direction immediately.

He didn't. And he wasn't.

To Wes's amazement, the cat leaped into the air, landed on the lip of an open oil drum being used as a garbage can, vaulted onto the hot tin roof of a Quonset hut being used as a rest stop, then launched himself six inches over the tip of the highest piece of razor wire.

That nearly stopped Wes in his tracks until he saw the woman wasn't slowing either.

"Hey!" he managed to shout. "Don't, you'll never—"

But she did, following the animal's path like a copycat. However, she wasn't a ten-pound feline. Wes couldn't help but picture her slamming the oil drum over, smashing face-first on the corrugated, galvanized steel of the hut roof, then slicing herself to ribbons on the razorwire.

He slid to a stop while, as if in slow motion, the woman's first jump took her off the ground. Her right boot landed on the oil drum lip perfectly, causing it neither to topple nor even to wobble. She jumped up to the roof of the Quonset hut. Rather than try the second leap there, she ran across its entire length along the very apex of the structure, then sprang at the top of the fence.

Wes found himself holding his breath. *She'll never make it!* he thought as her body arched and turned toward what seemed to be certain disfigurement. But then, to his wonder, she twisted in midair like a champion high jumper and cleared the tip of the highest razor wire by maybe a millimeter.

In fact, Wes could've sworn that, as she turned her head, bringing her freckled face toward him, a tiny lock of her fluttering red hair was snagged and zipped off by the razor-sharp steel.

Then, to Wes's eyes and ears, everything sped back up again as the young woman landed outside the camp fence, and the first of the military contractors jumped after her.

Wes hissed through his teeth as the Ring of Fire operative did what Wes had thought would happen before. His foot hit the barrel's lip and, of course, his weight slammed the barrel down on its side, spewing foul, self-composting garbage everywhere, and sending the man into the side of the hut. But that wasn't all. Before Wes's horrified eyes, the prefab, pliant metal bounced the man forward, right into the bottom two strips of razor wire.

Wes's reactive grunt was drowned by the man's shrieks, while his eyes snapped back to the two streaks of red racing on the other side of the fence toward the top of Wall X. Wes spun his body in that direction, toward the front gate of the camp, ignoring the stares of survivors. The other two military contractors noticed too quickly. They left their screeching, entangled comrade and started in the same direction, apparently after Wes now as well.

The FEMA agent momentarily considered stopping to talk with them, but the men hadn't stopped at the fence until one of them was shredded on it. That meant their adrenaline was cooking their brains, and he probably couldn't reason with them. They would either speed past him or one would detain him while the other kept up the chase. If the young woman was caught, she might not get a chance to explain herself unless someone neutral made sure of it. Wes had to get to her before they did. He yanked his official ID out of his jacket and held it high as he charged the shack they all called Checkpoint Charlie after the famed crossing in the infamous Berlin Wall of the Cold War.

"Named for me," his pilot had joked weeks ago.

Wes was in "luck," since actual National Guardsmen, not Ring of Fire operatives, were out and on duty, checking a shipment of Red Cross supplies. The gate was open and unlocked.

"FEMA emergency!" Wes called to them as he slipped between the side of the Red Cross truck and the edge of the gate.

"Hey!" called one of the National Guardsmen. "You shouldn't go out without backup!"

Wes raised his arms in a what-choice-do-I-have? shrug and then, after glimpsing the military contractors coming after him, stabbed his forefinger in their direction.

"They do not have clearance!" he called, then turned and kept running as the Guardsmen blocked the helmeted, flak-jacketed, gun-toting men from slipping out the same way he had. He guessed that Passarelles's men actually had clearance to go anywhere they wanted, but at least determining that would slow them down.

As they started arguing with the National Guard and Red Cross personnel to clear the way, Wes concentrated on finding the woman's trail. He was outside the protective gates of the camp without Charlie and his chopper for the first time ever, where the ground was unsteady and the population hungry, displaced, and violent. His senses sharpened quickly, and his eyes flicked to the ground more frequently, checking for obstacles. The wreckage of LA could turn his ankle faster than rain on Astroturf.

He glanced at the top of Wall X in time to see a wisp of red disappear over its top. Scanning in both directions, he saw nothing but rubble. But one pile of rubble to his right seemed to create a makeshift stairway toward the crest of the wall, so that was where he ran.

Wes started up as fast as he could, but unavoidably, the black names, dates, religious symbols, and messages penned, penciled, marked, painted, and even scratched there started to seep into his senses. The words of loss and longing were bad enough, but some people had even drawn pictures of their missing and dead. The children's drawings were the worst . . . and the best.

The weight of the tragedy began to slow him down, but Wes knew that if he let it get to him—if he let the drowning drag him into the deep with them—he might never stop crying. So he lowered his head, closed down his brain, dug in his hands and feet, and scrambled to the top of the wall.

He stood, panting, fully intending to scour the area for any sign of the girl or the cat. Instead, the desolation of the city hit him in the face like a hot blast from a brick oven. It actually seared his eyes. He stood, knees bent, arms slightly out, staring at what should have been a bright, colorful, internationally famous scene. Instead, it was a dream in ruins.

The Hollywood sign was a burned skeleton. The Capitol Records Tower looked like a collapsed, broken stack of dishes. The famed streets were deeply pocked, widely cracked, and thickly overgrown. The Crossroads of the World now marked the border between Earth and Hell. There was nothing that was not broken, torn, burned, or shattered. Even the buildings that had managed to stay upright seemed to lean on one another for support, like stumbling drunks.

But incredibly, between all these broken bones flowed life-blood. There were people. Furtive, hunched, stained, bruised, rag-covered people, who scurried from makeshift shelter to makeshift shelter, often tracked by dogs and even a goat or two.

Why aren't you heading for the camp? he couldn't help but wonder. *Why are you still hiding out here?*

As he stared at them, they began to turn their faces toward him as well. They slowed. A few stopped. But then their eyes widened, and they seemed to disappear like cockroaches caught in the light.

They saw something, Wes realized. *Something that isn't me, something that spooked them. Something—behind me?*

Wes leaped forward just as the two military contractors jumped at him.

As he scrambled down the incline on the other side of the wall, he caught sight of the woman as well as the cat, deep within a low-level labyrinth of crevasses that were once roads and sidewalks. He wanted to call out to her but didn't dare—not when the ones who labeled her as a looter were close behind.

So he just kept sliding, running, zigging, and zagging in an eerie, wordless chase through what had once been the streets of Tinseltown.

Sunset Boulevard was right there, he couldn't help thinking as he raced toward who-knows-what. *Little Armenia was right down there.* Just beyond was where Route 101 interchanged with the Ventura Freeway—long known as the "Hollywood Split"—the road that always took him home. The broken paths were there, but their utility was gone.

He didn't dare turn around to check the jackboots' progress. That would slow him down. What he really needed was a way to slow *them* down again. But there was nothing out here but rubble.

He looked to where the woman was scrambling up another incline thirty feet ahead. That was it.

Wes hunkered down and willed all his strength to his legs. They started moving like pistons, and memories of his father's football drills splashed across his mind's eye.

"I can't, I can't!" he had cried as a nine-year-old kid when his legs felt like rubber and his throat burned from the effort.

"Yes, you can," his father had said as an encouraging statement of fact. "All you have to do is believe it. Become a partner with your body and it will do what you ask. Now run, Wes, run!"

Wes ran, his willing, cooperative legs going up the silty incline as if he were scaling a slide. By the time he reached the last few feet, he had actually caught up to the woman, who was crawling on all fours. Grabbing her under one arm, he all but catapulted over the top of the incline—taking a quick glance behind them to see the military contractors huffing and puffing twenty feet away.

Then he was on the other side with the woman, sliding and twisting down the hill on a shifting bed of sediment. The combination of liquefied earth, fetid water, and spilled oil had turned the hill into the mother of all slippery slopes. No matter how Wes tried to slow his plunge, his body only picked up speed.

He glanced to his right to see the woman in the same predicament. She glanced back with an expression of mixed resentment and relief. He wobbled, almost lost his balance, flung out his arms like a surfer and concentrated on controlling his descent as best he could.

He heard a noise from her that might have been a snort or might have been a laugh, which inspired him to hazard another look at her. But this time she wasn't looking back. She was glaring forward, stabbing her finger in that direction. Wes looked where she was urgently pointing. The cat was racing ahead of them as if the slip-and-slide was Velcro. And two more Ring of Fire operatives in full gear were at the bottom of the hill, preparing to grab them all.

"Holy—!" Wes blurted.

He started searching wildly to find some way out. Then the woman was gripping his right shoulder. She pointed to where the cat had taken a sharp left into a crumbling building beside the new military contractors. Then she all but tackled Wes. The two started tumbling—but thankfully to the left, away from the waiting men.

"Protect your head!" he heard in his ear.

He whipped his arms across his head as the crumpled lower floors of the building loomed in his vision. All he could see was masonry, brick, concrete, and broken glass. It looked as if they were going to splatter on the side of a collapsing building that, upon impact, might fall on them as well.

But then, just as it seemed they would be tossed hard into the wall, the slide suddenly dipped into a hole that threw them through a crack in the side of the building. They disappeared into the place as if it had swallowed them.

Wes landed on a pile of dirt, broken furniture, and dust-covered carpet. He only had a moment to hear a cat's surprised screech before the woman landed on top of him, sending up a cloud of dust shaped like a mushroom cloud, visible in the dim, filtered sunlight.

Under normal circumstances he would not have pushed off the fit, cute redhead. One-night stands had never appealed to him. He wasn't necessarily looking for love, but he was looking for a connection. Ironically, FEMA had spoiled him: he wanted to bond with a woman the same close, fast way he bonded with the guys he served with.

But these were not ordinary circumstances. He rolled her off of him as gently as he could manage, but rapidly, and got to his feet. He didn't know if the new Ring of Fire agents were in pursuit, so he didn't take more than a moment to assess his damage—which was, happily, minimal. Lumps would rise and the scrapes he'd sustained burned like hell, but he was otherwise fine.

"You okay?" he asked his companion.

She had already scrambled up and was chasing the cat, which was tearing up a crooked staircase on the far side of the area.

"Wait!" he called after her. "Wait a second!"

At that moment, bullets began to riddle the east wall of the building.

"No!" he shouted, snapping around to face the drone of the guns. "Don't shoot!"

Then he was running after the woman as their pursuers tried to shoot open a new entrance to the place.

What the hell is it with these guys? he couldn't help but wonder as he found himself navigating what used to be a grand staircase. When did guns become the way for lunatics to mark their territory? Gripping tightly what was left of a wide banister, he propelled himself to a dusty, cratered landing that used to be a mezzanine.

He got there just in time to see the woman climbing up a former escalator. She was using the twisted, splayed metal stairwell like a ladder.

Wes turned his head as he heard a section of the wall below them collapse from gunfire. The building gave an ominous groan as he spun his head back toward the girl. Snapping his mouth shut, he quickly followed.

He reached the top of the escalator just seconds after she did. They both stood, scanning the area: her for the cat, him for options. The third floor was covered with structural debris that had fallen from above and been coughed up from below. There was no trouble seeing: sunlight punched its way through dozens of holes and fissures in the outside walls and what was left of windows.

She started to move toward the widest open space, but he grabbed her elbow. She looked angrily at him, but he just motioned with his head back the other way. He used his other hand to signal "take it easy" and even "trust me."

She looked ready to yank her arm away, but then they heard boots thundering up the escalator. She lowered her gaze in thought, then nodded and stepped in Wes's direction.

In deference to her survival so far, he let go of her arm and led her to a shattered doorway near the very end of the collapsed side of the expanse. Lying flat on the remains of the floor, he snaked into the narrow opening.

She followed and stood up beside him in what had once been a salon. Shattered mirrors covered the room. A large rolling bar was twisted and scattered, with intermingled shards of expensive bottles of alcohol glinting in the refracted light.

The woman looked at Wes quizzically.

"I know this place," he whispered, listening closely for the sound of the boots. "It was an old residential hotel near the El Capitan Theater. The cheaper high schools used it for proms. Families used it for budget weddings. This was the girls' prep room."

She gave him a look that seemed to say, What were you doing in the ladies' room? But they both froze as the sound of nearby gunfire ripped through the space. It was coming from down the hall.

"Assholes." The woman seethed. "They'll bring this whole place down on us."

"Come on," he urged, waving her toward the opposite exit.

She didn't budge. "Not without the cat."

He looked at her as if she were insane. Worse, he looked at her as if she were sane, and serious.

"Look," he hissed urgently, "I know pets are a big deal, but your cat—"

"He's not my cat," she snapped. "That's the point."

He was about to confess his confusion when there was a conversation-ending whump, and the wall beside them caved in, sending them stumbling into the opposite wall. Both scrambled to their knees in time to see four helmeted, flak-jacketed, armed men standing in the dusty, smoking opening with smug grins on their big mouths. Wes immediately spotted the specially formed breaching charges that looked like disc-shaped grenades, clipped to each of their belts.

"This building is off-limits, civvies," one said, sneering, using the slang for civilians. "You just broke the unwritten law."

"Unwritten law?" the woman echoed. "Why don't you enforce the written—"

Wes shot out one arm to silence her and held up his badge with the other hand. "FEMA agent," he declared. "This is a sanctioned, warranted operation."

The men started laughing.

"FEMA?" one scoffed. "You mean, 'Fails Every Major Assignment'? You don't carry weight here, civvie. This is our building, get it?"

When the hell did the military start owning *LA?* Wes thought, but he kept his mouth shut. He saw fear growing behind the girl's defiant stare and felt it welling up inside himself too.

"Got it, got it," he replied with a heavily apologetic tone. "Sorry. We'll get back to camp right away."

He cupped the woman's elbow again, but before he could take a step, two of the contractors raised their guns.

"You aren't going anywhere, FEMA," said the third. "You broke the unwritten law, too."

"What unwritten law is that?" Wes pressed.

"You're consorting with looters, fuck up."

"And you're trespassing in our building, lame-ass," the first gunman said, sneering.

"Another unwritten law," interrupted the fourth man, bringing up his own weapon, "is that if you fuck with us, we fuck with—"

He never finished, because he fell through the floor. His heavily equipped uniform and weapon were too much for the already weakened, cracked boards beneath his feet.

He dropped, the bottom of his flak jacket smacking the hole edge. He managed a yowl of pain, surprise, and distress, then like a crack of lightning, the floor began to give way under them all.

The guns went off, but only into the upper walls and ceiling as the men dropped: two straight down and two in diving leaps. Wes grabbed the woman and dragged her into the far corner, hoping the hole the men were making wouldn't extend to the edges of the floor. They watched as the first two men disappeared, and then the two leapers scrambling for handholds as the ground beneath them fell away.

The first leaper bellowed as the floorboards he was clutching cracked like a trapdoor opening. But the second leaper—the first man—tried to bring his weapon around to aim between Wes's eyes. Wes could only cower there, but the barrel wavered, the man toppled, and then all four soldiers disappeared. Wes and the woman heard crashes and bellows of pain from below.

Wes leaned forward, trying to see what had happened. He saw two men lying in motionless heaps three stories below. Another man was hanging from an escalator tine like a lumpy work of modern art. The fourth was nowhere in sight.

Wes leaned further over, getting the impression of a new, man-sized hole in the building's outer wall, but his sudden shift seemed to attract the cracks in the floor. He saw a major break knife toward them, then grabbed the woman in one arm and wrapped a dirty, dusty curtain around his other arm.

She shrieked as the floor gave way, then grunted as her full weight thumped against his arm. He only hoped the curtain wouldn't tear, because he knew that it was anchored in the very maw of the entire building itself. Incredibly, the old, thick curtain didn't rip, and it swung the two of them like Tarzan and Jane through broken French doors between the barroom and ballroom below.

Even more incredibly, they landed on their feet, and slid as far as they could on what was once beautiful parquet flooring . . . until earthquake wreckage interrupted their equilibrium. The two fell in a heap and rolled until they stopped beneath the shelter of a one-legged table.

They lay there, recovering mentally and physically, in a tawny cloud of dirt. The woman managed to get herself back together first, and struggled to sit up. She looked down at Wes, who was blinking incredulously, and seemed about to smile. But that didn't last long.

"Omigod," she gasped.

"Fun, right?" Wes gasped in return. "I saw Kev Kelleher do that once during prom. I never thought I'd get a chance—"

"No!" she spat. "Not you. That!"

He finally noticed that she was pointing behind him. He turned around, afraid that he would be looking down another assault rifle barrel. It wasn't that, but what he saw instead wasn't much better.

It was the cat. Sniffing at a corpse. A fresh corpse, a man's corpse. But not with a bullet hole between his eyes. He was lying on his back, clothes splayed out, chest ripped open, and his ribs pulled back, sticking straight up like fingers.

3

CAT'S EYES

The air near the body reeked of dusty metal as the FEMA agent and the redhead crept forward to join the cat. Only it wasn't iron they smelled; it was the scent of oxidizing blood.

From opposite sides of the exploded torso, they looked down into the torn-open chest cavity. Sadly, both had to acknowledge that after all these weeks since the earthquake, they had become inured to this type of gore, to all but the initial hit of the odor. Before the Ring of Fire tore Earth's crust a new one—many, in fact—they would have been paralyzed and revolted by the scene. Now—

"More flies than I've seen before," the woman murmured.

"They're reproducing pretty quick in all this," Wes said. He glanced at the woman. Her gaze at the body was more than cursory or just morbid curiosity.

"You recognize him," he realized.

Her nod was almost imperceptible. Her whisper was almost inaudible. The corpse's face, although twisted in a rictus of pain, was not mutilated.

"Mr. McGuinness," she said.

Wes jerked with surprise. He recognized the name. "249 Baldwin Avenue?"

She met his gaze, and they shared a moment of shock. McGuinness was the husband that had been reported missing to Wes that morning. His mind reeled at this seeming coincidence. This man had not died in any earthquake-related accident. Desperately trying to figure out the pieces, let alone put them together, Wes started to mumble to himself as he glanced around.

"Something's missing," he said.

"The smell," she said. "And maggots. There are no maggots."

He nodded. "This just happened."

Steeling himself, he looked closer. Then closer still. Although the inside of the chest cavity was coated in blackening blood, the torso wasn't as full as it should have been. All but lowering his head into the corpse's chest, he saw that the dead man's heart was just sprawled there like a pale, discarded sponge. It shouldn't have been.

"Something else is missing," he said.

The woman had been looking at the man's face. Her eyes drifted to Wes then followed his blue eyes down.

"The lungs," she said with surprise. "They're gone!"

"Yeah."

Wes straightened up in confusion and concern. The two humans, and one cat, sat like a triangle of high priests, as though they were praying for the corpse's soul to make a peaceful transition to the afterlife.

The woman's mouth opened, but before any words could emerge, the wall adjoining the street began to whump in circles of detonation, like low-level fireworks. Both instantly guessed that the first military contractor, the one who was obviously the leader—the one who had been lofted out of the building—had planted all his breaching charges along the outside wall.

"It can't be!" Wes blurted.

"It *can*," the woman replied, already in motion.

"But he's—!"

"Trying to squash us!" she yelled.

The man was tearing holes in the wall, not to get in but to bring the entire building down on them. It didn't make sense. First they claimed the location, then one of them was going to destroy it? The contractor had gone from adrenalized bully to insane.

The woman grabbed the cat, and Wes grabbed one of her arms so he wouldn't lose her in the thickening cloud of dust. With a tug, he urged her toward the hole through which they had entered.

"No!" she boomed. "You idiot! If we go down, we'll be crushed for sure."

"And if we stay here—"

"We're not! We'll follow the cat!"

"Where?" Wes demanded.

In response, the woman released the feline. It hit the uneven floor running, but it didn't race for any of the large or small openings on the first floor. It sped upward.

The hell? Wes thought.

They ran after the cat faster than Wes ever thought possible, football-style drills notwithstanding. Just as they reached the grand staircase, the ballroom collapsed behind them with a whump, flattened like a car in a junkyard crusher. The sound of breaking glass filled their ears as they scrambled back up the twist-o-whirl escalator.

The sharp, overpowering noise made them go faster. The body of the military contractor who had been hanging from the escalator slammed sickeningly onto the steps in front of them, but even the spray of blood didn't stop them. It didn't even slow them. They leaped over it, reached the landing, and followed the cat as he shot down the hall and jumped through a crack in a door at the end. The door was still there, askew on its hinges; Wes went through it shoulder-first like a battering ram, in time to see the cat jumping through a broken window on the far side of the building, onto an old fire escape.

Wes and the woman ran toward the shattered window as the entire building drunkenly lurched in the opposite direction. They started to slide back toward the grand staircase as if the floor were ice. Still holding her hand, and grunting with the effort, Wes heaved her forward at the window with all his might. She grabbed the window frame with one hand as, with the other, she held his fingers tightly and reeled him toward her. As the building continued its slow, moaning topple, she pulled with a strength that surprised him until they both had their feet on the fire escape. It all took little more than a second, and then they were outside on a building that was dropping in the other direction. The trick was to get to whatever part of the building was facing the sky, atop the collapsing structure and not below it. Right now, that was the top of the fire escape.

The world seemed to move in slow motion as the two started clawing upward, following the cat that navigated the tilted iron staircase like a mountain goat. Though Wes's instincts shouted *Go down!*, the bottom of the fire escape was already being swallowed by the collapsing foundation. It was obscured by growing clouds of powdered brick that would have left them blind and unable to breathe.

The cat reached the top of the shaking, shuddering iron framework. Then he leaped, but the humans didn't have time to see where he landed, because the building was still dropping. It was not dying the way older structures cracked and came apart during the earthquake. This fall was slow and defiant, like a giant whose ankles had been roped.

The building inclined at a forty-five-degree angle to the street and was listing faster and faster. In a second or two, the edifice would be rubble, and the top of the fire escape would snap to a hard stop, either on the ground or pointed at some ugly angle. The duo would be on top, all right, but they'd hit with a velocity that would most likely snap their spines or impale them with a piece of the fire escape or both.

How did I get here again? Wes's brain asked incongruously.

He saw the woman twist toward the outside of the framework and, motioning quickly for him to follow, she jumped like a superhero. He was already nearly airborne as the fire escape bolts snapped from the building, and the stairway followed its own twisting path earthward. He saw sky and pushed himself toward it hard, hurled into the air just as everything hit the ground in a deafening, blinding explosion. For an instant he felt like a human bullet. The sky and earth danced in his vision, a whirlpool of light and dark; then he dropped, spinning, disoriented, no longer weightless. The kaleidoscopic display ended as a wave of blackness engulfed him.

Heaven looked exactly the way Wes hoped it would: a green-eyed redhead gazing down at him solicitously.

Wes had no idea if he was hurt, if there were still bad guys in pursuit, or where he was, exactly. Hell, he didn't know anything except that for the first time, he was getting a good look at the woman. Mid-twenties. Light freckles across the bridge of her straight, small nose. Eyes like the Teodora Emerald, an unusually dark shade of green. Pink lips, remarkably unchapped despite the dry heat and finally released from the tight pursing she'd held throughout the chase and flight for their lives. And hair the color of new embers.

Her lips moved. "You okay?"

"I don't know," he said with unfiltered honesty. "Give me a sec."

A quick internal inspection flooded him with relief and gratitude: no broken bones. But as he started to sit up, the big bruise of his entire body slowed his movements considerably. He eased back down.

She sat back on her heels, then stood. While she did, he looked past her. The rest of Heaven could certainly stand some improvement. He was back in post-disaster LA, outside East 101 in what was considered to be "no-man's-land," between a collapsed building and a crevasse.

Propping himself up on one badly scraped hand, he turned to look at the woman again. The cat in her arms certainly looked like he was smiling, and he was purring as if nothing had happened.

"After careful consideration," Wes groaned, his voice hoarse, "I'm naming that cat 'Miracle.'"

"His name is Bunter," the woman replied flatly.

That cinched it: Wes was alive. If he were dead, the comment wouldn't have surprised him. "You're a baseball fan?"

She gave him a look that was the opposite of whimsy. "Not that kind of bunter," she answered. "He hits things with his head." She demonstrated with a kind of gentle ramming motion.

"Oh," Wes said, still struggling to get his strength and bearings. "How long have you owned him?"

"I don't."

"Sorry?"

"He isn't mine. He belonged to a neighbor."

"Oh," Wes repeated, his brain still a little sluggish from the fall. "I figured no one would be so fanatical about finding a pet unless—"

"I haven't found mine yet," she interrupted softly, her eyes downcast. "So I find others."

The emotion in those soft, forlorn words seemed bottomless. Wes could immediately picture her post-disaster life. Lost, confused, desperate, she found a way to help those around her in order to help herself.

"So you're a pet-finder in this brave new world?" He tried to say it supportively, and thankfully it seemed to work.

She allowed herself a wan smile. "Freelance pet-finder for hire," she elaborated.

"You got a business card?" he asked.

She laughed softly and shook her head.

Wow, Wes thought. *We're almost actual human beings again.* Even amidst the ruin of their world and lives, he realized that was the true mark of civilization: sharing a smile, and trying to do something beyond just looking out for themselves.

"No problem." He smiled warmly at her. "I'm fresh out myself."

"Good printers are hard to find nowadays, don't ya know!"

He laughed quietly, suddenly happy to be alive, and happy she was too.

"Ready to get back on your feet, uh . . ." she started. She seemed to want to call him something other than "idiot."

"I'm Wes," he told her. "Wes Harding."

"Hannah," she reciprocated, hoisting her free hand up his armpit to help him stand. "Hannah Lonnegin." She surveyed the devastation all around them. "Of the smoking ruin Lonnegins," she said, both sadly and sardonically.

"Where's Bunter's owner?" Wes asked.

"In there," she answered, nodding toward the weird warren of makeshift hovels, lean-tos, holes, crevasses, and squats he had spied from the top of Wall X. "Like Mr. McGuinness used to be."

The mention of the name of the flayed-open corpse brought Wes fully back to reality, effectively destroying their flirty oasis.

"Let's go, then," he told her with conviction.

"Where to?" she retorted a little too sharply.

"Well, you want to return Bunter to his owner, don't you?"

She nodded, and he could practically feel her defensiveness returning.

"I'll help," he said, "and then maybe we can get all three of you back to camp where you'll be safe."

Her reaction was not what he was expecting.

"Camp?" she spluttered. *"Safe?"*

"Well, yeah. I mean—you just saw. There's no—no account-ability out here. You'll be safer there than here!"

He was thankful she didn't simply turn and bolt, but the way she hunched and stared at him with open hostility didn't make him feel upbeat about the direction this was headed.

"Did the fall give you amnesia? Have you already forgotten what happened in there?" She stabbed her hand at the collapsed building dozens of feet away from them. Her tension made the cat tense as well.

"No, I haven't forgotten," Wes said patiently. "But that was an aberration. Those guys were the exception, not the rule."

She leaned back from him, her expression now filling with de-risive disbelief. If they hadn't just saved each other's lives, Wes had no doubt she would have run again—and he would have been on his knees in agony, gripping where she kicked him to prevent him from following.

"You have *got* to be kidding me!" she said. "Wake up, idiot! Don't you know what's going on in your precious East 101?"

"Why don't you tell him?" they heard from behind them. "Looter."

Wes and Hannah stiffened, her in anger, him in shock. They knew what they were going to see when they turned, but that didn't make seeing it any better.

The first military contractor, the one they surmised was the leader—the one catapulted out of the crumbling building—stood twenty feet away from them. His uniform was ripped and stained, his helmet visor cracked, but his gun was undamaged and its barrel was hovering lazily between Wes and Hannah.

The cat hissed.

Now you hiss, Wes thought above the bedlam of his racing mind. He was about to cop an attitude of "enough is enough"—the natural extension of the bluffing he showed the contractors inside—when an inner voice came marching up to his ear and snarled, *There's a reason he hasn't already killed you. Figure it out, fast!*

It came to Wes like a thunderclap. *He wants to know how much she knows.*

"Too late, soldier," Wes snapped, yanking his smartphone from its Velcroed pocket. "She's already told me enough, and I've already reported in."

He held up his phone, quickly shifting it so the back was toward the contractor. Only he and Hannah could see that the front was shattered.

Wes noted Hannah's expression in his peripheral vision: a combination of fear and appreciation for his quick thinking. They didn't have to read the gunman's eyes to see the gambit was working. His shoulders and knees showed them that he was stymied and thinking furiously.

But they also saw that while his gun barrel wavered, it did not drop. Try as he might, Wes couldn't think of anything definitive to seal the deal.

"They're on their way," Wes added. "Shooting us will only make things much worse for you. Your only chance—"

Wes clapped his mouth shut, but he had already gone three words too far. Logic had transitioned to a warning, a threat, and that was the wrong way to play this goon.

"Up yours," the man drawled with his gun coming up level with Wes's face. "The boss has got my back. He'll sign off on whatever I tell him, especially if *you're* not there to argue on your behalf—"

Wes felt himself going down backward, then heard the cracking whoomp of the assault rifle—in that order. Flat on his back, his head craned up to discover that he wasn't dead.

Hannah had leaped on Wes, knocking them both down just as the gunman was pulling the trigger. The bullets passed more than two feet over them.

It didn't matter if Wes lived another second or a hundred years. He would never forget the look on her face. It was a look that said she knew she had only delayed the inevitable . . . but it was worth it, just to surprise him.

Wes embraced Hannah protectively. He closed his eyes and waited for the end.

He heard another whoomp, then another, and another. They were still alive, so these couldn't be coming from the gunman's weapon. Wes peered around Hannah and looked up into the whirling, descending blades of Charlie Dewey's helicopter. The gunman was nowhere to be seen.

Wes eased Hannah aside and leaped to his feet, hurting all over but cheering. Nobody could hear him over the noise of the chopper, but that didn't matter.

"How's that for timing!" he yelled, turning back to Hannah. His mouth snapped shut.

She was no longer there either.

For a sickening second he thought the gunman might've taken her, but he quickly realized that was impossible. The killer had been too far away from them, and Wes had held her until the moment he stood up.

Wes turned back toward the chopper as the pilot vaulted out with a relieved grin on his face.

"Charlie, thank God!" Wes cried over the sound of the idling blades. "How did you find me?"

Dewey clapped him on the shoulder. "Homing device in your uniform, kid. All you FEMAs have them sewn in, didn't you know that?" When Wes's expression clearly stated he didn't, the pilot shrugged and grinned. "Guess Doc Malloy figured you'd all be wandering around with your heads up your asses."

"But—" Wes stammered, trying to figure out everything since he left the camp. "How'd you know to look for me?"

"I didn't," Charlie admitted. "I needed to talk to you about some other shit. Then I found out you went AWOL outside the gate."

At the mention of "absent without leave," Wes's worries coalesced. "Does Doc know?" he asked intently.

"Yeah, he was notified immediately." Dewey's expression became clouded. "He's already gone to that briefing, and you've already been replaced at evac. Damn, the man looked crushed, Wes. What the hell were you doing out here?"

"Counterinsurgency," Wes muttered.

"What'd you say?" Dewey was incredulous.

"Bad joke. I've got to talk to him, Charlie." Wes pressed both hands onto Dewey's shoulders, staring seriously into the pilot's eyes. "Now."

At first Charlie looked conspiratorially at Wes, as if understanding that friends had to cover each other's asses, but then he saw how much more was going on in Harding's eyes.

"Well, what in the hell are we standing around for?" he said, catching whatever bug was giving Wes the fever. "Hop in."

4

CHECKPOINT CHARLIE

"The numbers don't add up," Charlie said through Wes's earphones. "The survivor numbers, I mean."

Wes's attention was torn between trying to read the papers Charlie had given him and keeping the wind from ripping them out of his hands as the chopper approached Griffith Observatory. Sitting on the south-facing slope of Mount Hollywood, the once three-domed landmark had been paradise for space and science nerds.

"That's why I was looking for you," Charlie went on. "It's been bothering me for days, but I thought I was missing something or misunderstanding something or erroneous pattern recognition, I don't know. Then those reports came out today. I grabbed a printout." He nodded at the papers in Wes's hands. "It's all in there. I pegged it, no mistake. And if the bureaucrats who wrote those reports can't be bothered to cover their own asses, damned if I will."

"I'm not sure what I'm looking at here," Wes said, holding up a fistful of papers. "Also, this bouncing seat isn't doing my bruised ass any good. Give me a minute."

Charlie gave him a thumbs-up and, pretending to study the papers, Wes settled gingerly into the thinly cushioned seat. Now that the danger had passed, he could take stock of his injuries. It wasn't just his backside that hurt from the fall; it was his entire back. And his sense of duty; that was bruised too. People were obviously out there, defenseless, at the mercy of those who were supposed to protect them. The physical injuries would heal. But what to do about those thugs?

And then there was Hannah. He felt most protective about her, maybe because she clearly didn't need it. He had to talk to her again, and finish that last conversation. What had a freelance pet-finder seen in the camp that he hadn't? It was obvious that the authorities' internal policing was failing on some level. He needed to know how much and how deep.

One objective at a time, he cautioned himself as the helicopter began its descent and he shifted uncomfortably in the seat. His eyes drifted to the window.

Wes knew the observatory, museum, and planetarium well. He had been there countless times as a kid—on both school and family trips. His father, despite being a jock, was also something of a geek, so for Wes it was cleats on the playing field, head in the stars. Yet both of those pursuits served the other; Wes's father insisted on an *orderly* pursuit of knowledge.

"First things first," he was fond of saying.

But no one would recognize the old place now, Wes thought as the copter approached. What the Ring of Fire hadn't changed, Passarelles's operatives had.

Once a bright and beautiful white, the observatory itself was singed dark, blending in with the burnt hillside below. It was still beautiful under the colors of the sunset—which the disaster-fueled fumes made even more wild and intense. But the west wing of the observatory was nearly gone. The east wing was completely collapsed, its telescope fractured like a bone broken in three places. The main building's planetarium dome had been torn open like a pomegranate.

The public was clearly no longer welcome. While National Guard units, FEMA agents, Red Cross workers, police, and firefighters milled around on the low roads, Passarelles had commandeered the high ground with razor wire, earthen berms, and T-walls. Its Checkpoint Charlie gate made East 101's checkpoint seem like sliding doors at a mall.

"Minute's up," Dewey said eagerly. "What do you think?"

Wes was annoyed at the interruption of his pleasant memories. Those precious moments of reflection were becoming more rare with each passing day.

"Yeah. Well . . ." Wes tried to get his mental bearings. To cover his confusion, he finally said, "It's a shame."

Charlie took a second to check out his partner's eyes. Maybe the fall off the building had done more than just shake him up.

"Just the numbers, man!" Charlie said, pointing two fingers at his eyes, telling his companion to focus.

Wes shook his head. "Sorry, Charlie. Help me out, would you?"

Charlie huffed with exasperation as well as understanding. "Survivor numbers, Wes. They don't *add up*, you get me? I heard some other stick monkeys grumbling about it because they don't want to get blamed for anything. Then my cousin gets evacced this week. A medtech sees him board one of the Stallions but, Wes, there's no record of him arriving, okay? I scanned the lists at evac against the Edwards Base check-ins. My cousin went up,, but he never came down. And there's no record of a crash or landing at another field. I checked. And then I read those reports and he's not the only one."

Wes's mind was still churning from his near-death in the collapsing hotel, but Dewey's last bit of anecdotal data got in. It was personal, a family member of a friend, and Wes forced himself to sharpen up. "How many?"

"At least fifty, man," Charlie told him. "I know that's nothing compared to the original RoF dead and missing lists, but—"

"It's not nothing," Wes insisted. "It's big. Why wasn't this reported before?"

"It *was*." Charlie chopped the air with his hand. "Some of the other pilots went as high up the ladder as they could, when they could find the time from our manic schedules. Each one was told in a few sweet and steely words, 'don't worry about it.'"

Wes appreciated the situation from the top of that ladder. Given the magnitude of the disaster, every worker with every organization was stretched thin. Normally, there had to be both a pilot and copilot in any military chopper, but these were not normal times. There were slips and oversights and agreements to look the other way.

Even so, more than four dozen unaccounted-for evacuees? he thought. That was absolutely something to worry about.

"Who exactly told them that?" Wes asked. "Not to worry, I mean."

Charlie jerked his head toward the observatory crown covered with razor wire. "Take a guess, win a prize."

"Passarelles?"

Charlie scoffed. "Of course not! Nobody would let rotorheads anywhere near the General. But it was one of his elite boys. God-damn jackboot 'Ring of Fire Riders.'"

"Which one?"

Charlie shook his head. "Who can tell? They all look the same in those storm trooper helmets. You ever notice none of them have ID tags?"

Wes had noticed. He had even mentioned it to several high-ranking officers. The nearest thing he got to an answer was something about "insufficient time" to outfit the new unit with nametags. There sure had been enough time to outfit them with assault rifles and concussion devices.

Wes was more than troubled now. He was determined. "Get Comm Center on the horn," he instructed Charlie. "Link me in on the call."

Charlie nodded, hit some switches, and suddenly, to their surprise, they heard a recording:

"This is US Army Communications. All comms are subject to monitoring."

Charlie snorted, "For what, quality assurance? Damn."

"Comm Sergeant," they heard. This time it was a live human voice.

"FEMA Agent Wesley Harding, Sergeant. I need to talk to Evac-Ops at Edwards."

"NCD, Agent Harding," was the immediate reply. *No Can Do.*

Wes was unfazed. In this post-disaster world, impede-and-obstruct was business as usual.

"Okay, get me the FEMA Edwards office."

"NG," was the flat reply. *No Go.*

"Why not?"

"Lines are down."

"WTF," Charlie interjected. "I did two tours in Baghdad, and we were never this locked down—"

He was about to start a ten-minute rant but felt a restraining hand on his arm. He looked over to see Wes looking especially grim.

"Everything okay, Sergeant?" Harding asked. "Anything we can do to help?"

A few seconds' pause followed. Wes suspected that the Army man was taken aback. He was used to barks and bites coming back at him, not consideration.

"No, thanks." Wes and Charlie heard a low mutter: "Everything's under control."

The FEMA agent nodded, exhaling deeply. "Thanks, Sergeant. That's all I needed to know."

Wes drew his forefinger across his throat, so Charlie cut off the communication link. The two shared an apprehensive look.

Then Charlie shook his head and stared out at the sky, saying, "When did it go from 'don't ask, don't tell' to 'don't ask, don't ask'?"

Wes had never heard his pilot sound less flippant. He felt profoundly uneasy too, like they were flying from a storm into something far worse. He'd never had warm feelings for Passarelles's jackbooted unit, but events today—deliberate detonations to bring down a building on living people, never mind the machine guns in their faces—had proven that the Riders were homicidal, no exaggeration. And then there was the corpse opened like a lobster and its lungs gone, a hell of a lot of missing evacuees, and now some sort of emergency protocol?

Wes had a lot of thinking to do and almost no time to do it. He looked down to see that they had come very close to the observatory. Through the ruined walls, they could even catch glimpses of "The Big Picture"—the largest, most astronomically accurate image ever constructed, depicting the Virgo Galaxy Cluster. Silhouetted against its extended, enameled glory was a growing congregation of uniformed men. That human cluster was looking in the direction of the helicopter. Wes suddenly recalled that if ordered, Air Force jets could appear in just a few minutes and knock them from the sky.

Wes and Dewey shifted their gazes to the huge, ragged crack in the planetarium's dome. Standing within, framed by the shattered Zeiss projector and looking up at their chopper, was General Passarelles himself. Wes realized that, all things considered, he would have felt safer back in the disintegrating hotel.

"Last chance to TTAR, boss," he heard his pilot hiss between clenched teeth. *Turn Tail And Run.*

Wes sighed. Doc Malloy was also below, flanking the General. That gave Wes a small, odd sense of surety. If there was one principle he'd learned from the disaster—and his father—it was that some things were worth risking everything.

Emergency protocols? Two can play at that game.

"Get me down there, Charlie," he told his pilot. "No matter what. I'll jump if I have to."

■ ■ ■

He didn't have to, but no one said it wasn't hairy.

Seconds after his instructions to Dewey, a nasty voice came on the radio demanding they identify themselves. Wes cut right to the chase, invoking VIRUS protocol—Vital Information Resources Under Siege—and demanding to speak with the General and the FEMA head as a matter of the highest national security.

After a breathless few moments, during which Charlie detailed how many decades they might spend in the brig, they were given a terse, seemingly disappointed "permission to land."

The two shared another significant look before Charlie brilliantly threaded the needle between the barely standing front entrance and the smashed remains of statues and a spire—the Astronomers Monument, its hewn stargazers now earthbound forever.

Wes braced himself for anything; anything, that is, but General J.C. Passarelles approaching the helicopter with a big smile on his face. He was followed by a crowd of his men as well as military police, National Guardsmen, Red Cross representatives, and high-ranking members of all the military branches. Wes was so nonplussed by the General's uncharacteristically friendly welcome that he actually felt relieved to see Doc Malloy's stricken, sickened expression behind Passarelles. It told him that the General's greeting was most definitely an act. Now that the man was closer, Wes could see a definite edge to that smile, like hungry steel.

Wes hopped onto the observatory's fried front lawn in the bloodred light of the encroaching evening. He was about to start a speech regarding his full responsibility for this unauthorized landing, ready to swear that he forced Charlie to do it if necessary.

But the man he was facing had not become the fastest promoted, most decorated military man in history for no reason. Passarelles beat him to the delivery, getting in the first words.

"Agent Harding. Now you are thinking outside the *fault* lines too?"

Suddenly the two of them were back in that FEMA HQ meeting room all those months ago. Only the circumstances—and dynamic—were clearly, palpably, very, very different.

"General," Wes said, "I wouldn't have done this if I didn't think it was of the highest importance—"

"Of course," Passarelles interrupted, in a tone of understanding and sympathy.

With that smile, though, it felt patronizing, almost mocking. Feeling even more cautious and alert, Wes sharpened his observations like a cornered cat. He realized that while he was nearly shouting to be heard over the copter's slowing engines, the General's voice was somehow settling into Wes's ears without effort, apparently normal in pitch and decibels.

This feeling of heightened awareness was getting to be a habit with Wes.

"General," he started, his eyes boring into Passarelles. "There are men in your unit who have violated military law egregiously—"

Passarelles's hand shot into a "stop" gesture. His disapproving look was strong. His words were stronger still. "Those are dangerous words, Agent Harding. Potentially as dangerous for the speaker as they are for the accused."

"I am not overstating this, sir!" Wes stressed, but the General's left hand cupped Harding's right elbow to lead the agent away.

Passarelles turned his head and commanded the others, "Return to your seats, ladies and gentlemen. I will be back presently and we will continue without further interruption."

He smiled conspiratorially at Wes as if that were some kind of private joke, while he waited for the rest of the crowd to move back inside. Only then did he motion for a hesitant Doc Malloy to follow him.

"No reason to embarrass this poor boy in front of his betters," Passarelles murmured to Malloy. "Let us go someplace where we will not be overheard."

Wes concentrated on breathing deeply and getting his thoughts in order as the three of them trudged down to the Checkpoint Charlie gate. There by the razor wire, about ten feet away from the guardhouse, the General turned. In the growing darkness of the evening and the compensating harshness of the gate lights, it was clear that all pretense of affability was gone from his face. It had been replaced by an intense concern and interest. He stared at Wes like the head of a secret service.

"Tell me," Passarelles ordered.

Wes told him how five of the General's unit had chased a young woman, threatened Wes himself, and seemed—no, unquestionably *were*—intent on killing them both.

"There seems to be something terrible going on outside the camp," Wes concluded. "I think there's a faction among your men that may be persecuting survivors. I don't know if it's motivated by a warped version of thrill-seeking or if some sort of cartel is forming, maybe siphoning supplies or worse, but the result is brutality and it has to stop."

Wes was about to discuss the splayed corpse and the missing evacuees, including Charlie's cousin, when Passarelles's expression and demeanor changed. His lips widened and his eyes narrowed. Wes paused warily.

"Agent Harding," Passarelles said soothingly, "I hope you will understand when I say you are not the only one with a story."

Wes's eyes snapped toward Doc. Malloy just stayed silent and looked sick. Wes turned back just in time to see Passarelles gesture "come forward" to the guardhouse. The RoF Rider who had shot at Wes in the hotel stepped from the guardhouse door. He was still wearing the helmet with the cracked visor.

He took two steps toward them, stopped, and pointed directly at Wes. "That's him!" he declared. "That's the man who killed them! Three of my good friends and this bastard didn't even blink an eye."

Wes's shoulders instinctively tightened like he was preparing for a tackle. Maybe other people would have gaped and stammered at such a twisted accusation, but Wes had learned in grade school never to back down from a bully—not when reality was on his side.

"Say that with your visor down," Wes snapped. "Show your damned eyes. You killed those men when you were trying to bring down the building on me!"

The man pulled off his helmet to reveal a smug, assured grin. "Nice try, you piece of shit. That building was brought down by an aftershock."

"There was no aftershock," Wes stated. "Since the Ring of Fire occurred, there has not been one single aftershock—"

"There was *now*," the man said with certainty. "Or maybe it was a gas explosion," he qualified. "But it was something."

His tongue had dug his grave, at least with Wes and Malloy. The silence that followed seemed endless, yet General Passarelles was remarkably unconcerned by the man's oddly shifting story. When he spoke, it was calmly, reasonably, quietly.

"You see my problem, Agent Harding?" Passarelles said vaguely.

Wes felt his eyes pulled hypnotically to the General. He finally realized where he was, whom he was with, and what was happening. He had walked straight into a trap. A premeditated, well-organized trap. One man's word against that of another. And there was no proof to back Wes's claims.

"I do indeed see your problem, General," Wes replied.

Malloy winced, but Passarelles's eyes flashed at the flint in Wes's words. He almost seemed to enjoy having someone to play with, someone who wasn't another pushover.

"Two stories, each from a credible source," the General said. Wes bit back a sarcastic comment while Passarelles widened his eyes with calculated suddenness. "If either of you had a witness—?"

Wes knowingly jumped at the bait. "I've got a witness."

The General smiled appreciatively. "Excellent," he encouraged. "And who would that be?"

A green-eyed, freckled face appeared in Wes's mind, but he put it behind him. He hardly knew her, let alone where to find her. But he did know someone he hoped was as smart as Wes thought he was.

"Chief Warrant Officer Charles Dewey III, sir," Wes replied. "My pilot. He saw that man preparing to shoot me."

Passarelles stared. Blinked. Turned back toward the guardhouse and snarled, "Get him here on the double!"

The RoF Rider ran to the helicopter. They saw him gesticulating wildly at Charlie, who nodded slowly, and started back with him toward the gate. Wes took the moment to look at Doc Malloy again. His skin was a nasty shade of mottled gray, and he was staring listlessly at the thick air between his prized employee and his commanding officer. Then Charlie was beside them.

Passarelles seemed eager to put this witness and his testimony behind him. "CWO Dewey, Agent Harding says you witnessed this soldier"—he pointed at the jackboot with the cracked visor —" about to use lethal force. Is that true?"

Charlie looked at Wes, his expression blank. Wes equaled the blankness of the stare. When the pilot turned back to the General, his expression was filled with concern.

"No, sir. When I was landing, I saw Agent Harding in the dirt and that's about it. I didn't see this soldier, I didn't see anybody else."

Wes felt his gut tighten. He swore he could feel Malloy's belly do the same.

"I'm sorry, Wes," Charlie said, not too quietly, "but I have to tell the truth. All I saw was you lying there, man."

Passarelles brightened, and he and the Rider grinned at each other. Wes fought the urge to nod or smile grimly or do anything else that might reassure Charlie.

The General raised his hands as if signaling helplessness. "Well, then, it seems as if we are back to square one, gentlemen."

Passarelles suddenly frowned at Malloy, with visible frustration. Wes couldn't help but feel it was the first wholly honest reaction he had shown thus far, and it was gone in an instant.

"We have wasted enough time on this!" the General announced. "We have thousands, if not millions, of survivors who must be found and taken care of." He turned sharply to Wes. "Now, you say my man is responsible for his comrades' deaths, and he says you are responsible, but I say, this terrible catastrophe is responsible. Is that understood, gentlemen?" He glared at his soldier, his eyes reiterating the words with an obvious threat.

"Yes, sir," the man snapped, his shoulders just barely slumping in disappointment. "Understood, sir."

Before Wes could say anything, Passarelles turned back on him. "Now you," he growled. "On the basis of Doctor Malloy's unyielding support and recommendation, I am going to give you every chance to prove your contention—"

Wes had the clear conviction that the General intended no such thing. The man was just using the prop of protocol for some other purpose, but Wes couldn't guess what that was.

"—but you cannot do it here," Passarelles continued. "I may command these men, but I cannot control their loose lips. The word has already traveled throughout my Riders that you were responsible, so if there is anyone who can corroborate your story— as I am informed there may be—I suggest you get her back here with all speed."

"Me, sir?" Wes asked.

"*You*, sir," Passarelles said mockingly.

"But, General," Malloy's strained voice interrupted, "you can't send him out there with no protection. It's . . . it's . . . suicide!"

"What choice do I have, Thomas?" Passarelles shot back. "We cannot afford to lose any more men on dangerous, uncertain terrain." He looked back at Wes with shady sympathy. "When you are out there, however, feel free to help anyone you find being persecuted, yes?"

Wes's eyes narrowed. It was an invitation to be executed, standing up to the jackboots. "Yes," he answered, unafraid. "I will certainly do that, sir."

The General turned his head toward the guardhouse. "Open the gate!" he ordered, then turned back to Wes. "And do not worry about this man you accuse," he said so only Wes could hear. "I will never let him out of my sight."

Over the General's shoulder, Wes saw the razor-wire fence being opened just enough to allow one man to exit through the earthen berms and T-walls. The gap seemed like the smile of a skull.

"What about Chief Warrant Officer Dewey?" were Wes's last words from within the safety of base command.

"Do not worry about him," General J.C. Passarelles assured. "We need all our pilots."

But when the FEMA agent and the commanding officer turned to look, both Charlie and his copter were gone, whirling off during the distraction Wes had created for him.

5

THE EIGHT WAYS

The General had said "her."

Wes Harding's mother raised no fools. Wes hadn't said who his other witness might be, so the only way the General could have known the gender was via his murderous jackbooted operative. Earlier, Wes was sure the RoF Rider wanted to know how much the redhead knew about—well, probably about whatever Hannah had hinted to Wes was going on in the camp. Did that need for interrogation still hold true? And was it the same for the General? Did they want to know how many others she may have told?

And then what? Eliminate her? And any others? Then Wes as well?

You're getting ahead of yourself, Wes thought. He remembered his father warning his players not to worry about the end zone while they were just breaking huddle.

Wes checked his pockets. Smartphone—broken. Pocket flash-light—broken. FEMA ID, three credit cards, thirty-six dollars and seventeen cents in bills and change—all pretty useless. But his pocket multi-tool and Swiss Army knife were still intact. He was all set if he needed pliers, wire cutters, a crimper, a serrated knife, a file, a screwdriver, an awl, a bottle opener, a can opener, a cork-screw, a wire stripper, scissors, tweezers, or a toothpick.

Thankful for small things, Wes made slow, cautious progress down what was left of the Roosevelt Municipal Golf Course that en-circled Griffith Park. What was once a beautiful, rolling landscape of immaculate fairways and greens was now pocked and cratered, with huge hunks of earth frozen in what looked like crashing waves.

The disaster fumes diffused the moonlight, casting a dusty gray pall over everything. It reminded Wes of the color of Doc's face. Try as he might, he couldn't help but wonder what was wrong with his mentor. He doubted it was just the stress and lack of sleep, but a worst-case scenario of some kind.

Of what kind? he wondered, immediately chastising himself for worrying about something other than his next few steps, any of which could be treacherous. He peered down at the ground to gauge where he could place his feet without twisting his ankles or tripping, and felt confident enough to double his speed. Still, his mind worked as he moved. It was only after his hundredth step that he noticed what was missing. No birdsongs ending the day. No insects chirping. It made the eeriness even worse.

He had heard the rumors the same as everyone: "No-man's-land is deadly. The street gangs have expanded their hoods and are running rampant. The motorcycle gangs, still running drugs, guns, and flesh, are refusing to go down quietly. There are mini-wars every day. If you go out there, your bones will be picked as clean as a piranha pork roast."

But that was rumor and hearsay. All Wes had seen from his helicopter was desolation, and the furtive movements of those warren dwellers beyond Wall X. He'd like to think that in reality, people would come together after any emergency. Up until today, it really looked as if they had.

As the command camp's Checkpoint Charlie diminished behind him, Wes kept his eyes sharp. He doubted a RoF Rider was going to pop up to take revenge just yet—but he didn't doubt that they would be trying to follow to see if he would lead them right to her. For the first time since meeting Hannah, he was glad he had no idea where she was.

Then a new concern hit him. Maybe they didn't need to follow him. Who besides Charlie might have access to Wes's homing device? Now that he thought of it, he wondered how Charlie had managed to show up on the other side of Wall X and take off from Griffith without raising alarms. Was he allowed to do that? Or worse, was he sent?

Wes refused to believe that. Charlie had so easily and thoroughly gone along with the ruse Wes had set up in front of Passarelles, and the pilot had trusted Wes with his appalling discovery about the missing survivors. He was not playing for two teams.

Wes was nearing the edge of the golf course. He'd have to see if he could find Northingham Avenue, which would lead him to Los Feliz Boulevard. From there it was a fairly straight line to North Western Avenue, which would bring him right to Hollywood Boulevard, near where East 101 crossed Wall X. From command camp to Wall X was normally three and a half miles, making for a one-hour walk. But, of course, he was far from "normally" and very much in the dark, literally and figuratively.

At least some things never change, he thought. Los Angelenos were always obsessed with the best ways to get from here to there. Figuring out how close he was to Wall X would be no problem, even after the catastrophe. He could guide himself via the Eight Ways—eight streets that connected North Hobart Boulevard and Winona Boulevard in a shape that was . . . well, eerily similar to the Ring of Fire, now that Wes was mentally picturing it.

Despite the danger, he smiled lightly as childhood memories flooded in on him, of driving past the Eight Ways on the road to Griffith. He and his sister would sing out the names of the streets as they went by, with their mother calling out translations from Spanish to English.

"Los Adornos Way—ornaments!"

"Los Bonitos Way—beautiful!"

"Los Caballeros Way—knights!"

"Los Encantos Way—charm!"

"Los Franciscos Way—Saint Francis!"

"Los Grandes Way—grand!"

And finally there was Los Hermosos Way—beautiful again, but a different kind than "bonitos." It was even *more* beautiful . . . gorgeous.

But not now, he thought, peering out at the ruined city. Perhaps never again.

Wes wasn't sure which appeared first, the lump in his throat or the jagged rock whistling by his head. His head snapped up.

Another stone hurtled toward him. It didn't drop from above, it was pitched, like a fastball, from somewhere ahead. Wes threw himself down, peering as far as he could into the gloom. More rocks thudded into the dirt and dead grass around him. He looked back the way he had come. He had made too much progress from the camp. He doubted that they would hear him shout for help, or that they'd send assistance if they did.

Whoever was throwing the rocks either wasn't using lights or didn't have any to use. There was only one reason Wes could think of to throw stones at all, and that was to make him back away. So Wes scuttled forward, in the direction from which the rocks were coming. His bold move paid off. The rocks continued to be aimed at where he had been standing. He couldn't see the attacker, but they couldn't see him either.

Wes crawled feverishly until his hands stopped touching earth and slid across cracked asphalt. He had made it to the crown of the boulevards, where Hobart met Winona. Then he heard it— motorcycle engines being revved.

Suddenly, Wes was blinded by headlights. Raising his hands and crossing his arms to protect himself from the glare or more rocks, he saw four men in cracked, ripped leather jackets and boots, with helmets obscuring their faces.

Wes didn't take more than a second to comprehend this new danger. They had been playing with him the way mean kids played with trapped insects. Survivors? Gang members? Rogue police? It made no difference to him. He had to get away from the lights.

Wes was off the burnt grass and onto the torn-up street like a sprinter who just heard the starting gun. He spotted four bright beams, and it was the bikers' turn to be surprised as he raced between the two in the center, causing one to wobble sideways into another.

"Hey!" he heard one bellow, a man. Then the night was full of revving engines and shouts.

Wes didn't look back. He concentrated on what was before him—a crumpled road, crumpled houses, cracked and collapsed trees, wires dropped everywhere like dead snakes. He saw a break in a once-tall, once-white fence. He twisted and dodged through it and kept going.

He heard two motorcycles blasting the fence to tinder behind him. Spying an enclosed back porch with ripped screened windows, he hurtled through the tear, keeping his legs high and his head low.

As he landed on the porch and sped toward the kitchen door, Wes heard a biker try the same thing—on his chopper. The screen wrapped around the bike, sending it and its rider into the wall of the house. The biker smashed through the weakened structure and landed on his side in the living room.

Wes didn't stop. He was through the kitchen and into the hall just as the remaining three lights slashed through the twisted venetian blinds of the front picture window.

Smart bikers, Wes thought without slowing. Some of them had circled the house to cut him off.

Wes instantly changed direction, racing down what was left of the hall to blast through an already shattered bedroom window. Bursting outside, he saw a biker alerting the others to his detour. He amped his speed even more and dodged between and through more houses. He was really starting to push his limits now. His lips were peeling back from his locked teeth with the effort.

Wes was nearing Bruna Place, a dead end near the start of Los Hermosos. He used to play baseball with friends who once lived there, and had accidentally broken a window of a nearby house with a foul ball. He hoped the huge oak, elm, and palm trees he had loved to climb then were still there.

They were: some upright, some fallen in a perfect labyrinth of branches blocking the road. By this time Wes's eyes had adjusted to the dark, so he instantly burned the branch and tree positions into his mind's eye. He only had a few seconds before the bikers appeared, so he made quick plans, grabbed a long, thin branch, and said a silent prayer.

When the second biker of the four appeared at Bruna Place, he swore with exasperation. His quarry was nowhere to be seen. But as far as the biker was concerned, there was only one clear path where the runner could have gone. He revved his engine and screeched up the street toward the intersection of Bruna and Winona.

The third biker appeared behind him. Wes couldn't wait for the third one to close the gap between the bikes. The second biker would be long gone by then. He released the long elm branch he had pulled back, the branch that left open the clear path for the second biker. It swung like a fly swatter and caught the biker in the chest. Wes was already running, so he didn't see the perfect result. The second biker was hurled backward off his bike. He collided with the third biker, both of them crashing in a rolling heap on the blacktop, tearing their leather jackets and cracking their shiny helmets like the San Andreas itself. Their motorcycles spun, flipped, tumbled, and crashed in two different directions.

Wes heard it, but his eyes were straining forward. The fourth biker came roaring onto the street from North Hobart, tearing in from the direction Wes was heading.

Wes pivoted and shot left, down what used to be Stanley Gold-farb's driveway. His childhood buddy had had a one-car garage that backed onto a small grove, where Wes could create more traps for any other bikers. But luck finally abandoned him. The garage was gone, replaced with a small mountain of debris that made an effective roadblock. To the right was a doorless, windowless, collapsed wall of shingles. To the left the Goldfarb house had imploded, creating a dune of jagged wood, metal, and glass. Running through that would be about the same as running through razor wire.

Slowing down, Wes turned just in time to see the fourth biker appear at the mouth of the driveway. Every possibility of charging the biker played out in his brain. None turned out well for him. This time Wes knew that he was well and truly trapped.

The biker knew it too. Wes couldn't see through the one-way visor on the man's helmet, but his entire body language was smirking. Wes shook out his arms and legs, stretched his neck, and looked for a branch or plank to use as a weapon. There was none. So he stood his ground, preparing to fight for his life.

"Wes!"

His chin tucked in and his eyebrows rose. He could have sworn the night wind had somehow whispered his name. Was he going crazy?

Then he heard another sound under the motorcycle engine's rapidly rising growl—the yowl of a cat.

The mouth of the FEMA agent dropped open and his head swung around at the sound. There, between the edge of the debris and the remains of the Goldfarb residence was a small triangle of open space, previously obscured by night shadows. In that space was the face of Hannah Lonnegin.

"Wes!" she hissed. "Here, idiot!"

Wes flung himself through dirt and shattered splinters as Hannah grabbed his arms and pulled. After scrambling back to his feet on the other side, sure that the biker couldn't get through, Wes didn't know whether to faint with relief or hug his savior. The former wasn't advisable and the latter wasn't possible. By then, Hannah had taken off after the cat. Wes sped after her. But with each swing of his legs, Wes cursed himself.

Idiot is right!

It had never occurred to him that the attack might have been planned to lure Hannah to the rescue. The bikers could be under orders—military orders—or working on commission as mercs. In either case, he was angrier with himself than he was at them.

Wes tried to catch up to Hannah as they sped through a maze of walls, crevasses, and fallen roofs, but there was no way. She was younger, lighter, and far more lithe, and he had been running for his life for a while now. He wanted to shout, "Go, leave me, hide," but he knew it was too late. She had shown herself.

Wes summoned the will to make his legs go faster. She was like the front car of a roller coaster, or a professional skier on a black diamond. She found twists, turns, drops, rises, and gaps that he never would have seen on his own, let alone navigated. But she was so intent on her mental map that she wasn't checking around them. Wes took a couple of split seconds as he ran to look on either side and behind them. They were in luck: no sound of motorcycle engines, no glare of motorcycle lights. Then he played a hunch and looked up. There on the slopes of Mount Hollywood he spotted them—dark little glints, almost like floating flakes of coal. No normal citizen would have noticed them, but Wes had been trained well. Someone was stationed on the hillside above command camp with a handheld, high-performance, long-range thermal-imaging camera that had target acquisition capabilities. Up close it looked like bloated binoculars—five different colored and shaped eyes on an oval housing, able to pinpoint anyone anywhere. They must have been tracking Wes from the moment he left Griffith's command post.

Wes felt a chill along his spine, but at least this meant that neither Doc nor Dewey had told anyone about the FEMA jacket's homing device. If he and Hannah kept moving with this speed and dexterity, they might actually find a way to lose their trackers. That was his last thought before running into a dead, sharply angled streetlight that Hannah had ducked.

His entire body bounced back and his shoulders slammed to the ground. The rest of him followed in a cloud of dirt and dust. His vision filled with a miasma that started to darken. He was heading for unconsciousness, but he had to protect Hannah, had to warn her—

He forced himself back to full awareness, but it was too late. She was cradling his head, kneeling beside him. Bunter was next to her, looking at Wes like he was the world's stupidest mouse.

"Déjà vu," Hannah said quietly before adding, "Idiot," though not without sympathy.

"Run," he grunted, pushing at her. "Hide."

"Too late for that, a-hole," they heard a voice say.

They looked over to see a biker on foot, moving into the clearing, holding an HK45 automatic with a silencer extension centered on the middle of Wes's forehead. The smart bastard had stalked them, obviously getting instructions on how to cut them off from the eyes behind the camera on the hillside.

As the biker took another step toward them, Wes got his bearings. They were near the junction of North Hobart and Los Diegos Way. Hannah had gotten them all the way across five streets until Wes had lost his concentration. He was lying on a blind corner near Fern Dell Drive. If only they had made it across, there were plenty of places they could have used to screw up thermal trackers. But he hadn't made it, and was now staring down yet another gun barrel.

"What do you want?" he asked, with defiance and exhaustion.

"What do you think I want, lame-ass?" came the reply as the helmeted biker took another step toward them. "I want you gone so I can have a chat with the little lady." He shifted the gun to her. She and the cat tensed. "You can still talk fine with a bullet in your leg, bitch," he reminded her. "Maybe better, in fact."

Wes recognized the voice. It was a man from East 101, the Rider who had interrupted his conversation with Doc when they were between the tents. Not that the knowledge would do him any good. He had screwed the pooch big time, and it had taken him—what, less than a half hour to do it?

"Can't we talk this out?" Wes tried.

"Too late." The man laughed. "And hey—what a lame last question *that* was!"

Wes pushed weakly at Hannah, but she refused to go. She just stared defiantly at the man who was lowering his eye to his sight, on the verge of shooting them.

But as the Rider was pulling the trigger, a long, gnarled shepherd's staff appeared from around the blind corner and jabbed into the fleshiest part of the Rider's forearm, sending the shot off course. The bullet slammed into the ground three feet from Wes and Hannah. Recognizing a reprieve when he saw one, Wes rolled hard and slammed into the Rider. The man stumbled, and the two fell into a scrambling heap as the owner of the shepherd's staff came around the corner. Bunter jumped into Hannah's arms as she stared back and forth between the struggling men and a tall, wild-haired man in a long lab coat.

"There's always time for another question in the new rustic age!" the craggy man cried. "Friends, they've come from the future to save us from ourselves! The new rustic age has begun! Join us in celebration!"

As he spoke, additional wild-haired, wide-eyed people in rags and robes came around the corner after him. The craggy man's steely gaze turned down.

"You two—you two scrapping down there, you've no need to fight anymore," he chided the FEMA agent and the Rider as they punched and kicked each other.

The Rider ignored the speaker and hit Wes in the ribs and on the shoulder with the butt of his gun, then tried to get a clear shot into his head or chest. Wes knocked the barrel away from killing targets but the bigger, stronger man was quickly getting the better of him.

Hannah started forward to grab at the Rider's gun arm when she was suddenly blocked by the man in the lab coat.

"I said," the man intoned, shifting his gaze from Hannah to the pair of fighters, "there's no need to fight anymore!" With that, he knocked the gun out of the Rider's hand with his shepherd's staff.

The hardened, well-trained Rider marveled at the ease of the disarmament, then pushed and kicked Wes away so he could scramble after the gun. With a nod of his head, the craggy-faced man sent four of his followers to pile onto the Rider.

One grabbed the Rider in a bear hug. "The new rustic age has begun!" he cried.

Another hugged his thighs. "Come celebrate with us!" he challenged.

A third got the man in a headlock while the fourth, a woman, grabbed his ankles. Together, they brought him face-down to the ground.

The craggy man crouched to look benevolently at the man's helmet. With the end of his shepherd's staff, he snapped up the visor as easily and neatly as crossing a "t" with a ballpoint. The man huffed and writhed, but he was pinned.

"That's better," the older man said amiably. "Now we can see eye-to-eye on this thing. For the future fathers will appear through the portals of darkness to smite the demons of chemicalia and plastica . . ."

The Rider struggled in anger and frustration as the laughing celebrants managed to hold him down. The craggy man stood and looked kindly at Wes and Hannah, who was kneeling and holding the agent again.

"For, in reality," he told them, "the city of angels was a land of steel and sin, where the human soul was lost."

The Rider caught a break and hurled the followers off him in a screeching rage. He sprang to his feet. "Shut up, you crazy asshole!" he yelled, surging forward. "I'll kill you, you goddamned—"

The craggy man jabbed the Rider's shin with the tip of his shepherd's staff. The Rider went down like a cut tree. The smack of his helmet hitting the ground sounded like a crack of lightning, and the visor shattered as if a bullet had gone through it. The Rider's body shivered once, then lay still.

The craggy man looked down upon him with apparent curiosity and surprise. Then he looked back to Wes, Hannah, and Bunter with a small, wise smile playing on his lips.

"For it was also said that the future fathers would appear with a velvet sledgehammer, my children. And that the future fathers would know human physiology very, very well."

By then the man's followers, at least a dozen in number, had gathered around him with grateful, worshipping smiles. He stood at the forefront, both hands atop his remarkable stick. Wes could see now that the gnarled shepherd's staff was covered with intricate carvings.

"But where are my manners?" the man inquired lightly. "Allow me to introduce myself. My name is Bernard Nigel Dumas. Professor Bernard Nigel Dumas." He pointed between Wes's eyes, his forefinger exactly where the gun barrel had been. "But you can call me Dumb Ass."

6

MAYER MEMORIAL

The Rider remained motionless on the refuse-strewn ground. A moment later Wes's FEMA jacket, with two holes ripped in it, was dropped over his upper body and smashed helmet. Professor Dumas had quickly and neatly torn two small devices from the jacket before using it as a shroud.

"So he's—dead?" Wes asked quietly. He was struggling to stand, but his limbs just wouldn't hold him yet.

Dumas looked over at the blond, blue-eyed young man as if noticing him for the first time. He considered the question, shifted his gaze to Bunter the cat, then shrugged and frowned.

"Possibly," he answered.

"I figure when you drop a cloth over a man's face . . ." Wes said, finally getting upright. "Shouldn't we check?"

"Why? If he is, there's nothing we can do. If he isn't, he'll see to himself."

Wes considered the strange logic of that. "What did you do to him?"

"Me?" Dumas responded innocently, his eyes intent on a small, rectangular device he held between the thumb and forefinger of his left hand as if it were a particularly interesting cockroach. "Not much. Just used a little acupressure on a major juncture in his nervous system." He crushed the small object between his fingers as if popping a pea, while slipping another small, flat device into his coat pocket with his right hand. "Creates a rather notable shock, as you could see."

"And what was that?" Wes continued, jabbing a forefinger at the craggy man.

"What was what?" Dumas was all innocence.

"What you just crushed in your hand."

"Oh, a standard tracking device, much like the ones they used to make for airline life jackets. That's how your bosses could find where you were."

"And the other one? The one you just put in your coat pocket?"

Dumas grinned and replied, "Now that was a nonstandard one. That's how *I* could find where you were."

Before Wes could pursue the matter further, a broad-shouldered young man dressed entirely in black appeared from around the corner at a fast trot. He tossed the Professor what looked like a lens-covered projector about the size of a binoculars case, then went to mingle with the other followers.

"Thanks, Rick," Dumas said as he neatly caught the device. He examined it with mild interest as Wes spluttered.

"That's the thermal imager! How did he get it?"

Dumas's head shifted back on his neck, examining Wes with solemnity. "You ask a lot of questions," he replied.

"Do I?" Wes said, annoyed. "You don't think your obtuseness has anything to do with that?"

The man's serious expression broke into another wide grin. "'Obtuseness,' eh? I like that. Actually, I like you too." He transferred his smile to the other young man, who might have been a prize college fullback in better times. "Rick knows a lot about all kinds of things. Ask him."

Rick Samuels looked up from where he was quietly chatting with the woman who had grabbed the Rider's feet. "Sure do. But not now. We have work to do."

"Yes, that's probably enough chitchat for now," Dumas said, and motioned for all his followers to come closer. "It's only a matter of time before the powers that be discover their sleeping wolves. We'd best not be nearby." As the others moved quickly to cover their tracks, Dumas stepped to where Hannah was still kneeling. "Don't you agree?"

Hannah considered this, then nodded curtly.

Dumas nodded with satisfaction. "Now you're talking." He looked at Wes. "She's a marvel, is she not?"

"Yes—"

"I actually believe either she's picked up skills from the pets she's tracked or—more likely—there was a preexisting simpatico."

"Both," Hannah said. "I've told you before, I like them better than I like people. We relate better."

"But you and I get along," Dumas said.

"You, sir, are—"

"Don't say it," he said. "A dumb ass. A mule."

Hannah smiled warmly.

Dumas turned to Wes. "You, my boy? Are you coming?"

"I don't really have anywhere else to go, do I?" Wes asked.

"No place better, I'll give you that," Dumas replied. He regarded Wes thoughtfully. "Yes, I like you. Feisty. And you've been through quite the ordeal here." He pointed his stick away from where the Rider lay. "Come on, everyone, let's get out of here."

Wes was expecting to walk for hours through every imaginable landscape to get as far away from the RoF Riders as possible. So even though Professor Dumas distracted him with scholarly chatter, he was surprised that they merely weaved this way and that, back and forth across the remains of Fern Dell and Black Oak.

"Ironic that I found you at Los Diego Way," the Professor was saying. "In the Renaissance era, Diego was Latinized as Didacus, from the Greek *didache*, meaning 'teaching.'"

"Fascinating," Wes said, trying not to be distracted by his myriad aches and bruises. At least the walk helped to shake them off.

As the man nattered on, Wes was able to study him more closely. His stick was more than just a walking device and weapon. It was a work of art. Intricate designs had been etched and whittled into its slightly shiny surface, over which a layer of shellac had been applied. From the way it thudded softly into the ground, Wes could tell it was strong. And very, very solid.

The lab coat, too, was intriguing. At first Wes thought it was just dirty and stained. Upon closer examination, he saw that it was akin to the stick: dark, intricate designs had been drawn onto it with paint, charcoal, and permanent marker. Some looked like tribal tattoos, some like the swirls from atmospheric pressure maps, and others like astrological star charts. But Wes could recognize none. He looked up to see Dumas looking back down at him.

"The coat interests you?" the Professor asked, but did not wait for Wes to respond. "Each of my new rustic agers gets to add something once they agree to join us," he explained. "Perhaps you will have the opportunity as well. Ah, here we are."

Wes was brought up short as the group stopped climbing upward, as they had been for several minutes. They had walked for less than a half hour and, as near as he could tell, for less than a mile. They emerged at the crest of a Hollywood hill at what remained of the Louis B. Mayer Memorial Library at the American Film Institute Campus. There, Dumas's dozen followers joined eight more within the crumbling walls of the darkened interior.

Dumas's chest inflated as he took in their new surroundings. "Highest altitude in the area," he boasted as he motioned Wes and Hannah in, scratching Bunter's head as she passed with him in her arms. "Naturally camouflaged, exceedingly defendable. No one can approach unseen, and we can remain unseen until any interloper is within a few feet."

Wes couldn't disagree. The collapsed structure looked completely empty, even uninhabitable, from the outside—and also from the inside. Dumas's followers all but melted into the darkness, and Wes thought he'd be lost until the Professor showed him around a blind corner.

The group had used the junk of the ravaged building to create architectural optical illusions. Even as Wes peered inches from the corner, it looked as if the structure had collapsed in on itself. Only when he bent down and twisted his head could he see an angled gap. And on the other side of that gap was a fairly large, igloo-shaped space held up by judicious use of bent beams and stacked books.

"The Conservatory Library," Dumas identified. "Useful before the quake, useful after."

Wes marveled at the living quarters as Dumas stepped past him. The twenty followers each had sleeping and study spaces created with papers and bindings. There was even a cooking area. Everything was lit by carefully placed candles.

"The pen is truly mightier than the sword," Dumas informed them with a certain amount of pleasure and pride. "We have even devised a more than adequate lavatory supplied with, as you might imagine, ample and very erudite bathroom tissue."

"Nice." Wes chuckled.

"Isn't it?" Dumas said. "I amuse myself by wondering which of the philosophers would applaud and which would be offended."

Wes shook his head, and stared around at the space. It had all the charm of a backyard fort, with all the resources of some very clever grown-ups. He marveled at how he and his FEMA teammates had missed this.

"It's remarkable, Professor, really. But why this settlement, this organization? I would have guessed for mutual self-protection, except it would work against that. If one member is found, everybody's found. The place could be declared a hazard, a haven for ne'er-do-wells . . . bombed, torched."

"What, by people whose mission it is to protect and preserve?" Dumas mocked.

"I think we've all learned that's not quite true," Wes admitted.

"His compadres brought a building down on us earlier," Hannah said.

"Yes, I know," Dumas noted.

"Not my compadres," Wes said quietly, surprising himself. The phrase felt a little heavier, a little wider, than just the RoF Riders he thought he was referring to.

"Believe me," Dumas replied, "we have taken those boys into profound consideration."

Wes gestured at the setup. "But even this large a group wouldn't be able to withstand a concerted, mechanized assault."

"You are correct, but your concern is misplaced." Dumas held up an understanding hand. "All will be revealed, Agent Harding. All in its own time." He looked from Wes's concerned, confused face to Hannah and Bunter's placid ones. "You two look like siblings," he commented. "Soul siblings."

Hannah smiled. "When I first started tracking him, he wouldn't go near me," she explained to Wes. Her smile disappeared and her green eyes grew dark. "But once we found out his owner had died, he refused to leave."

"Are you so certain he's the one who doesn't want to leave?" Dumas asked.

Hannah grinned.

Dumas returned her smile. "No matter. You have a sweet little family," he said, including Wes with a nod.

Hannah's mouth straightened noncommittally as Dumas put his big hand on her right shoulder. He stepped back and waved an arm toward the back wall of the enclosure. "Step into my office, would you?"

Wes joined in beside them as they moved toward the farthest wall. There, they found another architectural illusion. To move forward they had to step into a disguised recess that opened into a small but comfortable trailer. The makeshift corridor that connected the two was roofed with the windshield of a Metro Rapid bus. The glass was carefully shattered so as to refract and reflect lights in myriad different ways. Seeing beneath it would be impossible.

The interior of the six-foot-wide, six-foot-high, twenty-foot-long rectangle was lined with shelves on three sides. They were covered in the oddest assortment of homemade gizmos Wes had ever seen. Dumas, who had to hunch down to fit inside, pulled the other tracking device and the thermal imager out of his pockets and added them to the collection.

Above an assortment of car batteries were stool seats attached to the trailer wall that could be swung out. Dumas sat on one, and the two others joined him. The visitors noted that several low-wattage devices were being powered by one of the car batteries, bathing the area in soft, dim, yellow light.

Wes looked around at the small, curtained windows that lined the room and a plywood wall behind Dumas. "This looks familiar somehow," he mused.

Dumas nodded, pleased. "Might be a bit before your time," he suggested, "but it's a familiar space for anyone who went to college in the sixties."

"A Volkswagen bus!" Hannah realized.

"Oh, you've been in one before, have you? Modified double-cab pickup circa sixty-three." Dumas glanced at Wes as if the young man knew what he was talking about. "Wanted to go with a later model, but this was the tallest, widest, and longest I could find."

"Cozy," was all Wes could think to say.

"Ultra," Dumas replied. He sat back, his arms crossed. "My mobile lab ever since I came out here. It's never let me down."

Wes focused on the second tracking device. "Professor, how did you—"

"Find you?" Dumas finished.

"Find me, find Hannah, find this place?"

"So impatient." Dumas tut-tutted.

"Curious, sir," Wes replied. "It keeps me human." Dumas grinned, and Wes cocked a thumb behind him. "And after all, aren't we in the right place to seek answers?"

Dumas nodded slowly. "Very well played. Yes, this is a library. And I am a professor. But one question at a time, my boy. First things first."

Wes started at Dumas's coincidental invoking of his father's mantra. The Professor didn't seem to notice, however. He picked up the sophisticated surveillance device and held it up to Wes's eyes.

"This is not just a tracker," he said. "It's also an eavesdropper. This evening's fortuitous timing wasn't just one of my mistress's."

"Sorry?" Wes interjected.

"Dame Fortune," Dumas chuckled. "I woo her constantly as though my life, our lives, depend on her favor, which they do. Agent Harding, I've been following you since your hotel adventure with Ms. Lonnegin and the bike-riding thugs who tried to apprehend you."

"Kill us, you mean," Wes said. "Dewey and I call them RoF Riders."

"Nice," Dumas said. "Very Teddy Roosevelt."

It suddenly hit Wes, then, and he turned toward Hannah. "Hold on. You're one of them? One of these people?"

"I don't think I care for that tone of voice," Hannah said.

"It's not a 'tone,' I'm confused. I thought you were a loner."

"What is *that* supposed to mean?"

"Just that you didn't seem the kind of person who would be one of . . . who would need—well, let's call it what it is. A cult."

Dumas clapped his hands playfully. "This is precious. A cult. Go on, Mr. Harding. I love the hole your tongue is digging. How they have brainwashed you, back in civilization."

"This isn't 'them,' this isn't FEMA speaking. It's . . . I mean, a shepherd's staff, carvings, tattoos on your coat—"

"Technically, they're pictograms," Dumas said. "But do continue."

"I'm done," Wes said. "I appreciate everything you've done, but let's be frank about what you are."

Hannah was quietly livid. "What we are," she said. "We are a group of caring, capable people whose only concern is keeping survivors safe. If that's a cult, then yes, I'm a member! Who are you 'one of'?"

Instinctively, defiantly, he launched into the words he had said so often in the field. "The job of my team is to support our citizens and first responders in recovering from and mitigating all hazards—"

Wes stopped under the withering eyes of his two companions. His own bullshit detector would have clipped him in a few moments anyway: the words weren't true. Not for the group back at the base. Not anymore.

Dumas clucked in a calming, considerate way. "I'll chalk that outburst up to post-traumatic stress and exhaustion."

Hannah was not so immediately forgiving.

Wes met her gaze. "Yeah, I'm sorry, that didn't come out the way I wanted."

"There's a book back there that says something appropriate," Hannah said coolly. "Two words. 'Judge not.'"

"You're right," Wes said. "Again, I'm sorry. It's only that—this is a lot to take in all at once."

"And here I thought you were a quick study."

"It's a lot of information you've been doling out—"

"No," Dumas agreed. "It's more. It's dynamics. New people, new energy, hope instead of despair. An adult who's not barking orders at you."

"I've had that in my life," Wes protested, thinking of how grounded Malloy was compared to this borderline crackpot and his commune. "I'm just trying to fit all of these pieces."

Dumas lowered his forehead, and while his grin widened, his expression grew grimmer. "Then I'd say you're in for a long night, Agent Harding. Because you ain't heard nothin' yet. Say 'when' if it gets too much."

"I can take as much truth as you can give me." Wes regarded the Professor and leaned forward. "And I need it. I need to know what we've been turning a blind eye to, because I will personally make sure that we respond and assist."

Dumas pondered his wall of gadgets and seemed to go inward for the first time since Wes had met him. "My boy, I hope that's enough."

7

THE GENERAL'S NEW CLOTHES

Before Wes heard the part he was going to play, he had to look it.

With his jacket torn and left behind, the Professor thought it best that the agent blend in. Going through several trunks of clothes, Dumas left Wes dressed much like Hannah, in a long-sleeve T-shirt, hoodie, black jeans, and black running shoes. Much to Wes's surprise, it felt good against his skin.

"Only the best new rustic age materials." Dumas grinned. "They wick moisture to the outer layer where it can evaporate. They also regulate body temperature in all conditions, resist bacteria, and swallow odors." He raised his arms like a crane stretching. "In close confines like these, trust me, that is a very good thing."

While Hannah resumed her earlier mode of being stand-offish—Wes wished it were otherwise, but he didn't blame her—he joined the Professor in a wide circle of his followers. They all held wooden bowls, waiting for an old-fashioned covered pot atop what looked like a glowing, rectangular metal box resting on a flat rock in the middle of the library floor.

Dumas motioned at the ingeniously contained fire that was heating the soup. "Modeled on an induction oven. My own design. Collects the smoke, and little battery-run fans push it through a pipe under our feet to a series of pinholes in the outer wreckage."

"Clever," Wes said. "Blends in with the clouds of our ruptured world."

Dumas grinned appreciatively at Wes. "Exactly. Any passerby wouldn't give it a first thought, let alone a second."

Wes regarded him, his expression a mix of wonder and weirdness. "You've been doing this for how long?"

"Which part?" Dumas asked, picking up his own bowl and spoon. "Science? Forever. This settlement? Since a couple of weeks after the Ring of Fire kicked up its heels."

"What were you doing before that?" Wes asked.

"There were plenty of treasures to collect, eh, Prof?" Rick Samuels winked as he loomed over the stone, metal box, and pot.

Dumas nodded as he settled into a makeshift divan—a frame built from an overturned desk cushioned with stacked magazines. There was even a pillow for his neck made from an old state flag wrapped around crumpled newspapers.

"Indeed," Dumas agreed. He looked from Rick to Wes. "Some people collapse after disasters, becoming one with the catastrophe—human wreckage. Others blossom and grow stronger. Like trees sharing roots to help one another."

"God knows this old tree needed some new soil," Rick said. "I was afflicted with boredom."

The Professor tapped his bowl with a spoon, and everyone in the circle suddenly and silently shook their left hands next to their foreheads—as if they were fanning themselves. Then, just as abruptly, they stopped.

"Our new rustic age salute," Dumas answered Wes's questioning stare. "We use it to signal we're okay when we're out and about—"

"And we mock the uniformed martinets who lord it over the needy," Hannah interrupted from the shadows.

Dumas nodded solemnly then continued the conversation. "Yes, we have been traveling, planning, and collecting since before the disaster hit. When we found this place, we knew our journey was at an end, at least for now."

"Collecting?" Wes echoed. "Collecting what?"

"Oh," Dumas said distantly, waving his spoon. "The usual. Food, batteries, antiseptics, shoes, first-aid supplies . . . people."

"People?"

Dumas motioned to the circle. "People. People in need, people who tried, people who cared, people who sought safety."

"He collected me," Hannah said with special import. She was the only one without a bowl. She held Bunter the cat instead.

Wes looked at her, but she didn't look back. Instead, she stared into the darkness. "I was trapped in my building. It crushed my fiancé right in front of me. My cat—Zanzibar—escaped just before the walls collapsed. I heard her yowls, then her cries, then her pathetic mews getting quieter and more distant. Then I didn't hear anything at all."

Hannah grew silent and stared at the cat in her arms. Rick silently raised the pot lid and started ladling out some stew. He tenderly held out a bowl to Hannah, and she took it wordlessly.

"Hannah was noticed by us in the immediate recovery response after the cataclysm," Dumas informed Wes quietly as everyone was eating. "That was before we took her in. She was out searching for the pets of neighbors, ignoring her own well-being. We made sure she took care of herself first, cats, dogs, and turtles second."

Wes fixed Hannah with a curious look. "Pets," he said. "Just pets?"

"Yes," she said defiantly. "Just pets. Why?"

"Then why were those Riders after you?"

"Aha, they *weren't* after her," Dumas interrupted. "They were after me."

"Why you?"

Professor Dumas put down his stew bowl with certainty, as if steeling himself for what he was about to reveal. "Because, I'm both sorry and proud to say, I'm the one person on this entire planet whom General J.C. Passarelles fears."

Wes studied the ragged middle-aged man and thought about the powerful, assured military leader. The two just didn't match up. In fact, despite all the capable inventions that the man had accomplished here, Wes had to wonder whether the scholar was actually delusional.

"What would make him fear *you*?" Wes said aloud, unable to avoid emphasis on the last word.

Dumas was unfazed. "Because I'm the only one who knew him at JPL. Knew him before the accident."

"The Jet Propulsion Laboratory?" Wes pressed. "NASA's JPL?"

"Passarelles—no general then—was in charge after the Northridge quake in 1994. Did you know that?"

"No," Wes said. Then he added sarcastically, "The General didn't confide a whole lot in me. You trying to tell me that you were Army?"

"Heavens, no," Dumas said.

"So what would an Army man be doing running a science lab during an earthquake?"

"That's what we *all* wanted to know," Dumas said carefully. He stopped eating his stew. "I was part of 'The Pencil Crew' at JPL. The computer nerds called us a bunch of Neanderthal throwbacks because we wanted everything put on paper by our own hands. We developed the Mars Rover that way, Voyager, Cassini." His eyes grew distant. "That Crew, my friends—they're gone now. All of them." After a moment, he resumed his meal and his lecture. "Northridge had the highest ground acceleration ever recorded instrumentally in a North American urban area. After that, Passarelles was put in charge. His stated mission was to see if we could predict, or possibly prevent, another or an even worse disaster."

"The death toll," Rick solemnly interjected, "for the Northridge, California, area was more than fifty, with over five thousand injured. Property damage topped twenty billion dollars. It was the costliest natural disaster in US history at that time."

"Until now," Hannah added.

"Until now," Dumas agreed. "As our supervisor, Passarelles revealed his sole obsession: the fault systems beneath the Los Angeles basin."

"I'm still not getting it," Wes said. "Why did you report to a military man?"

"And I'm still getting to that," Dumas said patiently. "Now, you may ask why he was so obsessed with the fault lines here. Well, right before the accident, I discovered—the old-fashioned way, by eavesdropping outside his door—that the soon-to-be general was searching for a legendary geologic 'AH' spot."

"AH?"

"The Achilles Heel. The Ache. The Ack-Ack. We called it many things back then, but what it is, is the single spot that could set off, like dominoes, this entire planet's plate tectonic movements and epicenters."

Wes searched for any sign that Dumas was teasing him. There was none.

"He was searching in order to guard it, to close it," Wes said. "That has to be the reason."

"Does it?" Hannah said quietly. "You're a nice person, Wes. You have to have noticed by now how rare that is."

"Nice" and "rare" in the same breath, Wes had noticed that. He wasn't sure what it added up to, though. Hannah was concentrating on her soup again.

"Young man," Dumas picked up, "civilization exists by geologic consent, as it were, subject to change without notice. A tremor here or there we can deal with. Even a major earthquake now and then. But what about a dozen major events in a single day?"

Wes didn't like where this seemed to be headed. "Exactly," he said. "Even a madman has to realize he would die too, if it ever popped."

"The possibility of death versus the reality of supreme power? Which he could easily establish during the unparalleled chaos that would follow a full-strength, full-circumference Ring of

Power detonation," Dumas replied. "Son, how long have you been wearing a uniform? Can you think of no one in history who would have accepted that deal with the devil?"

"Fair enough, there are occasional lunatics. But there are also checks and balances. Forget Passarelles. How could the *government* sign off on something like that?"

Dumas had a ready answer. "Passarelles's 'official position' was that this spot would serve as a doomsday weapon. He maintained that no one would go to war if the United States could rattle the world to pieces." Dumas shook his head with an old bitterness. "You know how much money-grubbing senators love doomsday weapons."

"Actually, I don't."

"Well, they do," Dumas said.

Something Dumas had said a minute before suddenly popped back into Wes's brain. "Hold on. You said 'accident,'" he remembered. "You said 'before the accident.' *What* accident?"

Dumas exhaled slowly, easing his way back into a painful memory. "There was a fire," he said softly. "At the lab. Apparently, some substandard equipment Passarelles had us buy to cut costs gave off toxic fumes. For some unknown reason, the failsafe door-locking mechanisms failed."

"Or were sabotaged," Rick interjected.

Dumas waved the idea away. His big head slowly lowered to the left, and an analytical frown grew on his lips. "The windows were shatterproof. No surprise the Pencil Crew couldn't get out that way." He turned his head to focus on the still-bubbling stew in the pot on the glowing metal rectangle. "By the time the failsafe locking mechanism inexplicably became failsafe again, it was too late. My colleagues were dead. All my *friends* were dead."

"Like a pharaoh," Rick said, "entombing those who knew the route to his final resting place."

"Do you have proof of that?" Wes challenged.

"The man himself!" Hannah snapped. "*You're* the one who couldn't believe he'd knock down a building to kill us . . . even while he was knocking down a building to kill us!"

"We don't know that he ordered it," Wes protested.

"Who did, then? That dead body?"

"Obviously not," Wes said, "though maybe that's what they didn't want us to see."

"Why?" Hannah asked.

"I don't know," Wes said. "Just putting it out there. Didn't seem natural."

There was a heavy silence, made thicker by Hannah's obvious frustration with Wes.

Dumas shook off his sorrow and continued. "I should have died with them, of course. But—the mundane came to the rescue. I was in the men's room. I went into the hallway, smelled something off, realized the direction it was coming from, ran the other way. And I didn't stop running."

"Forgive me, Professor," Wes said, though he looked at Hannah as he said it. "But all of this is still supposition. You said yourself the toxic gas release happened because of faulty equipment."

"The equipment, yes," Dumas said. "Not the locking mechanism. Even so, even allowing the improbability that you are correct about this and I am not, Passarelles would still have wanted me for his obscene work, handing him and his sponsors a doomsday weapon. Those deaths gave me clarity. Sometimes the misfortune of others is the clearest, widest window into your own soul, your own priorities. I didn't want blood on my hands, so I disappeared. I went to Washington, went to work at Consolidated Power Corporation, changed my name, and buried my identity with the help of Jane, a helluva computer hacker."

A young woman in the circle waved her hand.

"That was where we met." Rick smiled. "Consolidated Power Corporation."

Dumas grinned at the couple. Then he shrugged. "Who knows? Maybe I should have stayed. Maybe I should have tried to get proof about the doomsday weapon, blown a few whistles. But I didn't. And now—now here we are."

"You're fighting now," Hannah said.

Wes wanted to know what the man's real name was, but there were more pressing concerns. "I'm still not clear about something. Are you saying that Passarelles succeeded anyway? That he found this Achilles Heel?"

"I don't know."

"What do you *think*?" Wes pushed him. "Do you believe that the spot somehow set off the Ring of Fire or a portion of it? Is that what you're trying to tell me?" He looked at the others, at Jane, at Hannah, at Rick for corroboration. He found none.

Dumas nodded. "What I think is that this"—he swept his arms around him—"was the epicenter, the trigger that set off a series of cataclysms around the globe. But I am not convinced it was a natural disaster."

Wes reacted sharply. "What then? There were no explosions, no fracking, no asteroid hits . . . I mean, that's a big leap of an assumption!"

"Which is why I'm investigating this event," Dumas said patiently. "I think there is something going on in which I believe the General is secretly involved, in which his team is involved, in which your friend Malloy is involved."

"More speculation," Wes retorted, stung by the reference to his friend and mentor. "Or do you have something concrete?"

"You want proof," Dumas said wearily. "Well, I suppose that's fair. We built a jurisprudence system around that idea. All right. You and your director Malloy made a good team, right?"

Wes nodded warily.

"Heart and soul, as they say," Dumas continued. "So why didn't he come to your rescue when you were in trouble before?"

"Something was wrong," Wes admitted. "They threatened him, I suspect. He looked scared."

"He was scared!" Dumas corrected him. "*Is* scared."

"Of what?" Wes asked.

"I'll answer your question with a question," Dumas said. "The answer will provide your proof."

All the sardonic mirth left Dumas's face, leaving him looking dead serious.

"What would anyone gain by killing an innocent man, tearing open his chest like a lobster, and ripping his lungs out? Oh, and Wes? Mr. McGuinness was not the only one."

8

THE WHITE PATCH

Wes decided to take a short nap. Though he was physically tired, it was his mind that needed a break from all the information the Professor had doled out. And in the darkness of the pod space he was led to for his rest, he admitted that he felt more than a little heartsick over the Professor's aspersions against Doc.

Dumas let him sleep until deep into the night, then had Hannah wake him. She led Wes outside with the lanky, lab-coated professor tagging along not far behind. The rest of the group, including Bunter, stayed behind, secure in the hideout.

Hannah led them through ragged shrubbery, then under a fallen tree trunk that spanned a shallow ditch. There, she swept aside some dirt, uncovering a rotting wood plank. She slid that aside as well, revealing an opening that sloped down into a dark tunnel.

"What's this?" Wes whispered softly.

She slipped inside without answering or looking back. Wes followed in her footsteps, and the Professor brought up the rear. He and Hannah took palm-sized, battery-powered lights from their pockets. Shaped like domes, their light coated the area in a soft yellow glow.

It was a crevasse formed by the quake and covered over with fallen debris, but that was only the start. Beyond a hundred yards or so, the rest had been dug out and supported by whatever wood and concrete had fallen through, rearranged. Water plinked loudly somewhere in the distance. Rats moved around them, scattering from their approach. Wes had gotten used to vermin since the disaster. They filled ecological niches previously occupied by humans, cats, and working mousetraps.

As the trio moved through the low, narrow passageway, it reminded Wes of the tunnel network his father said the Viet Cong had built during the Vietnam War. It was strange. He had visualized the tunnels but never imagined what they smelled like. This one had an odor of damp earth mixed with the smell of dead things.

Dumas closed the space between himself and Wes, his mouth nearly at the young man's ear.

"If you speak, do so very, very quietly," the Professor cautioned.

"Are Passarelles's people listening?" Wes whispered back.

"No," the Professor replied. "The ground is. Not much holding it up, as you see."

That sobered Wes more than he already was. He pulled in his elbows and ducked even lower to keep from brushing the ceiling or sides.

"As I was saying," Dumas went on, as though hours had not passed since their previous conversation, "Mr. McGuinness was not the only splayed corpse. My people and I found more and more of them, until we realized it could no longer be a coincidence."

"Animals?" Wes said, knowing it was a pointless question but curious what the answer would be.

Hannah turned her head. "Scavenging animals attack in a variety of ways," she said. "This is not one of them."

"And there was another matter," Dumas said. "Survivors would go into East 101, they'd be evacked to Edwards, and some didn't arrive. No, sir. But they were found, by us. They were in the condition you and Hannah discovered."

Oh Jesus, Wes thought. *Charlie's cousin.*

"Why wasn't it reported?" Wes demanded in a whisper.

"It was," Hannah snapped softly over her shoulder. "But every time a witness brought an official to the spot, the corpse was no longer there."

"Didn't the witnesses get themselves on tape about it, start the paper trail at least?"

"The witnesses disappeared," Hannah hissed. "We're guessing that what happened to them was what the Riders wanted to 'happen' to you and me."

"That's why many folks headed for the hills," Dumas said. "Literally. Despite rumors to the contrary, Passarelles's influence is not absolute, and his Riders' jurisdiction is localized. They seem interested only in controlling the Los Angeles basin and most especially Coldwater Canyon."

"That would be one hell of an operation," Wes said.

The canyon ran perpendicular to the Santa Monica Mountains, stretching three miles from the Upper Franklin Canyon Reservoir to the Lower Franklin Canyon Reservoir. That was almost a thousand acres, and all the razor wire the authorities had requisitioned wouldn't come close to covering that.

"The size of the canyon might account for the increased number of Riders," Dumas pointed out. "There seem to be more and more of them all the time—ah, here we are."

Wes looked up and stopped short as Hannah stepped into a small alcove. Beyond her, Wes could see that they had reached a juncture where several tunnels intersected. There were five access ways there, and as he had seen from the top of Wall X, several people were furtively moving from one to the next. In their shawls and rags, it wasn't clear if the hunched figures were men or women.

"The look of dedication," Dumas said, pondering the humble figures. "You'd be surprised what dedicated people can accomplish when the powers that be give them little choice."

"Dedicated to what?" Wes asked. "Survival?"

"God no," Dumas said. "Not just that. Some felt indebted to me for taking them in, others were next of kin of the splayed corpses. They want to get to the bottom of this."

"I still can't imagine any reason the General would do everything you said," Wes admitted, "or how he could have anything to do with those bodies. But I agree it's possible. Not likely, but possible, and we'd better figure out the answer."

"Is that what passes for commitment with you?" Hannah asked angrily.

"Now, now," Dumas said. "There's room for dissent in any group."

Wes didn't feel like discussing politics or sociology right now. Roots were brushing his face from above, and he didn't like the slushy feeling of the earth below him. And the most urgent matter needed to be addressed.

"The missing evacuees, do you know if you found all of them? Are they all dead?"

"We can't be sure," the Professor replied.

"Then let's plan to get sure," Wes said firmly. "Was there any logic in the location of the bodies? I mean, why the hell would there be one in a broken-down ruin of a hotel? Just for the privacy of it?"

"That one was largely an anomaly," the Professor replied. "I'm assuming the murderer ran out of time. As for the others, there were patterns. But for the purpose of gathering information, I suggest we take care of one piece of business before we formulate further plans. Are you willing?"

"Relevant information?" Wes asked.

"At the heart of the matter."

Wes nodded. "All right, what's the business?"

They emerged from the network of tunnels between Hollywood Boulevard and Franklin Avenue, close to where the Dolby and El Capitan Theaters had once stood. Wes didn't doubt this was where Hannah had escaped after impulsively planting the bug on him as Charlie's copter landed.

As before, the tunnel egress was camouflaged, this time with a crumpled row of mailboxes. Although Hannah and Wes emerged furtively from the warren, their hoods up and their heads down, Dumas stepped out into the pitch darkness as if for a brisk early-morning jaunt.

"Coldwater Canyon, five miles that way," he quietly announced, pointing his left hand west.

"Five miles?" Wes echoed. "That'll take hours to walk, even with the tunnel's head start."

"Who said anything about walking?" Dumas replied.

Hannah led the way to the remains of a parking lot at the corner of Franklin and North Highland Avenue. Wes vaguely remembered it as an innocuous spot the family would pass on the way back and forth from the Hollywood Bowl—the cracked shards of which were just up Route 170.

At first glance, the site looked like any other patch of destroyed real estate within the surrounding fifty square miles. Wes could imagine the way it must've looked just before the Ring of Fire struck—painted asphalt covered in vehicles, surrounded on three sides by hydraulic parking shelves that allowed the parking company to stack cars three levels high without the need of a garage. That wasn't how it looked now. The parking shelves were twisted like lightning-blasted trees, the cars and trucks crushing one another while, in turn, being crushed by chunks of the destroyed buildings around them.

Hannah stepped up to a four-wheel-drive Ford Explorer 500, painted in dark shades of camouflage. The Ford's doors had been replaced with thick, heavy shades. The Professor pulled back the one on the passenger side and motioned for Wes to enter.

"Wouldn't do to have the sound of a door closing give away our presence or position," he explained. "And they're bulletproof. Goes well with the combat tires."

Wes found that the rear section was without seats, but it was far from empty. More gizmos and gadgets were strewn everywhere. Dumas sidled by him, pulling the thermal imager and "nonstandard" tracking device from his lab coat pockets.

"You ride shotgun," Dumas instructed. "The back is better suited to old dogs like me." He sat cross-legged on the vehicle floor and started tinkering happily,

Wes settled in next to Hannah, who was giving him a dubious look.

"Okay, enough with the evil eye already," he groused. "I *am* fully committed, in every sense of the word. Just start the engine and let's get going."

"It is started," she informed him, with the hint of a smile.

"Battery-run electric motor," the Professor said in his ear.

"Nice," Wes said.

"Thanks," Hannah replied, putting the vehicle into gear. "It was my idea."

The five-mile ride toward Beverly Hills was not much faster than walking, but Wes was glad they weren't on foot. Hannah guided the Explorer along slowly, cautiously, weaving up, over, and around wreckage, fissures, fractures, and ravines. Once or twice she even navigated through collapsed buildings when there was no better choice.

They finally passed through the ruins of West Hollywood and Wes heard Dumas snort like a bull. He turned to see the Professor kneeling between the driver and passenger seats. The thermal-imaging device was in his hands.

"We're clear behind and on either side of us," he reported. "But from here on it should be pretty hairy. I'll guide you away from any guards or patrols."

Peering through the windshield, Wes spotted a warning sign almost fifty yards ahead. Judging by its unblemished paint job and erect mounting, it had obviously been set up post–Ring of Fire.

"A Checkpoint Charlie can't be too far off," he cautioned.

"Screw them," Hannah replied. "I know this town."

"She's been scouting," Dumas informed Wes. "Almost daily, with Bunter as her bloodhound."

Hannah guided the vehicle off Sunset Boulevard and away from the mangled Beverly Hills Gate—up into the hills of Doheny. Then she slowed beside a curtain of scrub.

"Behind that is an old drainpipe, six feet around," she said. "It's stuck in the bottom of the canyon wall. There used to be a reservoir up there," she added, pointing. "And I'd watch for rattlers if I were you."

Wes looked to Dumas. He nodded. "You're on point, my boy. I'll be right behind you."

"And I'll be here watching your back," Hannah added.

"Thanks," Wes said, peering ahead. "So what the hell are we looking for?"

"I'll show you when we get there," Dumas said.

Wes exited quietly, followed by the Professor. The young man slipped easily into FEMA mode, moving as though this were an active disaster site that could collapse, flood, erupt, or present a live electric wire at any moment.

Thankfully, the walk through the drainage pipe was relatively short and rattler-free. They completed the cautious march in the dark because it wouldn't do to have the glow of their lamps getting brighter and brighter out the other side. Not when they didn't know who might be there to see it.

Wes and the Professor kneeled at the end and took their first look from this vantage point at the post-apocalyptic Coldwater Canyon. It was far less threatening than they imagined. Although it was covered in cracks and fissures that, with landslides and fires, had laid waste to at least a thousand homes, it was free of any razor wire or prowling Riders—as far as they could tell.

Wes looked over to where the Professor was scanning the area with the thermal-imaging device.

"Anything?" Wes asked him.

"Not even a raccoon," Dumas replied. "Which is good."

He handed the thermal imager to Wes and started digging through his pockets. He pulled out two pairs of sleek black earbuds, each with a microphone that looked like a rolled adhesive strip. He gave one to Wes as he stuck the other pair in his ears.

"Hannah," Dumas whispered.

"Here," Wes heard through his earbuds. "Wes, FYI, there's a miniature video feed just above the mike. What you see, I see on the SUV's dashboard computer monitor."

"Good to know," Wes replied softly. Then to the Professor, he said, "I'm still waiting on the relevance of all this."

Dumas pulled his bugging device out of the lab coat's breast pocket and pointed down the valley. "There. I want you to attach this to a security camera."

Wes brought up the thermal imager. He found the night vision switch easily and held the device to his eyes. Through it he saw, half-buried by a landslide, a house that had fallen onto a telephone pole in such a way that the shaft stabbed through the roof. Though the house was at an angle, the pole pointed straight up. At the top of the pole was what remained of a security camera.

"Yeesh," Wes understated. "It looks like the whole place will collapse if I even breathe on it."

"I understand, but I can't overstate how important it is. And while we of the new rustic age are all daring and brave," Dumas added with a flourish, "none of us is quite limber enough to make it up there."

"I tried," Hannah added. "It requires a bit of monkey, I think."

It wasn't an insult. She almost sounded playful.

"Well, if it'll help . . ." Wes took the bugging device from the Professor.

"Son, my colleagues at CPC saddled me with the epithet 'Damus'—as in Nostradamus—for trying to explain crazy theories before I could prove they weren't crazy. You attach this to the camera and you will not only validate my theories, you'll get your explanation."

"Fair enough." Wes examined the bug. "How the hell do I attach this thing?"

"It's magnetic and wireless. It'll attach itself."

Wes left the drainpipe. The next few minutes were tense, but not as tense as they could have been. As Wes moved through the dark, picking his way across fallen trees, split ground, wickedly clinging wreckage, vines, and wire, Dumas lay flat on his stomach in the pipe opening, scanning the area with the thermal imager while Hannah watched the periphery.

Upon reaching the crushed house, Wes moved along the front, trying to decide the safest way to enter. He finally decided to make his way up a challenging slope of broken wood, glass, and plaster. They all heard the house creak with every step.

The creak became a groan, and Wes reached up and grabbed a jutting beam. He tested it, found it sturdy, and gripped it hand-over-hand as the pile of wreckage began to shift and slide.

"Good news," Dumas said suddenly.

"Eager to hear it," Wes said.

"The shifting rippled through the house. It opened a hole to the roof and the top of the pole. I can see it from here."

"Right," Wes agreed, looking up through the hole while digging in his pocket for the bug.

"When you get there, look for a small patch of white on the security cam's base that may still be marked 'closed circuit' or 'c.c.'"

"Got it," Wes replied.

The young man found a low-hanging eave and, after testing it, half pulled, half leaped onto the roof and grabbed the telephone pole. He shimmied his way to the top, collecting splinters on the inside of his thighs and arms. Hanging out over the valley, he was glad for the little pricks of pain: they kept him from thinking about how perilous his situation was.

"Do you see the white patch?"

Wes reached for the security camera housing and tried to wipe it free from weeks of disaster dust.

"Yeah," he wheezed through the thick cloud. "Yeah, I think so."

Wes couldn't be sure which came first: his snapping the bug onto the white patch, or the pole collapsing from his weight.

With a screeching crash, the pole started dropping, ripping open a bigger and bigger chasm in the roof.

Wes heard Hannah gasp, which was fortunate: it snapped him from his sudden paralyzed panic. He gripped the pole, with arms and legs twining around it. While the pole chopped through the roof on its way down to the ground, Wes peered through the dark to try to spot the softest place to land.

That was when he realized that there was no ground at the end of the fall. It was the canyon wall.

Dumas saw him jump, just as the pole crashed amongst an avalanche of debris. It broke in two, sending the part that Wes had been holding into a long, ugly tumble along the debris-covered slope. Then there was silence.

"Hannah?" Dumas asked.

"Not sure," she said.

Then he heard her sigh, a sound that was almost a laugh.

"He's okay," she said. "I see his hands moving."

Wes pushed himself up from the pile of junk, quickly checking the damage. "Barely okay," he corrected. "The good news is, the cuts and scrapes knocked most of the splinters out. Professor?"

"The camera's working!" Dumas said with a smile.

Wes was about to ask why that mattered, now that the pole had dropped through the roof, but suddenly a deafening sound roared above them. Dumas's head snapped up just as Wes whirled, blinking up into the lights of a huge chopper. It wasn't Charlie Dewey's bird, and it was rocketing in low, right on top of him.

9

FIRE TEAM FOUR

"They saw me! We've got to go!"

Wes ran as fast as he could to get behind the crumpled house so he wouldn't give away the Professor's position. He wished he could be sure that Hannah had started the truck, but the electric motor was silent.

"Wes, wait!" Dumas grunted, but it was too late.

Having spotted an opening through some bent and cracked trees, Wes took off toward it. He hazarded a glance at the chopper as it shot past him overhead, then plunged through the thicket, burned and jagged brambles tearing at him. They were almost worse than the wires strung by the Riders, but he didn't dare slow down. The muted roar of the chopper drowned his muttered curses as he felt new scratches being added to the old ones.

"Wes, they didn't see you!" Dumas said in his ear.

"Gotta be sure," Wes replied, huffing.

The FEMA agent felt himself clamping his teeth—to prevent little cries of pain or any other sound a nearby patrol might hear. He could talk to Dumas and Hannah later—after he was sure they were all safe. He lowered his head and plunged on.

"I *am* sure, Wes!" Dumas all but boomed in his ear.

Wes ignored him. Maybe he was playing the decoy, maybe he was just running off the terror that had piled up inside of him. All he knew was that right now, he had to run.

Hannah, watching the Ford's dashboard monitor, saw nothing but brush and Wes's stabbing, clearing hands until suddenly, night sky filled the screen. She gasped as Wes slid to the edge of a precipice—a cliff at least a half a mile drop.

"Ledge!" Hannah shouted.

But Wes had already stopped, grinding his heels into the earth. He swallowed his breath and stared down at the chasm he had nearly dropped into. He ducked low, breathed hard. "Jesus."

"Wes," Dumas cut in, "it's not a patrol chopper—"

"It's evac," Wes interrupted. "I just realized." He looked up at the helicopter as it receded from him. "And I'd lay odds on where it's going."

Hannah was out of the truck and into the drainage pipe before the Professor invited her to join them. Within five minutes, their flesh pricked and raked, they lay on their stomachs beside Wes. Dumas stared into the thermal imager while Hannah used some binoculars from the truck that the Professor had modified. They were now hands-free and wrapped around her eyes like the goggles of a World War One flying ace.

From their vantage point, they stared at a clearing that had been, and was still being, leveled in the canyon. Wes felt sick, and angry. This had once been the home of dozens of different species of coniferous, deciduous, and evergreen trees. But what the Ring of Fire hadn't wrecked, the General's private army was now flattening. The trees, like the Professor's JPL colleagues, were gone.

The three observers saw chugging earthmovers and treading bulldozers, but didn't hear them. The bowl of the canyon was swallowing the sounds of the heavy machinery.

"Cunning," Dumas drawled quietly. "They found perfect, natural, organic valley acoustics. They took advantage of nature creating the opposite of the Hollywood Bowl. This noise isn't amplified, it's muffled."

"Professor," Wes said, pointing at the edge of the clearing.

Dumas looked over. A jagged crease in the mountainside looked like a fifty-foot-tall lightning bolt had torn it open from the ground up—making it narrow at the top, but big enough at the bottom to fit a train.

The Professor's face grew grave. He nodded and glanced at the thermal-imaging device.

"Chopper's landing," Hannah reported.

"That's a Sea Stallion, damn it," Wes muttered in frustration. "What's it doing out here?"

"Prepare for that question to be answered, Agent Harding," Dumas said grimly. "Prepare to not like the answer."

Wes stared at the chopper settling onto a small, slightly raised platform. It was a perfect touchdown, raising dust and dirt but no noise. In response to the landing, Riders poured from the opening in the mountain like roaches from a crack in the wall.

Wes quickly counted them, his twenty-twenty vision covering the distance. The Riders numbered an even dozen, and they surrounded the chopper as its rotors slowed. But the passenger of the helicopter wasn't Passarelles. Wes suppressed a curse as a Rider pulled open the bay door of the chopper. Earthquake survivors blinked and hunched in the opening, clinging to their belongings as they hesitantly emerged.

"Thirty," Wes said. "But that chopper holds fifty-five."

"Time must be running out for the General," Dumas said.

"What do you mean?" Hannah said.

"Careless security. There should be one guard for every two survivors. Only fifty survivors have disappeared so far. That's one or two a day, maximum, but this is thirty in one gulp."

"So," Wes said, "whatever he needs them for, it must be urgent. Professor, is he using them to dig down to the Achilles Heel? Is that your theory? Because the Riders would be stronger and better equipped to do it."

"No," the Professor said, "sadly."

Wes's attention jerked back to the scene below. The woman who had accosted him and Doc Malloy in the mess tent had just emerged from the chopper, as well as the man who had comforted her.

The Riders closed in, herding the thirty evacuees with silent shouts, sharp pointing motions, and physical threats from their assault rifles. Even at this distance, even without a scope, Wes could see the woman asking desperate questions, and the man shouting at the Riders—to cover his fear, Wes suspected. He had seen that kind of bravado before.

The survivors were pushed into a line and forced to start trudging back to the crack from which the Riders had emerged. Wes found himself grinding his teeth, his fingers clenching and unclenching.

Tragically, the Professor had been right. With one guard per two survivors, the Riders could have been utterly overcome. There were gaps in the line and that was what drew the prisoners' attention. The woman who had pleaded with Wes glanced quickly at what remained of the trees at the end of the clearing and impulsively broke from the line. The man who had backed her up also started running.

"Go!" Hannah whispered.

Wes was ready to plunge down the incline to help them when they got close enough, but even before Dumas could restrain him, two Riders turned, steadied their weapons, and pulled the triggers. The man and woman jerked in the air then flopped to the ground like marionettes with their strings snapped. Blood spattered on the dirt.

The leader of the Riders ran over. He ignored the fallen woman and stared at the man. Wes noticed Dumas rolling over onto his back just as the Rider leader inexplicably punched the head of the shooter—his own man—with the butt of his rifle.

The Professor was now holding the thermal imager in the direction of the Ford. Wes glanced at it. On the screen he saw a mass of body heat outlines, moving quickly toward them.

He grabbed Dumas and Hannah by their elbows, hauled them up, and started running. His mind furiously replayed his previous run, his memory spotting places where they might avoid the pursuers. His mind also separated and counted the heat signatures he'd seen: four. Special Operations usually consisted of two-man reconnaissance units, eight-man squads, and twelve-man platoons. Four meant a fire team, no doubt equipped with night-vision goggles and orders to shoot to kill.

Wes pushed Dumas and Hannah toward the drainage pipe, turned, and raced back to the cliff. He didn't check to see if they followed him, but he hoped they hadn't. They had to know that the only way to improve their chances was to split up.

Wes plunged back into the miserable thicket, moving as fast and as loudly as he could. He stood upright, breathed loudly, moved his arms with exaggerated chugging motions. He was a man who wanted to be noticed.

To his relief—and then fear—he heard at least one of the fire team crackling after him. Now it was just a matter of timing. Wes pretended that the brush was slowing him down. He twisted, grunted, swore, and flailed his arms whenever they encountered dead, noisy leaves. The crackling behind him picked up speed. By then Wes felt secure that the Rider wanted to grab him, not shoot him.

For a split second, he regretted what he was trying to do. Then he remembered the faces of the woman and man he had met in the mess tent.

Wes waited until he all but felt the soldier's breath on his neck. Only then did he accelerate to full speed toward the cliff edge. The crackling behind him sounded like a forest fire as the soldier, concerned that his quarry might elude him at the last second, matched then topped Wes's speed.

Wes's foot met the cliff edge. He twisted his body and spun to the left, away from the edge.

The fire team soldier did not. He yowled, his foot slipped on some loose gravel, and then he went over. The organic acoustics swallowed his scream.

Wes didn't have time to watch him hit the ground. As he turned to run back to Hannah and the Professor, another fire team soldier jumped out of the thicket. His gun barrel was aimed at the middle of Wes's chest. Luckily, Dumas's stick flew through the air and smashed into the side of the man's helmet.

There was a crack louder than a gunshot, then, as if in slow motion, the soldier followed his comrade over the cliff. The Professor's stick bounced back like a javelin hitting a steel wall, and Dumas emerged from the thicket. He caught the stick in midair as if it had been lazily lobbed to him.

Hannah was just behind him. Together, the trio ran toward the other two fire team soldiers, motionless on the ground.

"What happened to them?" Wes hissed.

"Hannah happened," Dumas replied.

Wes was about to ask how when he nearly tripped over the thick, bloody branch that had taken them down.

"I don't poke pressure points like the Prof," she whispered as they ran.

The three jumped the bodies and raced back down the drainage pipe. Dumas held back Wes as Hannah kept moving ahead. She raised her arms and with a strong yank downward revealed the Ford beneath a thin, camouflaged tarp. Wes hadn't seen it despite being just four or five feet away.

He jumped into the passenger seat as Hannah started the Ford, and the Professor scrambled amongst the gizmos on the rear compartment's floor.

"I'd guess there are four to eight men still out there searching for us," Wes said, peering through the windshield.

"Let's not find out," Hannah said and drove the Ford straight down what was left of Sunset Boulevard, superbly avoiding the cracks and crevasses. Before they got a hundred yards, there was a roar from behind and above them. Wes craned his neck to see through the upper windshield.

They were being pursued by a cross between a military all-terrain vehicle and a monster truck with giant wheels. It was soaring over a concrete barrier, dropping onto the road right at them.

"That's new." Hannah gasped, looking in the rearview mirror as she wrenched the wheel to the right.

Wes was almost thrown from the curtain-covered door. He held on, righting himself just as the Explorer smashed through an already broken store window and sped out the other side. The monster truck slammed into the roadway right next to them so Wes could clearly see its powerful struts and shocks absorb the landing. It bounced up a few feet, its massively treaded tires shrieking. Then it tried to land on them again.

Hannah wrenched the wheel left, barely dodging the crash, then fishtailed back onto the roadway. The monster truck was still on them.

"I was expecting this from Passarelles!" Dumas shouted, sitting in a lotus position on the floor, furiously fiddling with some device on his lap.

"You *were*?" Wes shouted.

"Know your enemy," Dumas replied, "but more than that, anticipate your enemy's wish list and prepare. That beast is perfect for the post-apocalyptic terrain! Four-link suspension!"

"And it looks like four feet of clearance, plus a seriously supercharged engine," Wes added.

"Probably fueled on alcohol," the Professor called.

"We won't be able to keep ahead for long!" Hannah shouted. She was twisting the wheel back and forth, her eyes darting from the side mirrors to the windshield. "What about the tires? Any way we can—"

"No, those are Terra tires!" Wes yelled, as one came perilously close to the Explorer's fender. "We had them on fertilizer spreaders at my granddad's farm! They can take anything."

The Professor's fingers were still dancing across a squat machine. He seemed to be ignoring the snarling beast bearing down on them, but then his head snapped up, his eyes bright. He held up the thing in his hands. It looked like an old-fashioned typewriter case.

"You can do it, Hannah," he urged. "Just a few seconds more!"

"Till what?" Wes demanded.

In response, Dumas slid back, threw open the rear curtain, and thrust the machine toward the looming monstrosity. The device in his hand beeped, then suddenly emitted a torrent of beeps. The monster truck bounced at them—then skidded, as if all of its wheels had locked at once.

"Gun it, Hannah!" Dumas boomed, holding the machine out the back of the Ford.

The monster truck lost speed, then lost control altogether and flipped over. The Explorer lurched ahead, sending Dumas almost perpendicular to the ground. Wes flung himself back and grabbed the Professor's lab coat, tugged, and brought Dumas almost upright. Then Dumas embraced the passenger seat from behind as Hannah sped straight forward. There was no guessing which way the beast would roll, no time to guess where to steer. Hannah hoped the Professor's batteries were as good as he said they were.

One of the massive tires slammed down on the road just inches from the Explorer, but then distance opened between their truck and the beast, and rapidly increased. The monster truck smashed down a final time and slid to a stop, a twisted, silent wreck.

"Those things all have kill switches," Dumas said placidly. "Three, in fact. It's so easy for a driver to lose control, they're necessary."

Wes grinned as he climbed back into the passenger seat. "So you engaged a little electronic warfare, I'm guessing."

"Oh yes." The Professor held up the device. "Once my kill switch killer finds the right wavelength, it can lock on and take over." He looked upon it with fondness. "I can modify it to control the computers of most modern cars."

Wes peered out the windshield. "How much farther to the parking lot?" he asked Hannah.

"Just a couple of minutes," she replied. "Why?"

"Those monster trucks usually just hold one person, right?" Wes asked.

"Two, tops," Hannah answered. In response to Wes's glance, she added, "My fiancé was a car nerd."

"Four on the cliff," Wes murmured. "Two here, maybe . . ."

As if reading his mind, Dumas shook his head. "If there had been others close by, they would have pounced already."

"Not necessarily," Wes replied. "Not if Passarelles took over when the fire team failed to report." He scanned the area ahead for alternate routes but could find none. This part of the make-shift road seemed to hem them in. "He's too smart to pounce. He would have thought ahead and—"

The Ford hit the final turn before the Hollywood Bowl junction.

"Stop!" Wes shouted. "Stop now!"

Hannah slammed the brake to the floor. The Professor slid

across the back of the Explorer and had to grab a side curtain to keep from falling out.

Two concrete wedges were blocking what was left of the road. Two more monster trucks flanked them, accompanied by a flatbed truck and three Humvees. Every vehicle hit their headlight high beams at the same time, filling the area and the Ford with blinding light. Then came the bullets.

Hannah screamed and ducked. Wes's hands jerked up as assault rifle shells slammed into the windshield, pumping out of the MP7s at a thousand rounds per minute. The 12mm cartridges tore into the vehicle's steel body, filling the interior with a deafening sound of punctures and ricochets.

Wes pulled Hannah further down and clambered over her to grab the wheel. He stomped on the accelerator, and the lights and bullets seemed to spin around them as the engines of the waiting vehicles roared in. Wes scanned the blur of their surroundings, made a split-second decision—and then they were weightless. The only way out he saw was a sheer twenty-foot drop onto De Longpre Avenue.

The Explorer slammed down hard, and the Professor slapped around the cabin like a dropped squid. The vehicle kept going, Wes tucked hard into the driver's seat, his foot jammed on the accelerator, his hands tight on the wheel. Hannah lay beside him, unconscious, her face bloody, eyes shut.

Looming over De Longpre Avenue was a crumbling concrete blockhouse covered in razor wire, which had been used as a detention center for overpopulated state prisons.

"Keep going!" Dumas yelled. "Full speed!"

"Are you nuts?!" Wes shouted.

"I'd like it to look that way, son!"

Wes met the Professor's eyes for one moment. Then he shook his head but aimed the Ford directly at the blockhouse. As he yelled in a mix of euphoria and panic, the Ford Explorer smashed into the cracked side wall of the building, sending concrete and iron shrapnel everywhere. The second floor and ceiling of the blockhouse gave way, smashing the front of the Explorer. The specially modified vehicle had brought down a behemoth the earthquake hadn't quite been able to vanquish.

"Hurry!" Dumas said.

Gathering Hannah gently in his arms, Wes followed the Professor's lead.

Less than a minute later, the three Humvees and two monster trucks roared up to a stop. Gun-toting Riders poured out. But before they could reach the back of the Ford, it exploded in their faces.

10

TERRAPHAGE

Wes carried Hannah the entire way, cold dread stabbing him every time he glanced at the blood on her face. He didn't know if she'd been hit by a bullet or if his driving had knocked her out or worse, and though he'd had no other options with the Ford, he still felt guilty.

The Professor was staggering beside him, less than superhuman for the first time since Wes had met him. He seemed to be struggling to breathe, gasping a little.

"Broken rib?" Wes asked.

Dumas only shook his head, and Wes let it go for now, adding just a "Thank you." The Professor waved it away.

Just before the crash, Dumas had reached forward and pulled Wes down over Hannah on the SUV floor between the seats and the dashboard. Just after the crash, he had hauled them back into the rear compartment. Ripping a recessed trapdoor panel off the rear compartment's floor, he slipped Hannah and Wes onto the ground beneath the vehicle, then used his staff to prod and shove them clear of the SUV. Now they were inside the building that was groaning and screeching all around them. Wes hoisted Hannah and hurried after Dumas to an opening opposite the crash site. They stepped clear of the building just as their pursuers pulled up to it.

The Professor frantically dug around in his lab coat pockets and came up with something that looked like a car-locking device. But when Dumas pressed the recessed button, Wes didn't hear a reassuring beep. He heard an explosion, and he felt the concussion through the wall, but he was already rocketing toward the tunnels.

It was only after the explosion that the Professor started gasping for breath.

Wes hated to add another problem for the man but, "Professor," he said. "Hannah needs help as close as you can find it. The library might be too far away."

Suddenly Dumas straightened up, gave Wes a smile, took a sharp turn, and picked up his pace. "Sensible assessment," he said, his voice and breath normalized. "I've got just the spot."

To Wes's surprise, they hurried less than fourteen hundred feet to the remains of the Cinerama Dome on Sunset Boulevard. The moonlight revealed that its majestic geodesic roof had been split like a grapefruit.

Once they were inside, Dumas guided them to the large projection booth, where Wes laid Hannah on the floor. Almost at once they were joined by Jane, holding Bunter. She released the cat and knelt next to the unconscious young woman.

Out of the blue, Dumas said quietly, "I think a lot."

He absently gave a small new rustic age wave at his own prodigious forehead. The woman automatically mirrored him.

"He not only thinks," Jane told Wes, "he thinks ahead. Told me to be here, just in case." Then she went back to examining Hannah. "No internal bleeding or permanent damage," she informed them.

So somewhere in her hacker background, she'd learned some seriously efficient nursing, Wes pondered. The Professor had surrounded himself with the best of the best—or the best had seen good reason to shun the organized relief effort, Wes remembered. The latter was looking more likely with every new attack the General leveled at them.

"You've learned the hard way not to hope for the best," Wes directed at Dumas.

Dumas nodded. "Instead, I plan for the worst."

"Like installing a self-destruct device in Hannah's ride," Wes said.

"Like installing a self-destruct device in Hannah's ride." The Professor grinned.

Wes looked from the Professor to Bunter, who lay at Hannah's side. He had been surprised when Jane showed up with the cat in her arms, but now he was grateful.

"They must be searching for us like crazy," Wes muttered.

Dumas shook his head, wandering toward the projector. "The Riders are still few in number and being stretched increasingly thin. That's why the General is being bolder in waylaying the evacked survivors."

That reminded Wes of the deaths he had witnessed, making him feel sick.

"You need any first aid?" Jane asked Wes.

"I don't think so," he said. "Just some bruises and sprains. And splinters. And ripped-up skin."

She smiled. "To me, that's the sign of a *good* day."

Wes looked over at the Professor fiddling with the projector. His face was so intent that Wes doubted a gunshot would distract him, so Wes moved toward Hannah. He hadn't gone two steps when her eyes opened. Her left hand rose to rest on Bunter and, to Wes's surprise, her right hand searched out his. He dropped to his knees, entwining their fingers. It wasn't exactly a romantic touch, but it was warm and welcome, and he was happy for it.

"We're even," she said quietly.

He was trying to figure out what she meant when she explained.

"You woke up and saw me. I wake up to see you. That's how I knew I wasn't dead. Oh," she groaned, trying to sit up. "Did you get the number of that truck?"

And just like that, the feeling Wes thought they were sharing was gone, as if he'd dropped down on De Longpre all over again.

"Yeah," he chuckled to cover the jolt. "It's Minus-One."

He helped her lie back down more comfortably, then updated her on what had happened after she was knocked out. Hannah glanced at the Professor with gratitude, then gazed around the projection booth.

"Here's irony," she said. "This is the first place I ever saw a movie. My mom brought me here when I was six."

"Your folks make it out?" Wes asked gently.

She seemed confused by the question for a moment, then nodded. "Oh. Yeah. They're safe in Kansas. I was the one who wanted to try to make it in the big city after visiting here with my mom." She looked up at him. "You?"

"My folks were just up the road. Ventura County."

"Are they all right?"

Wes shook his head. "They were long gone before the Ring of Fire. I was a freshman in college. My father had a massive heart attack at the wheel. Mom died with him in the crash." He tried to shrug, but couldn't. "You know what's ironic? My father wanted me to find a job where I could help people."

"You know what? You've got one," Hannah pointed out.

That caught Wes off guard. He suddenly felt very close to his father . . . and his new friends.

Their heads turned in unison when they heard a polite cough. Professor Dumas was looking down at them from a stool beside the projector.

"Something you should see," he told them regretfully.

Wes helped Hannah to her feet, and they stepped to either side of Dumas as he put on his magic lantern show. He had plugged a six-by-one-inch rectangular battery into the projector unit, which he had removed and was now holding like a movie camera. The battery allowed him to send light through the lens onto a white towel that Jane had brought, which she was now holding up to catch the Professor's flickering images.

"The bug you placed, Wes, nearly at the cost of your life, is doing you proud. It sucked the security footage dry, and it's been feeding the data to processors back at my office. Rick and the others have been watching the footage and forwarded this."

The Professor nodded toward the towel. Wes and Hannah moved closer so they could study the images. What they saw looked like the Coldwater Canyon mountainside sprouting a growth. First it was flat, and then the landscape seemed to swell.

"The first image was from January 20, 1994," Dumas informed them.

"Three days after the Northridge quake!" Wes realized.

Dumas nodded. "The second is from last year. Before the Ring of Fire erupted."

Hannah looked back at the Professor. "What is it? It's not natural."

Dumas shook his head. "No, it definitely is not. I think it's evidence of construction inside the Coldwater mountains long before the General took over the Los Angeles basin." The import of that statement hit Hannah and Wes like electric shocks. "I told you he's been working on this for a while," the Professor reminded them. "I just didn't know how far along he had gotten."

"My god, what are they doing with the survivors up there?" Hannah wondered.

"Whatever it is," Wes said, "Passarelles is more than willing to kill for it."

A muffled, tuneless tone suddenly filled the air.

"What?" Wes said, as perplexed as anyone.

The noise kept coming, though. Suddenly galvanized, Wes stabbed a hand into his pocket and yanked out what he had thought was a broken smartphone. It vibrated in his hand thanks to the operational FEMA tower. Its glass casing may have been shattered, but its workings were not. Behind the web of cracks on its face, an alert stated who was calling him. They all saw the name and the friendly, smiling face in the photo.

Doctor Thomas Malloy.

The ringtone continued. Wes glanced at Dumas but didn't wait to read permission or dissuasion on his face. He pressed the green "connect" button, carefully so as not to cut his finger on the shattered glass. Then he cautiously placed the device near his ear.

"Hello?"

He heard two hoarse words that sounded like they were being torn out of the speaker's soul.

"Help me."

The cavalry took an hour to arrive, which worked since Doc needed time to cover his tracks.

"I'm behind the observatory," Malloy had assured Wes, gasping and rushed. "The General isn't here, but some of his men are still around, so I can't go far. I certainly can't get away, and I need to."

"Why?" Wes asked.

"I'm on the ledge. Just get here as fast as you can," he pleaded, then disconnected.

Wes was determined to leave at once, and the Professor concurred. Only Hannah dissented.

"Are you sure it's not a trap?" she asked Dumas.

"Of course not!" the Professor replied. "But when you're fighting lions, sometimes you must go to them."

"Not recklessly," she pointed out.

"Are we ever?" he asked, handing a fresh bug to Wes.

"Well, we took the Explorer, let's see—off a road, into a building, then blew it up."

"And we survived," Dumas reminded her, behind a wagging finger.

■ ■ ■

The tunnel network got Wes to the "Warren of Oaks," a labyrinth of roads all named for that tree—Red Oak, High Oak, Spreading Oak, Valley Oak, Park Oak, Spring Oak, Green Oak, and many more. They were all cuddling the edge of Griffith Park, around the side of the command camp.

Skirting what was left of Western Canyon Road brought Wes to a long disused access path, seared by fire on one side and half buried by landslides on the other. He nearly had to go on all fours to scale the veritable mountain there, but as the first slivers of sunrise began to crack the horizon, he reached Doc Malloy on the ledge of the craggy precipice.

Wes had to hand it to his FEMA superior. The remote location was precarious but also well designed for secrecy. Its peak blocked all view of the observatory, and the only thing visible in all the other directions was devastation. Malloy was doing his best to keep the cavalry—his friend and protégé—safe and unseen.

Malloy's back was turned to Wes, but when Doc turned, Wes's breath wheezed out of him in shock. He had expected his mentor to look concerned and conflicted, but the man he faced looked like a long-term insomniac. He appeared at least twenty years older.

"Doc?" Wes stepped forward, his hand out.

"Stay back," Malloy wheezed, sidling away. His eyes were sunken and red-rimmed, his jowls practically flapping in the wind and his mouth slackly slavering.

"Not gonna happen," Wes said, reaching for his elbow. "Come on, I'm getting you out of here—"

"No!" the man screeched, wrenching his arm away and all but slamming himself against the landslide-created cliff. "Stay away from me!"

Wes froze, trying to comprehend what was happening. Rescuing, he could do that. He was also prepared for Doc to be bait for a trap, involuntarily of course. Wes still rebelled at the idea that Doc could be working with Passarelles of his own free will. Now he didn't know what to think. All he knew was that something was horribly wrong with the man who had become like a father to him. Even though Malloy had failed to defend him from Passarelles earlier, that might have been because something much larger was going on. Something Wes had to help him through.

"Why did you call me here?" Wes asked softly. "What is going on?"

The voice, when it came, was almost imperceptible, sounding like scraping sand. "You must . . . listen to me . . . while I can still . . . speak!"

"All right, Doc. Of course."

Spittle flecked the man's white mouth. "Passarelles—came with the last orbit," Malloy gasped. "Twenty-one years ago. He's worked since then—found the target point!"

"Found what? And what 'orbit'?"

Malloy appeared not to have heard. Or if he had, the words weren't registering. "He got the Joint Chiefs out here for a meeting. They're all . . . all buried . . . in Coldwater . . ."

Wes was staggered and confused. Not just by the words, but how they sounded. Something was bubbling in Malloy's throat, as if he were gargling. Something awful was invading his eyes, but they weren't bloodshot. The cracks in the pupils weren't red, but black.

"Doc, I saw what Passarelles is building inside Coldwater Canyon, in the mountain. I know he's looking for the seismic Achilles Heel."

"Yes," Malloy choked. "But you need the why! I would have . . . told you before . . . but you were too . . . easy to get. He would have . . . gotten you."

"He's been trying," Wes said grimly.

Malloy gave out a horrible groan and started shaking violently in some sort of seizure.

"Doc!" Wes started to cry. "Doc—"

Malloy slammed his back against the wall of the dirt cliff, as far away as he could get from Wes. His fingers clawed the earth behind him, digging as though he were trying to find the heart of the cliff. As Wes watched, Malloy's face started to contort. Improbably, monstrously, the man's face started to *expand*, as if inflated from inside.

Wes wanted to yell, to recoil, to run, but he couldn't—he wouldn't. His mentor, his friend, was going through hell to tell him something. The words, when they came, were slurred, as if Doc had just suffered a stroke.

"He needs this place—this planet—for *his kind*!"

"His kind?" Wes echoed with alarm. "He wants a military dictatorship?"

"*No!*" Malloy howled, his throat swelling, his chest ballooning, his fingers clawing the air as black blood began to pour out of his eyes, ears, nostrils, mouth, and from under his fingernails. "His species—his *alien* species—Terraphage!"

Before Wes could react, Malloy threw himself to the ground and, open-armed, literally clamped onto the dirt. His arms dug furiously, and his mouth opened and shut feverishly.

"Down!" a voice commanded. "Get down, on his level. Watch carefully!"

It was the Professor, talking through Wes's bug. Wes immediately crouched, not caring what risk there might be. He stared as Malloy's eyes filled with blackness and expanded, just barely contained in their sockets.

"What do you see?" Dumas demanded.

"His mouth," Wes said. "Christ, his mouth—"

Wes concentrated on Malloy's distended lips, told the others what he saw. With each quick, gasping breath, the man's jawline was getting bigger. Wes suddenly noticed a sharp movement of Malloy's right hand. It grabbed a fistful of dirt and shoved it into his mouth.

Wes felt like crawling backward as the black eyes locked with his, as the thing that was once Thomas Malloy fervently chewed on the earth in his mouth. He choked, then swallowed, mud dripping down his chin. Something between a smile and a grimace twisted his lips.

"*They—made—me join them,*" Malloy gasped. "*They're inside me!*"

"Doc," Wes pleaded mournfully. "No."

Malloy's answer wheezed through his teeth, using the man's larynx as a vessel: "Doc. Is. Dead."

Then Malloy's body shot forward, his blackened hands clamping onto Wes's throat. Their bodies hurtled toward the ledge, Wes's head hanging over, Malloy on top of him, squeezing with unearthly strength.

"Your whole world will shatter!" the possessed man croaked. "Most will die. The rest will be harvested!"

Wes clawed at the hands on his throat as he gasped for breath, kicked frenetically, feeling the capillaries in his eyes starting to rupture. But as he struggled against the creature's supernatural strength, he saw something change. The blackness of Malloy's bulging eyes began to swirl milky, cloudy white.

"No!" a voice screamed, but this time it sounded like Doc again.

The pressure on Wes's larynx eased just enough so he could breathe, and he saw something in the corner of Malloy's right eye. Something clear.

A teardrop fell onto Wes's cheek.

"No!" Doc wept, then sprang up off Wes's body, scrambled to his feet, and screeched at the sky. "I will not kill my own!"

Then with one certain step, Doc Thomas Malloy hurled himself off the edge of the precipice.

11

DIRT EATERS

Wes rolled over just in time to see Doc Malloy's body plummet toward the rocky incline, bounce, slam again, and then slide the rest of the way to flat earth. Wes was oblivious to the brown and dark blue Volkswagen bus that skidded up alongside him. All he could think about was Doc . . . the Doc who had mentored him, become his second father, talked him through the worst nights after Wes had been cataloguing earthquake corpses, who put his arm around him while Wes cried—not the thing that had just tried to kill him.

Wes had no cognizance of getting down the slope. The next thing he knew, he was scrambling across the incline to where Doc's body lay, reaching out protectively for it. The man was dead, wide-eyed, broken and bent in ugly ways. Wes wanted to fix him so at least he *looked* like a man—

"Don't touch him!" Dumas warned as he followed Wes.

"Go away!" Wes barked, focused on the body.

"Damnit, I mean it!" Doc said, his big hand out, grabbing for the FEMA agent.

Wes yanked out of reach. "I meant what I said too!" he yelled back, wrenching around in place so he was kneeling between Malloy's body and the approaching Professor. "You manipulative, lying—"

He wasn't able to finish because Hannah was suddenly there on her knees beside him. He had never seen her so intensely present and caring. Her gentle manner shut him up.

"Wes, it's okay," she said softly. "He's just trying to protect you, to protect *us*. Really."

Wes relaxed slightly, letting go of the horror of what he'd witnessed, the grotesqueness of the broken body at his feet. He turned to where Dumas had been, but the Professor was already past them, hovering cautiously over Malloy's body.

"It's too late, he's dead," Wes said.

"Be grateful for that," the Professor said.

"What?" Wes was about to lunge at the insensitive old man when Hannah grabbed his sleeve and shook her head.

"Let him be, Wes."

Huffing like a bull, Wes watched as the Professor pulled another device from a lab coat pocket.

"Yes," Dumas said, distracted, holding what looked like a remote control device over Malloy's head. "Son, I'm sorry for my seeming callousness, but there's no more time to be treading softly."

"What are you talking about?"

"You heard him," Dumas reminded Wes, pointing at Doc. "You saw it. There's something inside him. Something unnatural. Something alien—which might still be alive."

"*'Terraphage,'*" Wes muttered. "That's what he called it. *Terra* means 'dirt.'"

"And *'phage'* means 'eat.' Latin, loose translation. So, 'eat dirt.'" Dumas lowered his head to peer inside Malloy's mouth. "Didn't scream as he fell," he muttered to himself. "Killed instantly? Or didn't feel the impacts. No nervous system—"

"Doc seemed to be saying it's an alien invasion of some kind," Wes interrupted him. "I don't understand. They want to conquer Earth—to eat it?"

"There's time for explanations later," Dumas said. "He was also talking about shattering the world, which I take to mean that after the Achilles Heel is set off, any survivors will be harvested."

"But Doctor Malloy doesn't look like the corpses we've found," Hannah said.

"Not yet," Dumas replied, turning toward Wes and Hannah. "I think it's safe enough. Help me get Doc's body into my bus. Then we'll—"

Before he could finish his instructions, MP7 assault rifle rounds slammed into Malloy's corpse and the Professor's office-on-wheels.

Dumas leaped and the others fell back, looking up to see a line of Riders climbing over the peak of the landslide. Standing on the ledge sixty feet above them was General J.C. Passarelles, flanked by a man holding a grenade launcher and another holding a flamethrower.

"Run!" Wes cried, already in motion himself. Understanding that they needed to split the Riders' targets, he pushed Hannah west around the base of the landslide, and Dumas east, then took off to the south. Each runner tried to get as many trees, mounds, and thickets between them and the guns as possible. Despite their heavy breathing, despite their boots crunching on rock and exposed roots, they all heard Passarelles's word, like a thunderclap:

"Fire!"

Flame licked down the incline like an impossibly long tongue, but not at them: the fire consumed Malloy's body in an 1800-degree flash. At the same moment the grenade launcher bucked, and a stream of yellow-white streaked across the top of the landslide and punched the Volkswagen. It jerked, leaped, and exploded in a crystalline ball of glass, metal, and gizmo shrapnel.

Wes was hurled from his feet by the concussive shock wave, sending him tumbling down a hill toward Western Canyon and the base of Mount Hollywood. Hannah and Dumas looked back without stopping; they knew they could do nothing for him except stay safe themselves. And that was increasingly a challenge as Riders began to jump, fall, skid, and roll down the landslide, doing their best to aim their weapons.

Dumas counted eight of them over his shoulder—eleven including the General, flamethrower, and grenade launcher—more than enough to round up, or mow down, the desperate trio. Two went after Hannah, two after the Professor, and three loped toward the stunned, scrambling FEMA agent.

Wes's vision cleared just as the three Riders got to within twenty feet of him. He willed his body to spring up and take off, but it was not listening to him. All his arms and legs did was scrabble in the dirt.

"Hey, remember me, asshole?" laughed one, bringing his MP7 to bear. It was the lead man back at the collapsing hotel—the one who had accused Wes of killing the soldiers. "Guess I get to kill you after all!"

Wes peered down the barrel of the gun, ready to try jumping away, when the Rider suddenly spasmed, his assault rifle spinning out of his hands. As the Rider fell, his limbs still twitching violently, Wes could see behind the fallen man a series of what he could only describe as "fire-streaks" slicing from the sky. Each hit a Rider dead on. And each Rider seemed to suffer a seizure before collapsing.

Passarelles's laughter turned to bellowing rage, before all his noise was swallowed up by another noise—a sound Wes knew well. He watched Charlie Dewey's copter rise up from behind the landslide-created peak. The Chief Warrant Officer was at the stick, but seated beside him, shouldering some sort of metal pipe, was Dumas's aide-de-camp, Rick. Wes had made Charlie part of the plan for Doc's cavalry, on call nearby if needed. Dumas must have hit the panic button on his comm with Rick as soon as Passarelles appeared.

The Professor, Hannah, and Wes stood to see the General stab his forefinger at the copter. But before the grenade launcher could reload, Rick pointed the end of the pipe at the Rider raising the tip of the flamethrower toward him. The flame only got six feet before a fire-streak knocked the Rider down, sending the General and his remaining Rider scrambling away. Within seconds they were out of sight, vanishing as fast as they had appeared.

"Son of a bitch!" Wes cheered.

But no one was under the misapprehension that they had time to relax. Wes and Hannah did, however, have time to hug their rescuers with relief and gratitude once Charlie had nimbly touched down.

"What the hell have you been doing, man?" Wes asked.

"Ostensibly, making reconnaissance runs. In fact, looking for you." He nodded toward Rick. "Found this guy instead, and he filled me in."

"He liked the cut of my jib," Rick joked, raising what he cradled in his arms. "Had to find out what it was, when he was sure I wasn't gonna shoot him."

They *all* wanted to ask about the weapon Rick held—*that* hadn't been part of Wes's plan—but they suddenly realized that the Professor was not with them. Looking around, they saw him moving from the charred body of Malloy to the charred chassis of his mobile office before, finally, standing over the still form of the Rider who had repeatedly tried to kill Wes.

"I loved that van," they heard him say as they ran over to him. He looked at his aide. "What did you have the Electrolight set to?"

Rick raised his eyebrows and half smiled. "I don't know, Professor. I just pointed and pushed the recessed trigger button. You told me that was all it would need, remember?"

Dumas nodded darkly. "Then it was at nearly full power." He nudged the Rider's body with his toe. "He'll be out for quite some time then." He looked at Wes and Hannah, answered their querying eyes. "It's the human physiology version of my car-killer device. Overloads the internal nervous system." He looked from the fallen Riders back to the husks of the van and Malloy. "Clever General. Got rid of any evidence and my armory first."

"Evidence?" Wes echoed. "Evidence of what?"

"A new horror, perpetrated on people who have seen horror enough," Dumas replied. "Human-Terraphage hybrids." Dumas turned sharply to his aide. "Are the others ready?"

Rick nodded.

"Then lead my friends here to a place of relative safety. Take them all the way back to the Yakima River if you have to."

"Just a hot second there," Charlie said. "Human-Terra-what?"

"Human-alien hybrids," Dumas explained. "Doc was invaded. Others will be harvested." He looked at Wes and Hannah. "Can you guess for what?"

Hannah was the quickest to realize. "The only organ missing from those splayed-open corpses," she said with horror. "The lungs."

"Correct," Dumas said. "It would be presumptive and naïve to assume that aliens would arrive on this planet, on *any* planet, with all the body parts they need to survive . . . especially in a microbe-rich environment like Earth. So, yes. The lungs. Use them, gum them up with gases and toxins if you're working underground, then rip out some more." Dumas turned to Dewey. "What's the status at East 101?"

"Not so good," Charlie said succinctly. The pilot turned to Wes. "I didn't have time to tell you. After you amscrayed, the General locked down every facility like a straight-up lunatic. Fences sealed. Two Sea Stallions crammed with survivors and they evacked 'em to God-knows-where."

Hannah and Wes shared a glance. They knew where—the crack in the mountain in Coldwater Canyon. And Wes knew that meant at least a hundred new hostages, if some trigger-happy Rider didn't get them first.

"All the other copter rotors were sabotaged," Charlie continued. "No Riders in sight. But anyone who tried to leave the camp, or approach the fence, snipers took them out—snipers no one's been able to pinpoint. My rotorheads told me the survivors who remained got scared, then hunkered down like prisoners, which now they are. At least there's still enough food." He looked back to Dumas. "No comm now either, in or out, just shut the hell down. We can't get help from, or give warning to, anyone, anywhere. No way to tell Washington."

Wes was flabbergasted. Charlie hadn't mentioned any of this when they arranged the plan earlier, although admittedly, Wes hadn't given him any time to. "Why do I get the feeling this is just an opening gambit?" Wes directed toward the Professor.

Dumas frowned, rubbing the AA-battery-sized communicator between his thumb and forefinger. "Because you're learning the ways and means of Passarelles."

"How did you get out?" Hannah asked Charlie.

"He was never in," said Rick with a knowing grin.

Charlie smiled back and nodded. "The moment I left command camp, I stayed out. My cousin going missing, the Riders going postal, the way Passarelles was double-talking to you, it was all just noxious. So, Wes, when you were thrown into the forbidden zone, I got well and truly gone."

"Lucky for us," Wes said. "But we'd better set our next move before Passarelles sets his."

Dumas nodded and said, "Rick, time to go."

The young man did as instructed, tossing Dumas the fire-streak pipe and running toward Mount Hollywood. "We'll take good care of Bunter," he promised Hannah from over his shoulder.

"If he lets you," she called back.

"Won't Passarelles's troopers pick him off?" Wes asked.

"Doubt it." Dumas frowned as he examined the pipe. "The General thought he had us. He didn't. Now he can't afford to waste any more time or soldiers. So he'll just wait for us to come to him."

"And we're doing that?" Charlie asked dubiously.

Dumas leaned on his shepherd's staff and pinned the pilot with a deadly serious stare. "That's exactly what we're going to do. Make no mistake, Chief Warrant Officer Dewey. General J.C. Passarelles wants to rip this planet open like a melon and grow nasty little things inside us with the seeds."

"But what can we do?" Dewey asked incredulously, looking after Rick as if he desperately wanted to join him. "With one chopper and a bunch of demoralized hostages? The guns would cut them down before they got within fifty feet."

"You have any more of those?" Hannah asked hopefully, pointing at the Electrolight pipe.

"Sadly, no," the Professor replied, tossing it to Hannah. "This was a prototype, untested before Rick used it." He looked over to Wes, who had already started moving down into the trees. "Where are you going?"

Wes stopped. "Coldwater," he said.

Dumas shook his head. "Library. You and Hannah head back there and find anything that could be useful in a fight."

Hannah's surprised face matched Wes's affronted expression. "While you take on Passarelles by yourself?"

"Who said anything about taking on the General by myself?" Dumas cocked a thumb at Dewey. "He's taking me back to the Jet Propulsion Laboratory. With Passarelles escalating his operation, we need to find *his* Achilles Heel."

12

ISO

"I am?" Charlie asked skeptically.

"You are," Dumas assured him. "The General had a special building constructed there, then killed all my friends and tried to kill me."

"He did?" Charlie said with somewhat less skepticism.

Hannah confirmed the Professor's statement with a nod.

The Professor went on. "Tackling him directly inside Coldwater would be a hundred-to-one suicide mission. But that special JPL lab might be where the answer lies."

"That's a pretty big 'might be,' Professor," Wes worried. "Even for you."

The smile Dumas bestowed on Harding was the kindest he had seen for days. "Your granddad probably spent his life dealing with invasive species on his farm. So I bet he would say you can't do squat until you know what kind of bug you're dealing with. And you can't get that kind of information by asking the bug. If the key to beating General Passarelles is anywhere, it'll be in that lab."

Wes still looked doubtful, but Charlie shrugged.

"*I'm* convinced," he said simply, then started to climb back into his copter.

Wes knew there was no arguing once Dewey had made a decision, so he quickly joined Hannah. The Professor gave them both reassuring nods, then climbed into the copter, sitting where Rick had been. He maneuvered the shepherd's staff between his legs then looked down just as Hannah held the Electrolight up to him, as if presenting a sword to a revered samurai.

Dewey's eyes lit up at the sight of it, and he quickly reached across the Professor to grab it. But Dumas neatly prevented him with a nimble twist of his stick. Not only did the top half deflect Dewey's arm, the bottom simultaneously pressed the pipe back into Hannah's hands.

"I'm certain it will be more useful to you than to us," he assured her. "I know where we're going, what we're likely to encounter. Who knows what *you'll* find on your way back to HQ?"

She withdrew the offering and nodded gratefully.

Wes stepped back, and they studied Dewey's takeoff technique as the chopper lifted, drifted into a clearing between the gnarled, uprooted, and burnt trees, then shot up as if yanked by a puppeteer.

Hannah and Wes watched it head northeast toward Pasadena in the gathering sunrise. Despite each other's company, they had never felt more alone. The two took a moment to scan their surroundings in silence, then cautiously headed back toward the tunnel network. The area was quiet, an eerie counterpoint to the loud, ferocious firefight.

That didn't make them less watchful, however, or their minds less full. Several times Wes thought Hannah was going to say something, and several times Hannah thought Wes was about to speak, but then both went back to watching intently and thinking their way into dead ends.

For Wes's part, Hannah was still a deep and frustrating mystery. She was desirable and she seemed to be warming to him as a sister—nothing more. There was a strong element of frustration in that, but at the same time, he liked being around her. However it went, he'd let her run the show.

As if I have a choice, he thought wryly.

It seemed like forever, but they had only gone a few hundred yards before Hannah finally broke the silence.

"How do you feel?" she asked. "I mean, about—"

"Doc?" he said.

She nodded.

Wes shook his head. "I can't go there right now." He paused, then added, "But I'm also proud of him. What it took to fight through whatever was in control of him . . ."

"I know," Hannah agreed.

"What about you?" Wes asked. "Any thoughts?"

"I've been thinking about Doc too," she admitted. "I haven't been around many Eagle Scouts, but if your friend wanted you to earn your save-the-world badge, then there had to be a way to do it, right? He must've believed you could."

"Good point," Wes agreed.

"But it hit me another way," Hannah went on. "I've never much believed in anything. I had my life, my boyfriend, my animals. But the world beyond that? Didn't care. Yet here I am, *doing* something. What he did back there . . . that only makes me want to do it better."

Wes gave her a crooked smile. "I don't think anyone could ask for a better legacy."

She smiled back. "One thing more," she said.

"What's that?"

"We're not going back to the library, are we?"

"Yes, we are," Wes answered. "Probably for a few minutes." He scoured the horizon for any sign of trouble. "Just long enough to see if there are any more of those." He nodded at the Electrolight. "Or something like it."

They trudged in silence until they reached the mouth of the tunnel network. Making sure they weren't seen, they slipped inside. Hannah stopped there, bestowing on Wes a smile more sly than kind.

"Hey, Wes?" she asked quietly. "After the library"—she held the Electrolight tighter—"how would you feel about a little hundred-to-one hike?"

By all rights, Dewey and Dumas should have been dead a dozen times over, set upon by jet fighters or other choppers and blown out of the sky. But Passarelles had his secrets, and he didn't want any of his own fliers stumbling upon them. The less anyone could see from the air, or the ground, the better he obviously liked it, so he let the sole chopper pass unmolested.

To Dumas, the very emptiness and stillness around and below them was a shrieking alarm. It signaled that the General was applying everything he had toward his goal as fast as he could.

"Site spotted," Charlie murmured in his ear.

Dumas looked in the direction Charlie was nodding. The remarkable pilot had come in lower and faster than Dumas had thought possible, darting and hiding behind hills, groves, and rubble. Almost before the Professor knew it, he was looking down at what was left of La Cañada Flintridge, California—home of the California Institute of Technology's NASA research and development center.

Dumas remembered when he had first approached it all those years ago. The mountains beyond, flanked by hills, made a natural, rocky, two-hundred-acre floodplain basin for the federally owned property. It was as if the land itself was holding up the shining campus in its palm for all to admire. The Professor had marveled at the ten sports fields on the north side near the Children's and Wellness Centers. Just beyond were the theater, art museum, and science buildings, along with one of his favorite places, the Sojourner Truth Library. Now, it all looked like a burnt, black question mark scarred in the ruptured ground.

"All that knowledge," Dumas muttered. "All that experience —lost."

"Not all of it," Dewey said. "Just disbursed to new homes. Where to now?"

Dumas pointed straight ahead. "In the middle of the crest. Building Five-O."

That got a quick glance from the pilot. "You're kidding, right?"

Dumas shook his head. "One day the JPL campus had forty-nine buildings, not counting parking lots and garages. Then seemingly the next, it had fifty—a building that was never on any map."

Dewey peered ahead. "All I see is scorched earth."

Dumas nodded. "Yes. Look for the flat, shining, rectangular scorched earth."

As soon as he said it, Charlie saw it. There, sitting on the seam between the campus and hills beyond, was Building 50.

Dewey landed quickly and neatly, finding the one patch of level ground in a mass of ruins. By the time the pilot had unstrapped himself and hopped out, the Professor was already making his way to the dark bunker of concrete and steel. With his long, decorated lab coat and walking stick, to Dewey's eyes he looked like Moses.

Carefully studying the ground to make sure he didn't trip, the pilot noticed strange markings in the dirt all around the edges of the building's base. If he didn't know better, he could've sworn it looked like long teeth marks in the ground. He had seen markings like that in the corncobs and cakes at his last family reunion.

His thoughts were disrupted by a sharp, creaking sound. He hurried to where Dumas was pushing on an "Authorized Personnel Only" sign. Dewey could see cracks in this entrance portal, and quickly added his strength to the effort. With their combined weight, they moved the partition just enough to slip through.

They went from growing sunlight to veritable darkness in the space of two steps. Reaching into one of his coat pockets, Dumas pulled out his palm-sized domed light. In its soft glow, the two peered down a dark corridor.

"What is that?" Dewey wondered, peering as far as he could.

"Shhh," Dumas cautioned as he put the light back into his pocket. The pilot was referring to a dull red radiance pulsing on and off at the far end of the space. "Just head toward it with me," he quietly advised Charlie. "I didn't notice any breaks in the floor, so we shouldn't slip or trip."

The two came to the end of the hallway to find a wide, rectangular doorway without a door. Sticking their heads through it, they discovered a circular research chamber a hundred feet across, bathed in warm red light.

Charlie gave a slow, soft, wheezing whistle. The walls, ceiling, and floor contained utter chaos. Everything that wasn't nailed down—tables, computers, equipment—was piled together in a twenty-foot-high pyramid.

"Like a future bonfire." Dewey breathed.

"Or a sacrificial totem," Dumas added.

They approached slowly, seeing that the dim, pulsing red light was coming from inside the pile, through the cracks in the debris. The pilot looked at the Professor, who shrugged, then nodded as if to say "nothing ventured, nothing gained." Dewey hesitated, as if saying "better safe than sorry." Then he joined Dumas in picking off pieces of the tower.

Dewey recognized some of the things that passed through his hands. There were slide rules, folders, and graphite pens, but he paused when he came across a fracking hose. He turned toward Dumas to show him but was distracted by what the Professor held.

"What's that?" he asked.

"Sonic cannon."

"It looks a bit like the pipe Rick was shooting."

"A bit." Dumas nodded and started walking around the pyramid, peering at it. "This uses concentrated sound, while I used light and electricity. My weapon knocks people out. This, and that"—he pointed at the hose Dewey held—"are used for drill—"

Before he could finish the sentence, Dumas went down as if he'd slipped on a banana peel. Charlie gave out a little yelp and jumped to help him. Dumas stood up with the cause of his fall in his hands. It was a small, portable oxygen cylinder, complete with a face mask attached to it by an elastic hose.

The two men looked around their feet to see at least five others.

"If there's one with oxygen left, put it on," Dumas suggested.

"What for?" Dewey wondered, wanting to feel as cavalier as he sounded. He took a big breath. "There's plenty of air in here."

"Also plenty of oxygen tanks," Dumas replied. "That tells me they're here for a reason."

The Professor realized his other hand was propped on the smooth surface of the object that was glowing. He jerked his fingers away as if the thing might bite, then looked around to see what else he might be missing. His eyes locked on a fallen bookcase.

"Ah." He breathed.

"'Ah' what?" Dewey asked as the Professor hurried toward the bookcase that was flat on the floor, its back to the ceiling. "Shouldn't we be more concerned about the flashing red thing?"

"That means more questions," Dumas informed him as he leaned down to grab the edge of the shelves. "A bookcase always means more answers. Unless it's empty."

It wasn't. As Dumas yanked the bookcase off the floor, dozens of research journals spilled out. Dewey stepped over to check them. Every journal that faced upward was marked with the letters "PC" and a number: PC-4, PC-11, all the way up to PC-23.

"Personal computers?" Dewey theorized. "Politically correct?"

"Pencil Crew," Dumas said hollowly.

To Dewey's surprise, Dumas plopped cross-legged on the floor and opened the journal marked PC-1. Dewey could tell he was speed-reading by the way his eyes, head, and fingers moved, as well as how rapidly he turned the pages.

"'JCP only allows us cursory examination of ISO,'" he read aloud. "'More intent on new faults exposed by Northridge.'"

He tossed that book aside and scrabbled around until he found PC-2. More rapid eye movement, more page turning, then, "'Localized vacuum defense mechanism triggered by sharp impact, not by organic or alien biological matter.'"

Dewey was listening hard. "'Localized vacuum defense mechanism triggered by sharp impact, not by organic or alien biological matter,'" he repeated helplessly. "I could begin to guess but I'm sure I'd be wrong."

"It means, as it says here, that we must work with air supply."

"Still don't understand."

Dumas only grunted, then flung the journal after the first, followed by more searching on his hands and knees until he came upon PC-3.

"'JCP has cut off all further ISO research as soon as X reported gravity component of localized vacuum.'"

"Can you help me with the acronyms?" Dewey asked.

"J.C. Passarelles," Dumas explained absently as he located PC-4. "Our fearless leader."

"Who's X?"

"X is the unknown," Dumas informed him. "Whichever of the Pencil Crew wrote this didn't want to reveal who discovered the gravity component of the localized vacuum—the discovery that made the General shut this inquiry down."

"Gravity component? Localized vacuum? What were they going for, a frictionless chamber for some kind of ultra bullet?"

Dumas dropped PC-4 onto his lap and looked up at Dewey. "You've heard of UFOs, Charlie?"

"Unidentified Flying Objects? You'd be hard put to find someone who hasn't heard of them."

"Well, this," Dumas said, pointing at the glowing red thing under the pile of debris, "is an ISO. An Identified Stationary Object."

Dewey turned to stare at it while taking a step back. "You mean it's a spaceship?"

Dumas nodded, letting his eyes scan the journal in his lap. "Seems like it," he concurred. "A spaceship with a defense mechanism that reportedly sucks the air, and maybe the gravity, from a room." Dumas studied the journal with renewed vigor. "It apparently can re-create the vacuum and gravity-free environment of outer space outside its shell and within Earth's atmospheric space." He glanced back at Dewey. "Do you know what that means?"

"All hell breaking loose?"

"It means that whoever its pilot was, he might not have needed air to survive."

Dewey took a moment to process that. "So you're saying that for him, our air might have the effect on him that a vacuum has for us?"

Dumas nodded, a proud smile on his face. "You get a star, Charlie. Could very well be. Especially when we're chest-deep in lung-less human corpses."

Dewey stared at the glowing red thing covered by the debris, realizing that whatever it was, the pulsing red light meant it still had power. He snapped his mouth shut and strode to the scattered oxygen tanks, searching through them the way Dumas had searched amongst the journals.

As Dewey found one with some air left, Dumas sat hunched on the floor amidst the papers spread around him.

"All right, gentlemen," he intoned, grabbing PC-5. "Tell me everything you know."

He was so intent on reading the contents that he didn't react to a sudden clatter somewhere in the dark.

But Charlie Dewey did, behind the face mask of his oxygen tank. He also noticed a small shower of dirt that followed the noise. But as intently as he searched, he could see no cause. Not even a cat.

13

THREE CHAMBERS

Wes Harding and Hannah Lonnegin crawled to the top of the Cold-water Canyon mound that Passarelles had created.

The duo had not come from the drainage pipe. While pet-finding weeks before, Hannah had spotted an entry from the opposite direction: a deep crevasse that took them up and over the mountain, away from the entrance the Riders had used.

It took Wes and Hannah an hour of hard climbing, slowed by exhaustion and the fact that Hannah insisted on carrying the Electrolight the entire way.

"You planning to use that?" Wes had asked.

"Only if we have to," she answered. "We need to give the Professor all the intel we can, not start a fight we can't win. If all goes well, we should be back at the library before he is."

"Hell, what could go wrong?" Wes wondered.

Her sly grin had returned as her green eyes glittered in the shadow of the crevasse.

Once they reached the apex, they stayed very low, crawling to the back of the mound. To Wes's surprise, they saw steamy smoke sizzling from several cracks in the ground. Wes scuttled to the nearest one and tried to look down through it. Hannah joined him. First they tried using their eyes, but the steam effectively blinded them. Then they tried their ears, both hearing a cacophony of distant noises: the high-pitched whine of drills, the thudding of hydraulic presses, and some sick, pulpy sounds that neither could identify.

"What *is* that?" Wes wondered softly.

"I haven't a clue," she admitted.

They moved from one steaming fissure to another until they found the largest, one that was just wide and long enough to fit their bodies. Without hesitation, Hannah ducked her head down into the crack, emerging a moment later with her face beet red and her hair a mass of wet curls.

"I spotted a way to climb down," she gasped.

"There's a 'but' in your voice," Wes said.

She nodded. "We have to be quick or we'll be boiled."

They regretted having to leave the Electrolight behind, but there was no alternative. Hannah wasn't going to stand guard, waiting for Wes, nor did they have time to fashion a holster or back sling.

The two descended quickly, scuttling down on closely spaced outcroppings of rock. They emerged inside the cavern steamed and dripping. Wes dragged both sleeves over his eyes while Hannah literally shook off the droplets. Then they silently scanned the area, which was dappled in refracted morning light from the cavern opening. Rats scurried here and there, and Wes smelled, then saw, piles of bat guano. He was too alert to be disgusted.

The cavern itself was still out of their sight, as was the unidentified illumination coming from somewhere else below.

They moved forward, rats milling around their feet, the sounds of drilling, pounding, and whining growing louder. They felt the steady shuddering of the ground beneath their feet; the sensation was like one long, low aftershock. Then they stopped. Around a turn, the cave ceiling had collapsed, leaving a passageway just two feet high.

"I'll go," Wes said.

"I don't need protecting—"

"I know it," he assured her. "I'm narrower, that's all."

"Not by much."

But she tilted her head with resignation as Wes dropped to his knees and wormed his way through. Inside, he found himself on a small ledge. Below it was a chasm that plummeted into darkness. Four feet across the divide, the passageway continued.

"I can jump that," he said through the opening.

Hannah was about to say that she'd try to find another way to join him when a distant scream paralyzed them. It was suddenly cut off, but the echo made a mocking monument to its existence.

The silent look they gave each other combined a convulsive desire to retreat with a fearful conviction to find the source. Wes scoured the catacombs and spotted a place ahead that created a rat's maze of dark passages. He signaled that Hannah should see if she could make it there from the other side of where he was. She nodded and her head disappeared.

He pushed off the wall, hard, and cleared the chasm easily. He waited breathlessly on the other side, dreading another scream, then saw Hannah's head emerge from a large crack in the passageway some twenty feet ahead.

"How?" he asked.

"I followed the rats to a solid old water channel," she said, maneuvering through. "You learn a lot about animals, tracking them."

Wes made his way through the larger tunnel and soon they were crouching side by side. From below came a strange wheezing that resurrected their recent fears.

There was only enough room to crawl up ahead, so that was what they did, Wes leading the way. At the end of this tunnel was a ledge broad and wide enough for both of them to lie on. They gripped the lip at the edge and pulled themselves forward until they could peer down.

Hannah clamped her hands across her mouth to keep from gasping. Wes did the same to keep from retching.

East 101 survivors were scattered on the ground below them, hog-tied hand and foot outside a translucent dome with a thirty-foot circumference. As they watched, two Riders grabbed one man and cut his bonds. Before the man could run or fight, they threw him at the side of the dome.

Wes and Hannah thought he would hit, bounce off, and fall. Instead, the man seemed to sink into the milky side of the dome, as if it were made of pudding. As they watched, he sank all the way through and popped out the other side, into the dome's interior. They could no longer see his face, but they could see his body. He staggered, tensed as if he were surprised, and then, horrified, started clawing at his own throat.

"He's choking," Wes hissed.

Hannah exhaled hard through her nose with anger at what they were watching.

Suddenly, their heads snapped to the right as a shadow appeared outside the far side of the dome. It looked and moved differently than the human had. It seemed to contract, then ooze through the dome. It was an amorphous black thing that rolled like a cresting wave into a vaguely human shape on the other side.

Wes and Hannah held their breaths, then lost them as the thing shot across the dome interior to slap against the choking survivor like a hurled barrel of tar. It wrapped around him, then completely enveloped him, a black, oily tarp.

Wes wanted to look away as the thing started to sink into the man, but he couldn't. The black oil poured into the man's ears, nose, throat, and even around his eyes. It seemed to drool into his pores, with drops coursing down his pants to his feet. Even from their distance, Wes and Hannah could see shapes and shadows. They saw the silhouette of the thing pouring down the survivor's throat, as his mouth was held open in a frozen, silent scream.

The witnesses fought the bile rising in their own throats as the victim staggered, twisted, and spasmed. The survivors outside the dome screeched, bellowed, and cried as the attacked man lurched back through the dome's wall to contort among them.

Making it all worse, the Riders looked on dispassionately. The troopers studied the scene like bored sports fans until the attacked survivor slowed, then stilled—standing unsteadily, blinking. Only then did the Riders approach him. He grabbed one of them by the shoulders, but the Rider didn't flinch.

Then it spoke, in a voice that sounded like Doc Malloy just before the end.

"Bring me to—"

The invaded survivor said something—something that must have been a name, but it was a sound unlike anything Wes or Hannah had ever heard. It was a combination of a grunt and moan that never quite formed into vowels or consonants.

Wes and Hannah continued to stare at the unsteady man and at the Rider who was keeping him upright. They watched as the two left the chamber, and saw on either side of the entrance opening, a pile of what looked like black mounds. Black mounds with human bones sticking out.

Wes shook his head hard. "I've seen enough," he choked.

"No, you haven't," Hannah replied. "You said a Stallion could fit over fifty, and there were two Stallions. I count fifteen people. Where are all the others?"

Before she finished the question, Hannah rose into a crouch and started creeping along the ledge above the killing floor. Wes followed quickly, just in time to clamber after her through another narrow fissure at the far side.

The moment the two entered, their nostrils filled with a nearly overwhelming smell like something big and dead. They clamped their hands over their mouths and noses, dragging their hoodies and T-shirts to cover their lips and nostrils.

"Where?" Wes asked, looking around. He didn't understand how no hint of the smell had reached them before they entered.

They looked ahead, stumbling in that direction as they fought unconsciousness, and came to another cavern. The odor was even more powerful here. They held their breath and looked down.

They were forever changed. Wes's face crumpled with disgust. Hannah went blank. He realized it was shock, protecting her—or else she would never have stopped crying.

Below them were the rest of the survivors. These appeared to be older captives, less hardy. They were living, dying, or already dead, all of them lying on the cave floor, many with their chests carved open by Riders with scalpels and bone saws. One Rider pulled out a victim's lungs and plunged them into a central vat of viscous liquid that was both milky white and oily black.

"We—we've got to go back," Wes whispered.

Hannah couldn't. She fell to her knees and propped her head on the sharp, rocky wall. She curtly shook her head.

"No," she muttered, clawing the word from her stunned state. "We've got to learn as much as we can." She pointed to the left. A shadowy ledge led to another cavern.

Wes pulled his hoodie neckline tighter across his nose and mouth and nodded. Not looking down this time, they went on all fours so their watering eyes, stung by the acidic stench of whatever viscous liquid was in the lung vat, wouldn't send them screaming into empty air just to make it stop.

There was a third cavern that had no other egress. They were thankful, if they could say so, that the atmosphere here wasn't poisonous. There was no ledge here, so they peered in. They looked down just in time to see another black, oily, vaguely human-shaped thing emerge from another translucent dome that was surrounded by what looked like torn, twisted, black garbage bags. This time, though, it was the oily thing outside this second dome that reacted as if it were choking.

"A vacuum," Wes said softly. "These things live without air of any kind!"

"That's why they choke in our atmosphere," Hannah remarked.

They studied the creature, the being, whatever it was. Almost ten feet long, with a body like melted wax. Its "face" shifted constantly, almost but never quite forming eyes or a mouth. Not searching for air but rather for a lack of it, the black shape writhed and contorted as two hybrids, including the one they had seen meld in the first chamber, jumped on either side of it. They grabbed it and wrestled it to the ground, holding it down. Then a third ran forward, holding out a freshly harvested set of human lungs.

The hybrid tried to ram the lungs into the widest part of the Terraphage's morphing body, but the oily thing reacted as if they were trying to stab it. It struggled, trying to hurl the hybrids off, but then a section of its head seemed to clamp onto the thyroid cartilage at the top of the trachea.

Wes saw the lungs expand like bagpipes, and suddenly the Terraphage rippled, as if in pleasure. The hybrids backed away as the thing sucked the lungs into its own shape.

Wes, thinking they had seen enough, started to turn, but he felt Hannah's fingers grip his arm as if she were trying to break the skin. His head snapped back just in time to see the three hybrids dragging the body of a human by his legs toward the Terraphage. A body with its chest ripped open. A body with its lungs torn out. A body that, incredibly, was not yet dead.

Wes stared in disbelief, bug-eyed and agape. The human must have been harvested milliseconds ago. The lungs in this Terraphage were not his. His were going to go into another Terraphage. Even so, the hybrids must have thrown him from the killing floor toward this Terraphage in the moment between tortured life and devastating death.

In that moment, the Terraphage slammed itself into the man's chest cavity and spread like bubbling lava—expanding and sealing the human around it.

Wes and Hannah watched, awestruck and grief-stricken, as the human filled with the Terraphage began to retake his shape like a balloon being inflated. This new hybrid's expression mingled amazement, realization, disgust, and horror—before it was taken over with smug assurance.

"Doc," Wes said, thinking of what his mentor had endured. He turned away, doubled over, and quietly vomited.

14

REUNION

Once a vibrant hub of exploration and learning, of life and the promise of life, the Jet Propulsion Laboratory building they had entered was now a ruin. The earthquake had damaged the structure. and neglect and vermin had picked away at the sad carcass, leaving it dusty and dry.

And full of falling dust that didn't make sense. Like the large scratch marks they had seen outside the building, as if someone had dragged the edges of metal filing cabinets across the ground.

Charlie Dewey breathed deeply from the little oxygen remaining in the tank strapped to his back. He was studying every nook and cranny he could see in this circular research chamber, trying to find an explanation. Wes had pointed out several times that the Ring of Fire disaster had yet to include a single aftershock, so what would make something clatter, and a rain of dust shower down?

Something else that didn't make sense was the dome in the center of the room. Beneath the pyramid of upended chairs, overturned bookcases and cracked and crushed computers, the dim red light continued to illuminate the milky shape.

Dewey had both eyes on their dark surroundings as the Professor pored over his research journals, but he could hear what Dumas was doing.

"One, six, Y," the Professor muttered. "Two, M." He glanced up, apparently surprised that the pilot was not immediately nearby. "Sixteenth year, second month of research," he translated for Charlie. "Long after I left. Wonder who the General replaced me with to slave for him?" He shrugged and returned to reading. "Maybe no one. NGD."

"No Good Doc?" Dewey ventured.

Dumas grinned. "Very close, Charlie," he said, nodding. "You're getting better." He returned to the journal. "But I think it stands for No Go Dome. They wanted to study this thing." He poked a thumb at the half-buried dome. "Very clever," he said.

"What is?"

"The dome . . . not important now. The General only wanted the Crew to search for the Achilles Heel. So much so, apparently, that they started to mention it in their research journals, a major transgression in academic circles."

"What's a major transgression?" Charlie asked, keeping his eyes sharp on the shadows above them.

"Mentioning personal opinions in scientific journals," Dumas elaborated. "These are supposed to be pure research, for the edification of future generations, not personal, chatty diaries."

"Maybe they thought the personal opinions were important for future generations to know," Charlie mused.

The Professor snorted and pointed at the journal he was scanning, then read, "Quote: JCP smug, demanding we abandon formula V, seventeen, P, ninety-nine. Unquote."

"Formula V?" Charlie repeated. "They did twenty-one formulas before that?"

Dumas frowned. "I don't see how the General would give them the time."

"And formula for what? The amount of force needed to set off the Achilles Heel?"

"Presumably," the Professor muttered. "But V does not make sense."

"Maybe they meant Roman numeral V," Charlie suggested, holding up his hand in a high-five.

The Professor shook his head. "Not official research protocol. We didn't use Roman numerals, to avoid just that kind of misunderstanding." He scanned the rest of the journal, then tossed it aside for the next one.

"Which one are you at now?" Dewey asked, taking a step further away from the Professor. He was becoming more assured in their surroundings, and less certain that anything unnatural had made the clank and the dirt shower.

"PC-13," the Professor informed him. His finger danced across the pages. "Ah, yes, see here. Listen. 'V, seventeen, p, ninety-nine, failed to breach outer polymer shell.'" He kept rapidly scanning. "No more mention of it. Seems they never had the chance to create formula W."

Charlie shook his head. "So FV ends at PC-13? Very superstitious." He grinned.

Dumas chortled, tossing the journal over his shoulder and reaching for PC-14. "Yes, I suppose—" His head snapped up and he stared at his companion. "What did you say, Charlie?"

The pilot stopped scanning the ceiling and walls to look back at the Professor. "Me? Nothing."

"No, a moment ago," Dumas insisted. "FV what?"

Charlie tucked his chin and shrugged. "Just making a joke. Yet another acronym. Formula V ends at—"

"Charlie!" Dumas shook his hands on either side of his head in agitation. "Charlie, I am truly a Dumb Ass. I should have thought of it as soon as I saw the first numbers and letters!"

Charlie stepped away from the pile of refuse covering the dome and approached the Professor. "Thought of what?" he wondered.

A large, dark red shadow began growing on the wall behind Dewey.

"Scientists!" Dumas scoffed, now on all fours and shifting through the remaining journals. "Notoriously bad, inconsistent handwriting. There was no punctuation between the word 'formula' and the letter V. Or maybe there was one that faded out, or I just didn't see it, or maybe my fingertip was over it—"

"Over what?" Charlie pressed, stopping at the edge of the scattered journals.

Because his back was turned and the Professor's head was down, neither of them saw the red shadow expanding.

"It wasn't formula V!" Dumas declared. "They abandoned the formula, *period*. Then he wrote 'V17P99.'"

"Okay, okay," Charlie said encouragingly, his head turning this way and that to follow the Professor's frenetic search through the journals. "But what the hell is Victor one seven Papa nine nine?"

Dumas cried out in triumph. He sat back on his heels, holding up journal PC-17 in both hands like Moses with the tablets from God. "Not a formula, Charlie! V is for volume. Volume seventeen, page—"

Dumas's face fell.

"Ninety-nine?" Charlie completed helpfully.

Then he noticed that the Professor was staring at something behind him. Charlie started to turn just as Dumas whipped his illumination orb from his pocket. In its glow, they saw yellow eyes in the gloom no more than ten feet from them. Yellow eyes with streaks of red and black inside them.

"Please tell me you know what that is," Charlie muttered as he stepped backward, slipped on a journal, and began to fall. He yelped and his arms windmilled as his feet scrambled for purchase among the journals.

"I was about to say 'no,' and 'don't make any sudden moves,'" Dumas replied cautiously, "but that seems to be moot now."

Dumas stepped in front of the retreating pilot, holding up the illumination orb as if it were a weapon. The thing took on a more human shape, but the part that could be called a head was still huge and misshapen. Its wavering body loomed above them like a cresting wave. The black-and-red-streaked eyes moved forward as Dumas lunged at them, trying distract the owner with a swat from PC-17.

Before the journal could strike, Dumas was pulled backward. Charlie's fist had a tight grip on the sleeve of his lab coat, and the pilot was swinging his oxygen tank with all his might.

It landed with a wet, heavy *thunk*, and they heard an angry howl. The force of the swing wrenched the tank from Dewey's grip, and he dragged the Professor to the other side of the dome.

They heard scratching, scuttling sounds in retreat. Then everything was silent, save for their own heavy breathing.

"What the hell was that?" Dewey cried.

Instead of answering, the Professor pulled his arm free of Dewey's hand. He hurried back around the dome's base, aggressively peering into the light cast by the illumination orb. The thing was no longer there.

"Did we imagine it?" Dewey breathed. "A hallucination, brought on by toxic waste, or even this ship?" He looked at the pulsing dome warily. "Professor, I know it's against your scientific religion, but I *will* accept conjecture at this point!"

Dumas glanced at the pilot's tense form beside him. "I don't believe we imagined it, and I don't know what it was, except that it had eyes and a body," he said, in a tone that was part reassurance, part warning. "I *do* think that we should—"

He stopped, feeling something on his shoulder. Something like a drop. He saw fear and disgust on Dewey's face and looked down at his lapel. Something was dripping on his lab coat. Something black. Something from above.

They both looked up. Gazing down at them were ten yellow eyes, all streaked with black and red.

Dewey and Dumas ran. Dewey was hell-bent for the exit, but Dumas looked back at the five shapes attached to the debris around the glowing red dome. The Professor stopped moving. Charlie slowed, backtracked.

"Peter?" Dumas said.

"Shush."

The nearest shape was about twenty feet away. It rippled. The more it moved, the more it resembled a human figure. A maw opened beneath its eyes, and a wet, gravelly sound emerged from that orifice.

"Burn . . . hard."

The Professor was momentarily stunned but recovered quickly. "Yes!" he exclaimed. "It's me! Bernard." He squinted into the red light. "Jesus." He took a small step toward the thing.

Charlie grabbed his shoulder. "What the hell are you doing?"

"We know each other, from way back when. His name is— was—Peter Baker," Dumas explained to the pilot. "I was told that he had died."

Dewey looked around at their tomblike surroundings. "What makes you think he didn't?"

Dewey's grip on Dumas's lab coat tightened. Dumas tugged free and Dewey let him go.

"Peter?" Dumas said tentatively.

Dewey tried to distinguish features on Peter's shape. "How are you going to tell me you recognize that?" he said incredulously.

"You don't forget the Pencil Crew," Dumas said. "Five of the greatest minds of the century. There's something in the eyes. Or maybe I simply feel the power of their minds—"

The five shapes were moving slowly toward them.

"I was told they were all killed," Dumas said.

"I bet they wish they were," Charlie snapped.

Dumas's eyes pinned the shape wavering in front, a figure that was half walking, half lurching. "Did JCP do this to you?" he called.

The ten eyes began to narrow, and all the bodies started to quiver. As Dumas held up the illumination device, all five began to shrink into recognizably human shapes.

"Yes," croaked the lead creature, the one Dumas had called Peter. It sounded as if he were dragging the word out of himself, from somewhere down around his knees, with all his strength. "Terraphage!"

Dewey finally realized that their presence could explain the marks in the dirt they had seen outside. These tortured creatures were barely surviving by eating the ground around the building. Maybe they had been holding on to life in the hope that something like this would happen.

Dumas nodded at the Peter thing. "Yes. I've seen others like you."

The shapes rippled again, side to side.

"No," said the Peter thing. "No others."

The four shapes behind the Peter thing wavered. Each emitted only a few words, as if the sounds cost them more than they could pay.

"Us first."

"All others die."

"Explode."

"Yes, I understand," Dumas said. "He wanted to infiltrate the military and government with hybrids!"

The Terraphages seemed wracked by terrible pain.

"But fail!" said one.

"All fail!" gasped another.

"But JCP is nothing if not a single-minded officer," Dumas realized. "What does he know about science?" A terrible realization occurred to him. "He got you to work on the process?"

"Yes!" cried several of them, in an echo that sounded like damned souls.

"Some," Peter grunted.

"Some worked," said another.

"Some not."

Dumas reeled. "All right—the General wanted to create an army of hybrids, but it didn't work, he doesn't have one," he said rapidly.

"The Riders aren't hybrids?" Charlie asked incredulously.

"No, they're mercenaries, in it for the spoils, most likely. The General couldn't risk their bodies rejecting the Terraphages, even if their minds agreed with his twisted plans of conquest. So—my God."

"What?" Dewey pressed.

"As soon as JCP had a supply of 'expendable' subjects, he started testing the process again."

"The refugees," Dewey said with horror.

"Exactly. And people he was no longer sure he could trust, or people who were getting wise to him, like Doc Malloy," Dumas said bitterly. Then he spun back to the Peter thing, hit with a realization. "The General was in a hurry, wasn't he?"

The Terraphages rippled up and down. Even Dewey could see it meant yes.

"Left us."

"To die."

"He was in a hurry because he found the Achilles Heel?" Dumas asked urgently.

The Terraphages made horrid, tormented sounds. Worse, they started staggering toward the pilot and the Professor.

"Dumas?" Charlie warned.

"He found it," Dumas thought aloud. "He was ready to cripple the world and establish total dominance. He was under orders from his partners to pull the trigger. He had to hurry this . . . this hellish process along."

The silence of the creatures before them was a tacit "yes."

"Professor, we gotta go. This is big."

But the Professor was staring at the floor, intent on the new information. "Don't worry," Dumas said. "It's not that easy to just set off the Achilles Heel. Dumas would need massive firepower. And no matter how powerful he's become, I don't think he has that kind of armory available—"

"Crap."

"What?"

"We had a bunker buster bomb delivered to us before all this happened," Charlie said. "None of us could figure out why. 'For tests,' we were told."

"But that wasn't it," Dumas said. "It was used, but for another reason."

"Passarelles has obviously got gooey masses like these in high places," Charlie pointed out.

"I think even the pinheads in DC would notice Terraphages," Dumas remarked.

"Dumas!" Charlie yelled, jerking the man's attention.

They were now standing in a Terraphage tornado as the quintet of creatures moved around them.

The pilot tried to find an escape route, but the five undulating monsters blocked him no matter which way he turned. As the shapes passed them, Dumas moved closer to hear better, trying to translate their sounds into words.

"Peter," he pleaded. "David. Bill. Pat. Tom. Please. What are you trying to tell me?"

In his time, Dewey had heard some crackling comm voices and also a whole lot of drunken flyboys trying to make sense. He got it first.

"Professor," he said soberly. "They're apologizing. They're saying they're sorry!"

"Sorry?" Dumas echoed. "What could they be sorry for?" He called to his tormented friends again. "For finding a hybrid process? For finding the Achilles Heel?"

The things shrank even further into their human forms. They stepped from wavering black shadows, and as they came into the light, they looked much like the people they had been before Passarelles took over. Only now they were bent, tragic old men, who gazed at the pilot and their former colleague with sadness and pity.

Sadness, Dewey could understand. But why pity?

"Dumas?" Charlie said. "Remember what Doc Malloy said to Wes? When he could no longer control him—"

He wasn't able to finish. With a roar that sounded like the Ring of Fire blasting open, the five Terraphages finally shucked all semblance of clinging humanity and attacked.

15

DANCE AND DROP

The Joint Light Tactical Vehicle was parked on the concrete floor, tucked beside the entrance to the Coldwater Canyon cavern. From their vantage point thirty feet above, breathing heavily from the long, forced ascent, Wes and Hannah weren't interested in anything but the coils of rope that hung from its frame.

"Looks like an armored toad on tractor wheels," the redhead whispered sourly. Since witnessing what was happening in the three chambers, her disgusted expression hadn't changed.

"Improvised fighting vehicles were designed for function, not appearance," Wes said absently. "That's a Payload Category C—heaviest one they've got."

Hannah grunted and hugged the Electrolight tightly, not just for security but also for what they had in mind. Suddenly, a Rider emerged and took a look around. The two observers ducked low.

"Shit," she said simply, as the Rider lit a cigarette.

They watched, hunkered down. The plan was not elaborate, but Wes wanted to execute it quickly; lives were at stake. It had come to him while they hurried back up the fissure that had been their entry. As they exited, he turned his face from the sky to avoid the sudden brightness. He glimpsed sunlight glinting off metal, and suddenly he saw the source of the steam, a network of exhaust pipes that wound laboriously through the upper catacombs of the cave. They were obviously created to channel away the destructive steam. Here, flanking the three chambers, was where Wes and Hannah might cause the most damage—perhaps, possibly, fatal to the operation. As soon as they reached the top, he told Hannah what he was thinking.

Hannah hurt for the victims too, but she had implored him to retreat so they could team up with Dumas, or at least clear their heads for better planning, then go back. He wouldn't hear of it. They both knew that by then, most of the survivors would be dead, or assimilated.

Hannah had spotted something earlier, something they needed, so they had gone all the way around the secret enclosure until they reached the top of the incline. It had probably been created by a landslide caused by the construction that had hollowed out the cavern. Whatever had made the steep hill didn't matter. All that was important was that it created a sloping path down behind the vehicle.

"That Rider's not going anywhere soon." Hannah frowned. "And if it's break time, more may join him."

"I'm going," Wes said.

Wes looked down to where the Rider stood, well away from the vehicle's front bumper, leaning on a boulder as he smoked. Then

Wes slid onto the top of the incline and let gravity take him down. He only spread his arms to slow himself slightly near the bottom.

He landed almost soundlessly on his toes, let the momentum carry him forward, then jumped up to the back of the vehicle. Even before he settled into a crouch, Wes was grabbing the ropes and slinging them across his shoulders and under his arms, coiling them loosely in place.

All the while, Wes kept his ears alert for Hannah. She had agreed to screech like a cat if the guard moved, but she remained silent. When he was finished, he jumped back onto the incline, his trained legs chugging upward. Even with all his exercising, Wes felt his feet continually slip from under him. Toward the end, he had to lunge for the crest. But Hannah was there, grabbing his hand and gripping under his shoulder to haul him back to safety. The two tumbled out of sight, fretting slightly at how the dirt Wes had loosened with his climb slid down behind the vehicle.

The Rider looked back, then dropped his cigarette butt and ground it out with his boot. The General had made it very clear what would happen to anyone who risked immolation by bringing a flame within fifty feet of the machinery. They would become lubrication for the machinery. The Rider studied the area where the dirt on the incline was settling. He watched it slide to a stop for maybe a second longer than was necessary—then shrugged and went back to work. The General had also made it clear what would happen to anyone who took a break even a second longer than prescribed: his next break would be permanent.

Wes and Hannah had already moved back inside the cavern, returning to the ledge above the first of the three chambers. While Wes removed the ropes, Hannah peered down at the survivors, eight of them left. They were still lying on the floor, still hog-tied hand and foot.

Wes was noticing something else. The subjects seemed to be chosen for three things: their youth, strength, and masculinity. No one had seen a splayed-open female corpse, or a woman thrown into the dome. Maybe their society operated like ants, with one queen and countless drones. The woman who had accosted him and Doc in the mess tent was obviously evacked to shut her up about Coldwater. That, Wes bitterly supposed, was what made her so eminently executable.

Wes counted only three Riders standing guard. While he watched for others, Hannah tied the ends of three rope coils around firm sections of the catacomb openings. She nodded at him and then they crouched, waiting for the best time. It didn't take long.

The third Rider said something to his comrades, then left. The other two leaned against the wall, watching the trembling survivors dispassionately.

Wes and Hannah looked at each other. He pulled out his pocket multi-tool, and she leaned the end of the Electrolight on the bottom of the opening she was peering through.

"This better work," he heard her mutter, but he wasn't sure whether it was for his benefit or her own.

Wes threw down the loose end of one rope. It uncoiled in the air and slapped the cavern floor below. Everyone—Riders and survivors alike—looked over at the sound. Then they looked up as Wes slid down the rope. The Riders grunted with surprise and anger, but shut up as they focused their assault rifle sights on Wes's head and chest.

There was no sighting device of any kind on the Electrolight. Hannah simply shifted the pipe opening until it obscured the target from her vision—the Rider furthest from her, but closest to Wes—then pressed the recessed button to full power.

It was like turning on a flashlight, except that this beam coursed down to shock the Rider and then collapse him in a smoking pile of vaguely human ash.

Wes landed on the cavern floor, saw the one guard go down, then the second man sizzled, leaped, and collapsed like a torched marionette. Wes discovered that he had been holding his breath, so he exhaled with relief. Thanks to Dumas's ingenuity, the Electrolight seemed to have fail-safe targeting. Even a novice couldn't screw it up.

Wes's exhalation was cut off when he heard a survivor call out to him. He whirled on them, making a shushing motion. Bringing up the wire cutter on his utility tool, he stepped to the survivor closest to him. The tied young man's face showed a similar impatience toward whoever had started making noise.

"Strong enough to climb?" Wes whispered.

"Get me free and I'll run right through the walls," the man promised.

Wes gave him a reassuring but grim smile, then scuttled to each of the seven, cutting their wrists and ankles free. By then Hannah had thrown down the other two rope coils, and soon the men were all climbing, using the walls as footholds. The first three were the strongest and fastest, and they helped pull up the others.

Midway through the third group, which included Wes, the third Rider reappeared in the chamber's opening. Hannah had been waiting for him. He hardly had time to gape before the weapon in her hands made him dance and drop.

"Come on," Wes urged in a loud whisper, waving at the survivors to follow him. He led them toward the steam-opened fissures with Hannah taking up the rear, the Electrolight at the ready.

It was a quick, thankfully uneventful trip. But it didn't stay that way. Just as they reached the exit area, the steam-weakened ground started to shift and give under the weight of the ten people. Wes pushed the survivors away and fell back just as the rock beneath his feet began to crumble.

Some of the men cried out in confusion and fear, but then they were all scrambling on the end of a different craggy ledge. The fissure that was large enough to allow them to escape was now ten feet away—on the other side of a yawning chasm.

Wes cursed himself for not thinking to bring at least one of the rope coils with them. And the sound of the falling rock might bring someone to investigate—even if the three fallen guards hadn't already been discovered.

"We're going to have to jump," Wes told them, his voice firm. Some of the men reacted with hope, others with certainty, and some with fear. He didn't have time to deal with any of them. Turning back, he took two quick steps, then dove, thinking of the long jumps he had attempted on his father's football field.

His feet found nothing but air, but his fingers just managed to claw onto the opposite ledge. His body swung down, slamming against the wall. His grunt mingled with Hannah's gasp behind him.

"It's okay." He breathed, knowing she probably couldn't hear him. "It's okay."

Then he had to execute a painful pull-up, but he managed to drag himself onto the ledge. Gulping for breath, he crouched there and put his hand out. He nodded, hoping his face conveyed assurance. He motioned with his other hand for them to follow him quickly.

Before that could happen, the sky opened and the bottom dropped out.

Wes heard shrieks, not knowing if one of them was his. He felt jagged shards striking him on the side of the face and shoulders. He was blinded by sunlight that all but fell on him from above. Before he could look up, the stone beneath his feet disappeared and he was falling, tumbling, spinning, and sliding.

When he finally managed to collect his wits, he couldn't believe their bad luck. If he had been asked to imagine the worst possible result of their rescue attempt, it would be this.

He lay, propped up by the new landslide, on the cavern floor in front of the three chambers. The entrance to the cavern was to his far left. All the drilling and pounding was coming from far in front of him.

Riders toting assault rifles were all around him. The looks on their visored faces said that they had been waiting for him to exit one way or another. Maybe someone had noticed the ropes were missing from the Tactical Vehicle. Maybe the fallen chamber guards had been discovered.

None of it mattered now, because standing directly in front of him, flanked by two monstrous, vaguely human things, was General J.C. Passarelles himself. He was laughing.

"Oh, you should have seen your face, Agent Harding!" he boomed convivially. "So serious, so heroic, and then so—WTF!" He brought his hand down across his own face, changing his expression from comedy to tragedy. "What the *fuck* indeed."

Before Wes could even begin to formulate a response, let alone a strategy, he saw a lithe, redheaded figure step between him and their nemesis.

Unbroken, unfazed, Hannah Lonnegin brought up her long pipe. "I've been waiting a long time for this," she said, as she pressed the recessed button.

The Electrolight's beam speared Passarelles directly. In the glow of the light, Wes could see Hannah's satisfied, even smug smile. But it changed swiftly. The General did not drop. As Hannah's smile faded, Passarelles's smile grew.

Hannah pressed the button again. The light cannoned forth, this time enveloping the General, sparks flying from his fingers and hair. But, again, he did not spasm or even shiver. His smile only grew wider.

Hannah stared, dumbfounded, the Electrolight drooping. The Riders, who had seen what the thing could do to their fellows, were also taken aback.

The General spread his arms and commanded his men not to fire. He seemed happier than anyone had ever seen him.

"That tickles," he said. "Do it again."

16

"We're . . . sorry!"

The things howled the words over and over, gurgling it with varying levels of pitch and pain, out of sync with one another and quite out of their minds. They howled it as they tried to kill Charlie Dewey and Professor Dumas.

But they were neither human nor Terraphage enough to do it quickly and efficiently. They half walked, half oozed forward, their ill-formed hands extending with surprising speed and length to tighten around the men's throats. But just as it seemed they might succeed in strangling their victims, the ungainly limbs mutated back into oily black flaps. Their misshapen legs tried to kick but more often than not would slap, or even splash, against their targets. Even so, moving forward and circling the men, they still managed to trap their targets no matter how much Charlie punched and kicked.

"Stop it!" Dumas bellowed, backing up, slapping the appendages away. "Why do you want to kill us?"

"We . . . *don't!*" the one called Peter moaned as the others continued their groaned apology. "Hive mind—demanding!"

Hive mind? That's useful information, Dumas thought. If he ever got out of here to use it.

The thing that was once Peter covered Dumas like a net, using his weight to bear him down to his knees. It tried to seal the Professor's nostrils and mouth, but Dumas pulled it from his head, wiped it from his face, kept it at bay. He could no longer speak, for fear the gunk would pour into his mouth. He kept his lips tightly pressed, his eyes squinting, his nostrils turning to avoid the creature.

Then David, always the weakest-willed of the Pencil Crew, Dumas recalled—and therefore most susceptible to the invader—finally gave up the fight. As Charlie watched, the black, oily flaps that extended from his human limbs seemed to snap back inside him like rolled window shades. Suddenly, a recognizably human David Baker stood unsteadily before the copter pilot, blinking. Charlie blinked too, leaning forward in wonder, before David's reconstituted hands shot forward and clamped on his throat.

The other four men seemed to become demoralized from David's example—and the Terraphages within them seemed galvanized. From wavering ghosts they all started to turn back into frenzy-powered zombies.

"Need to . . . breathe!" they hissed.

Dumas fell back as the four overwhelmed him. Their hands ripped at his face and clawed at his chest.

"Lungs," Peter croaked. "Must have . . . working . . . lungs!"

"Charlie!" the Professor cried. "Help!"

But Dewey couldn't help. David was on top of him, crushing

his larynx with his ten tight fingers, powered by the great alien strength within. The young pilot couldn't believe he was about to be smothered by this pathetic, broken figure of a man—but he was. He felt his brain shutting down from lack of oxygen, his feet kicking weakly, uselessly.

Mere seconds before his death throes, his own fingers became spasming claws and scratched out at David's ribs. It was a purely reflexive action, desperate, unplanned—and entirely effective.

All Dewey knew was that he could suddenly breathe again. Then he felt something across his chest and legs. At first he thought that the Professor had fallen over, but then his vision cleared and he realized that what he felt was the black tar-like substance pouring from around David's eyes, out of his nostrils, his mouth, and even his ears. As the pilot watched, the miasmic pitch started to appear from under David's scalp, from under his fingernails, and finally through cracks in his skin that began to multiply—like gills appearing on a fish, but all over his body.

Charlie pushed at the thing and scrambled to his feet, looking down quizzically at the creature that was now neither human nor Terraphage. It was just a sickening, trembling, helpless pool of viscous flesh.

"Charlie!" he finally heard, and spun to see Dumas backing away from his former associates, all of them reconstituted into their powerful human-Terraphage hybrid stage. The Professor was holding them at bay—just barely—by swinging his shepherd's staff at them.

The Pencil Crew obviously didn't want to get hit, because they scrupulously dodged it; but neither did they retreat.

Charlie started toward them, but Dumas warned him off.

"Don't get near them!" he called. "Get clear!"

"Not without you!" Dewey yelled as he stepped to the side, looking for a way in.

"Give yourself to us, Bernard," Peter said in a burbling, gravelly voice that was not his alone. "Rejoin the team."

"I was born a human, from human cells—" Dumas said.

"You are delusional! You *still* have the DNA of our ancestors in those cells, ready to emerge when the planet is ours—"

"No! I am a human and I will die one!"

"True," Peter chortled. "Sadly true."

"Not today," Dumas said. "We will destroy *you*, you can be sure of that!"

Peter chortled. "How?"

Dumas fired a quick look at Dewey. "By getting intel *out*, damnit!"

"Not leaving you," Dewey said, finally just shouldering his way through the frail figures, who somehow felt as solid as linebackers. They parted to let the man in. Dumas saw what was left of the hybrid trembling on the floor beyond.

"Tell me what you did!" the Professor demanded.

"Dug my nails into his side," Dewey replied.

"Lucky," Peter informed him. "Not again."

Dumas swung his stick from side to side. "You're the ones who need luck! If either species rejects the other, the bodies disintegrate, don't they? Worse, they detonate, right? Conflicted gases, methane perhaps—an internal misfire, and boom!"

Dumas jabbed his stick forward like a lance. Bill stepped aside. Dumas drew it back and lunged once more at Bill's waist. The creature dodged it.

"They don't want to get hit by anything," Dumas said quietly so that only Dewey could hear. "The human bodies take a hell of a beating when they're invaded. They don't have a lot of cohesiveness left." He glanced around. "Find an oxygen tank. Then stand clear."

Charlie looked around, found a broken chair, and snatched up the seat. Holding it in front of him like a shield, he hunkered low and charged through the widest gap. He rammed one of the hybrids aside and collided with a bookcase, falling over it. Scrambling to his knees, he started scouring the area for unused tanks. As he crawled over them, he rapped each one with his knuckles to see which was the heaviest. He found one, then waited.

Ten feet away, Dumas was being backed into a corner. He bumped against it, lost his ability to jerk the staff back and jab forward hard. His eyes darted to his left.

The four remaining Pencil Crew hybrids moved in for the kill, but Dumas—still looking to his left—suddenly grinned.

Something human, fearful, appeared in Peter's eyes, and the four froze.

"The brain of David over there," Dumas said. "He just died, just this second, I was watching. You've got a blip in your hive connection."

The faces of the hybrids expressed their confusion and realization, as their own minds once more filtered through their alien arrogance and aggression.

"Fight . . . reintegration!" Peter admonished the others. It was the old Peter, the human Peter.

Dumas used the distraction to slip from the corner. "Charlie! Mask!" he cried, as he plunged the carved wooden staff through the outer wall of the dome.

Dewey snapped the oxygen mask over his mouth and turned the tank on, just as the entire room was bathed in white. A pulse rippled through the air, and then the air was gone.

Almost at once the Professor dropped, face forward, as though he'd been shot. Cradling the oxygen tank under his arm, Dewey ran toward him. He grabbed the man's coat, hoisted his face from the floor, slapped the mask on his face, and crouched beside him, sharing the air like ascending divers.

As Dumas greedily sucked down air, he watched the faces of the Pencil Crew begin to stretch like plastic masks being pulled apart. Skin split and entrails floated free, absurdly, like bloody streamers. Their sinew and skeletons remained intact as the flesh came away from them. Then the tendons split and the bones came apart, clattering to the floor. Dumas saw what was left of David's body begin to spread, the oily black parts lying there, inert.

The Professor indicated for Dewey to put the mask on and leave it. Reluctantly, Dewey did as he was ordered. He watched the Professor's staff shoot forward again. It sank into the wall of the dome just as it had before. Only this time the entire room was bathed in red, and the pulse that emerged brought back a rush of air.

The Professor turned his face toward the wind like a flower toward the rising sun.

Charlie Dewey yanked off his mask, then tore off his jacket and shirt to wipe himself clean of the gunk that had splashed everywhere.

"What the hell was that?!" the pilot demanded.

"A vacuum," Dumas informed him, breathing deeply as he ignored the blotches and rivulets that coated his own clothing.

"Yeah, I figured that," Dewey replied. "How did you know?"

"I took an educated guess," he admitted.

"You guessed . . . with our *lives*?"

"They weren't worth much as it was, were they?"

Dewey had to give him that.

"It was a good guess, though, very low risk," Dumas said. "How do the aliens breathe? Answer: they don't. How do aliens survive in our 14.7 pounds per square inch atmospheric pressure at sea level? In human bodies." He wagged a finger triumphantly. "But what if those bodies are really, really fragile—as your scratching demonstrated?"

Dewey reflected. "Change the pressure and kaboom!"

"Precisely. They explode," Dumas agreed.

"Okay, but what made you think—"

"That there was no air inside the dome?" Dumas replied. "Look at the aliens in their natural, oily form." He touched a glob of David with a toe. "Solid—designed to live in a vacuum. It stands to reason that they would re-create *their* environment inside, *our* environment outside."

"You were betting that those patchwork people, already stretched to the breaking point, couldn't stand it as long as we could."

"Exactly. It also explains the lung removal. When the creatures fill the chest cavity, the infusion damages the lung tissue irreparably. They have to protect the heart, or they'll suffer instant coronaries and death. But they can survive with damaged lungs until they can replace them."

The pilot thought for a moment. "All right . . . makes sense, I think. But that dome looked solid too. I don't understand how you figured it wasn't."

Dumas looked at him as if it were obvious. He motioned dismissively at all the journals, as he used his shepherd's staff to root around amongst them. When he found PC-13, he snapped it up from the floor. "Hmmm. Not too gunked up," he judged, then riffled the pages. "Before we were interrupted," he said returning to the page he had been reading, "I noted the research into self-sealing polymers. What would you need that for . . . except to pass one thing through environment A to environment B?"

Dewey grimaced. "Well, that's about a mile-wide assumption, Professor. One hell of a reach."

"That's what scientists do," Dumas replied. He continued flipping through the journal, compulsively searching for additional data, anything that might prove useful. "We reach. For books, for the stars, for answers. Sometimes you get lucky and win—" He stopped. Holding the journal, his expression grew thoughtful. His eyes were fixed on a hand-drawn map.

"Professor?" Dewey asked. "You catch your breath? Ready to get the hell outta here?"

"It seems, my friend, that now there's a bigger problem," he said.

"That's an understatement."

Dumas stared at the pilot. "You're thinking of the Terraphages," he said, "No. We have another enemy, one even closer."

"Passarelles," Dewey said confidently.

Dumas shook his head. "Time. I thought we had more of it," he said, his voice haunted. "I thought the General couldn't do anything until he got more ordnance. I was wrong."

"What do you mean?"

"Coldwater Canyon," Dumas said as he threw the journal to one side. He locked eyes with the pilot. "It's the site of a 'retired' nuclear weapon silo."

"*That's* why it's the Achilles Heel of the fault line," Dewey said.

"A blast with a conventional bunker buster bomb showed what could be done to the Ring of Fire," Dumas said. "Now the big gun comes out to tear the planet up exponentially!"

The two men started running back toward the copter, the pages of PC-13 fluttering to the floor like the Pencil Crew's blood, sweat, and tears.

17

THREE SETTINGS

Under the baleful gaze of Passarelles and his crew, Wes Harding eased in front of Hannah Lonnegin. He knew she didn't want or need his protection, and it was a useless gesture, because it was heroic but empty. What could his body do to stop MP7 bullets? But he did it anyway.

"Idiot," he heard her mutter behind him as the Riders leveled their assault rifles.

"Full-blooded and proud of it," he said without taking his eyes off the enemy.

She stepped beside him and, with a crackling sound, those enemies suddenly started dropping. Wes's depleted soul filled with admiration as the lady turned the Electrolight on everyone but Passarelles.

He really was an Idiot-with-a-capital-I, he thought. Just because the General surprised them by not falling, that didn't mean Hannah was going to drop the weapon, throw up her hands, and beg for her life. Even Passarelles looked surprised by her violent reaction. Judging from the look on his face, he obviously thought she would be so demoralized by his invulnerability that it would all be over.

But her surprise action did not mean the conflict was over. A moment after she started light-lancing the Riders, Wes tore into whichever guards she hadn't targeted, throwing roundhouses and uppercuts. He bought her enough time to neutralize the immediate threat.

"Come on!" Hannah cried.

She ran toward the utility vehicle parked ahead, and Wes raced alongside, keeping his head down but also twisted toward the General and the two things flanking him.

"*Trrllaggg . . .*" one of them gurgled.

These things were beyond hybrids. They seemed like some kind of Neanderthal form of Terraphages, bred for brutishness. The oily black gunk of the Terraphages formed bulging, lumpy masses within the bloated human limbs, necks, and shoulders. Even their heads seemed inflated outward, pumped to the breaking point, big balls of blackish rubber. They towered over Passarelles by a foot and a half, and they glared at Wes with wide, black-and-red-streaked eyes.

The General was raging at his fallen men, but Wes couldn't hear him through Hannah's shouting.

"You drive!" she yelled as she sped toward the armored transport. "Pray the keys are in the truck."

"Prayer not required," he assured her. "It's an 'MRAP,' a mine-resistant ambush-protected vehicle. Key not required."

"Then shut up and get it started!"

The remaining Riders were still firing in their direction. Wes vaulted toward the driver's side of the vehicle, knowing that once he got the armored door open, the bullets wouldn't be a concern. As he climbed in, he heard Passarelles yelling at his flanking brutes. He was pointing at the MRAP.

Hannah had her door open, but she was still firing at any Rider who came into her sight. The Electrolight continued to seek out whomever she pointed at. Like the best weapons, from swords to guns, it seemed a natural extension of her arm. Even if she didn't know that, she seemed to intuit it; she was a natural warrior.

Wes jumped into the driver's seat. He had seen these vehicles at East 101 and luckily Charlie had told him all about them. He knew what to do. He shoved his thumb into a metal collar on the lower dashboard. The vehicle throbbed to life.

Hannah snapped the bulletproof glass passenger window aside so she could keep firing.

"Cover me," Wes said, "I'm swinging around for the survivors." He clamped both hands on the wheel and slammed his foot on the accelerator as Passarelles's mutations roared their displeasure and stomped toward them. "And watch those monsters," he warned her. "The Electrolight might not work on them either."

"Way ahead of you," she said. "I was listening when Doc said they have no nervous system, nothing to overload."

"I was listening too," Wes insisted. "I just didn't know what he was talking about."

"Idiot," she muttered.

Wes wondered if she actually meant him. As the vehicle surged forward, Hannah got a bead on a Rider trying to flank them and brought him down.

The vehicle was spinning up dust, and, peering through it, Wes swore. The survivors were not going to be easy to reach. Passarelles was not the fastest promoted general in military history just because he was some kind of Terraphage Alpha. He was a clever tactician. He had retreated behind his brutes and ordered them to spread their arms to block any survivors.

"Mow those monsters down," Hannah snarled. "When they're on their backs, I'll see how much of a nervous system they have left!"

"Got it," Wes said. He felt a twinge of conscience, even though he knew it was misplaced. These were killers, not human beings. But neither was their will their own. Nonetheless, he centered the nearest brute in the driver's side windshield, and stomped the accelerator to the floor. The monster was struck hard and flopped to the side as they passed. Unfortunately, his big hands lashed out and grabbed the armor plating that stuck out from the side, supported by sturdy struts. He was dragged along with the MRAP . . . and pulling himself toward the cab.

"Hannah!"

"I see him," she said.

Hannah leaned over Wes's back, pushed the pipe end out the window, and tracked the giant. It was only a second before her forefinger danced on the recessed button like she was sending Morse code. The light lances stabbed into the creature over and over, from waist to scalp. The thing roared, reared up, and swung a big fist hard into the armored plating.

The impact was like the M-RAP sideswiping a tree. It lurched to the right and slammed into the side of the cavern, sending out whirling hunks of jagged rock. Wes and Hannah were thrown around the cab like socks in an industrial dryer.

Before Wes could get control of the vehicle again, the second monster slammed into the passenger's side of the vehicle, right into the fender, like a raging rhinoceros.

The MRAP spun again, this time in the other direction. Hannah screamed as she was thrown against Wes, the Electrolight bouncing against the ceiling then clattering into the rear compartment. There was nothing either of them could do as they realized, with growing shock, that the two beasts were tipping over the five-thousand-pound vehicle.

It crashed to its side like a dead elephant. Wes wished they were unconscious, to at least save them the brutality of what was certain to come next, but no such luck. He looked out the cracked windshield to see General J.C. Passarelles crouching outside, smiling philosophically at him—as if to say, "You dance, you pay the piper."

At least the Riders didn't test the bulletproofing. Instead, the passenger door was ripped open, and a long, ugly arm reached in, its craggy, lumpy fingers sinking deeply into Hannah's hair.

Wes only managed one fearful, angry shout before the woman was yanked from the vehicle. Then it was his turn. Only he was thrown down at Passarelles's feet at the mouth of the cavern, while the girl was placed down gently. The Electrolight was dutifully given to the General by one of the mutations—a creature that had been rammed, dragged, and light-lanced yet was unscathed.

Wes lay there, heaving, trying to push off the cement floor. He saw the survivors, the survivors they had hoped to save, laid out on the ground unmoving, like deer culled in a hunt. He watched as the Riders slowly reappeared, gripping their guns tight, apparently for reassurance. Now that the General had managed to create these monster hybrids, they had to be wondering how much longer they would retain their elite status as the General's shock troops.

"Traitors!" Wes heard, quickly realizing it was his own voice that was accusing the Riders. "How could you do this? To your own people!"

He felt a sudden sharp pain in his temple. He jerked back to see that Passarelles had "tapped" him with the side of the Electrolight pipe.

"Now, now, Agent Harding," the General said reasonably as he turned the silvery pipe this way and that, examining it with a professional eye. "Your history is full of traitors doing this to their own people."

Wes looked up at the martinet, as if for the first time. "Who are you?" he gasped. "*What* are you?"

Passarelles took a moment to study Wes. Then he prodded Hannah's limp body with a booted toe. When she didn't react, he returned his attention to Wes. "You heard Doctor Malloy, did you not? Your old boss, your old buddy, your old—daddy complex?" He kneeled so his face was almost level with Harding's. "I am your superior, and I am taking your planet."

Hannah groaned and started to stir. Passarelles looked over at her and straightened.

"Good timing, young lady," he said. "Rise and—do not shine," he taunted, wagging the Electrolight. Passarelles looked from her to his Riders, who had assumed positions around the intruders and the survivors. He stood with a fist on his hip, his boots wide. "Get them back to the chambers!" he bellowed. "And you get back to work! *Now* is when we make this our world . . . a new world!"

That was all the Riders needed: their marching orders. They did as they were told. The two brutes, returning to flank the General, made his words all the more motivational.

When Passarelles turned back to his two prisoners, Hannah was pushing her torso up from the ground at his feet. He shook the Electrolight nonchalantly at her.

"This thing has settings," the General said affably. "Did you know that?"

Before Wes was even sure what he was going to do, the General casually moved the mouth of the weapon toward Hannah and pressed the recessed button. The light lanced into the girl, who reacted as if defibrillated.

"No!" Wes cried, diving at Passarelles.

The General did nothing. And he reacted as if Wes had done nothing. Instead, the nearest of the giants swatted Wes out of the air with one impossibly fast backhand. Wes smashed into the wall on his back, then crashed to the floor. He lay there, gasping and sobbing, as Hannah cringed and moaned.

"It was your name," Wes croaked, writhing slowly, wanting to delay the man somehow.

Wes's words had the effect he wanted. The General paused, and turned from the girl. "What was?"

"The sound—the sound one of your hybrids made. It was a sound between a grunt and a moan. That's your name, isn't it? Your *real* name? The name you were given—out there," he gestured weakly, vaguely above.

Passarelles considered it, then cocked his head. "Sounds about right, Agent Harding." He stepped from Hannah, making Wes's heart leap, though he struggled not to show it.

"I was always amazed how no one picked up on the name I chose for *here*," the General mused. "Passarelles. Know what it means?"

"No," Wes mumbled, trying to draw as much attention as he could. "No."

"I did not think so," the General responded, then knowingly leered down at him. "They are boarding ramps. A way to get from one place to another. Excuse me a moment," he said, then turned and spoke rapidly to the recovering girl. "That was the lowest setting, stun. This is the second setting." He poked the pipe in Hannah's side and pressed the recessed button.

"No!" Wes cried out almost as loud as Hannah did. The girl writhed on the ground, her hands clawing concrete and air.

The General turned back to the young man. "You might wonder why I am telling you this." He waved a dismissive hand at Hannah. "Well, for one thing, it is a waste of time to tell her. She is in no condition to understand at the moment." He thought for a second. "Now, you wanted to know my name, Agent Harding? Was that it? Or were you just trying to distract me? No matter. You know I have always enjoyed our little exchanges."

"Why?" Wes gasped. "Why are you doing this to us?"

The General seemed to consider the question seriously.

"Because I can, I suppose," he answered, and checked his watch. The expression on his face told Wes that he was disappointed there was still excess time. Something was happening elsewhere in the complex. Something that had to be finished before Passarelles could carry out his plans. Wes dared to feel hope. But then the General was talking again and Wes had to concentrate.

"You should take it as an honor, Agent Harding, you really should. I should kill you right now but, as I was saying, I have always liked you. From that first moment back in the FEMA training center, with your intelligence and your ability to take a stand, I always thought more of you than the other animals I was going to harvest. Even more than your dear friend Malloy. After all, I made him one of the first Terraphages." He sighed. "Too bad he ended up tortured and twisted. I did not want that to happen to you. I wanted you to survive, to serve"—his voice became sinister—"to kneel."

The General checked on Hannah's condition. She was still twitching. Wes looked up at the two brutes, who looked down upon him as if studying a fly in a web.

"I made a mistake, I admit it," Passarelles went on. "I started this program trying to put my kind inside your kind. That way, I could infiltrate the government, the military, with human-looking invaders. Even until this very morning, I was still trying that. But *pop, pop, pop* went the bodies. I finally called it quits. Time ran out. I should have been trying to do it the other way around the whole time, humans tucked inside Terraphage shells! You must understand, though, gutting my own kind seemed wrong, disgusting."

"*You* are disgusting," was all Wes could come up with.

The General straightened. "Me? I was handcrafted, my boy, by scientists on the home world. I was the first one sent here. I am one of the few who should be anything *but* disgusting to your eyes!"

Something the General had said a moment before finally penetrated Wes's bruised skull. "*Time ran out.*" The bastard stopped trying to put aliens inside humans because he was ready to pull the trigger on Plan B: the Achilles Heel. It didn't matter what the end result of hybridization looked like anymore. With the world in devastation, easily conquered by Passarelles, the Terraphages wouldn't have to pass as human.

Wes was instantly distracted by Passarelles again checking on Hannah's recovery.

"Yes," he muttered. "Setting two is very effective at its stated purpose: 'stop.' It stopped her, all right. But setting three? Now that holds even more promise." He glanced at Wes. "I can see by the look on your face that you think setting three is 'kill.'" Passarelles frowned and shook his head. "Oh, no, not yet. Setting three is 'coma.'"

The General lazily swung the weapon back toward Hannah as Wes stiffened in anguish. He tried to launch himself at Passarelles again, but one of the giants simply stepped on him, its heel in the middle of Wes's back. Wes struggled like a butterfly pinned to paraffin as the General paused, then kneeled again to smile smugly in the young man's enraged face.

"A question for you," Passarelles said. "Let us see how clever you are. The 'J.C.' in my name. Can you guess what those initials stand for?"

"Jesus Christ?" Wes spat, thrashing.

Passarelles laughed. "Obvious choice, but no!" he exulted. "That man was a spokesperson for peace. I do not bring your planet peace, Agent Harding. And I will most certainly not be crucified by the very people I seek to save. No, I am a wager of war. I follow the human I was most inspired by: the conqueror, the dictator, the master of the earth, Julius Cae—!"

He never got to finish, because at that moment Chief Warrant Officer Charles Augustus Dewey III flew his helicopter right into the entrance of the Coldwater Canyon cavern.

18

HEART OF DARKNESS

Of all the landings Wes had seen Dewey make, this was the most welcome, not to mention the most spectacular. There wasn't enough room in the cavern opening to fit the chopper blades. By all rights, the rotors should have hit the sides, cracked off, and flamed into a crash. But Charlie brought in the bird almost sideways, banking hard to the right in the canyon then sweeping in with the blades spinning north and south rather than east and west.

And that wasn't all. Once he had swooped in, Dewey had to pull back just enough so that he did not crash into the stone wall in front of him, all the while setting down quickly and efficiently, compensating for prop backwash racing at him from every direction except overhead. Even through punch-swollen eyes, Wes could not help but marvel at the sweet piece of flying.

But it wasn't without casualty. Coming in low, a blade swiped through one of Passarelles's mutated brutes from shoulder to rib, sending off his top third like a pull-top tab. The creature's right arm and head splatted hard against the cavern top while the rest of its body knocked backward into the wall.

Luckily for Wes, it was the gorilla that had been standing on him. The creature's demise allowed Wes to scramble upright. He immediately clawed for Passarelles, but the General had turned heel, ordering his other brute to cover his retreat and dragging Hannah with him.

With both hands occupied pulling Hannah, there was one thing Passarelles couldn't take: the Electrolight. Wes ducked down, grabbed it and stood, frustrated, because he knew it wouldn't work on the General or the malformed henchman. He was also frustrated because he couldn't give chase—yet. He couldn't abandon his rescuer, who popped out of the copter door with his own MP7 blazing at the Riders who had charged back into the chamber at the sound of his arrival. Between the guns and the powering-down chopper, the noise was like being punched in both ears by heavyweights with horseshoes in their gloves. But Wes had to wince and bear it. The sight of that assault rifle in Charlie's hands told him which direction to turn as he brought up the Electrolight.

He started pumping light-lances into every Rider he saw. Even so, the troopers just kept coming, like ants pouring out to defend their hill.

And then there were the doubts, which he had in spite of himself: *How many bullets does Charlie have? How long will this gadget keep working?* Even now, Wes could feel the device heating up in his hands.

The Riders' bullets kept getting closer as Wes and Charlie stood their ground, firing as fast and accurately as they could. Worse, between the cavern walls and the copter, there was no real room to maneuver, and Wes wasn't going to take cover behind the crashed M-RAP while Charlie was still in the open.

Wes felt one bullet sizzle past his cheek. He felt another nearly flick his earlobe. The Riders were dodging and ducking, forcing Wes to lose precious firing time by tracking them and adjusting. And there were more behind them. Any second a bullet might find him, and even if they hit his arm or leg, it would be as good as over.

Wes wanted to retreat, but Charlie couldn't hear him if he yelled, and he dared not pause to gesture. Just then, Wes had a "duh" moment that perked his spirits. Charlie had an MP7. Where did he get it? There could only be one place! And that might mean—

The bullets that seemed to be moving in on him suddenly started to diminish in number and hit increasingly wide of the mark. The roar of the gunfire from Dewey seemed to increase in volume. And—Wes could just barely pick it out, probably because he was hoping to hear it—there was the sound of enraged, vengeful shouts and more gunfire coming from behind him.

Thank freaking God were the only words that came to mind.

He didn't have to look over to know that Dewey had not come by his lonesome. The first voice Wes recognized was Rick—also holding an appropriated MP7 and leading through the cavern opening dozens of police officers, firefighters, National Guardsmen, Wes's fellow FEMA agents, Charlie's fellow rotorheads, and even some brave Red Cross reps. Wes realized it was the East 101 survivors.

Rick must have disobeyed Professor Dumas. The new rustic agers used their experience and knowledge to find, disarm, and defuse the Rider snipers around the base camp. There hadn't been enough time to repair the sabotaged choppers, so Rick led them through the tunnels and drainpipe.

Wes felt elation unlike anything he had ever experienced. It seemed to supercharge his senses, speed them, sharpen them. Riders fell, along with the Riders behind them. Then Wes heard a sound close to his right ear. He whirled to face Charlie, who had leaped the space between them in a heartbeat. The two men fired side-by-side, hip-to-hip, taking out Riders from the flank as the East 101 team mowed them down from the front. Even though not all of the new arrivals had guns, they made savage, certain use of the hammers, knives, and bludgeons they could find or fashion. Wes even saw planks wrapped in razor wire being swung with merciless efficiency.

"I gotta go!" Wes shouted suddenly. Still firing, he started toward the rear of the cavern.

A tight hand on the crook of his arm stopped him. "The Prof says wait!" Dewey shouted over the din, before hastily grabbing a fallen Rider's gun to replace his empty one.

"Why?"

Dewey shrugged without altering the position of his weapon. "He didn't specify."

"Screw that!" Wes answered. He looked everywhere to spot Dumas, but the Professor was nowhere in sight. "Where the hell is he?"

"I don't know!" Charlie said, targeting and bringing down a Rider who was about to shoot a nurse. "He wouldn't get into my copter. He was going to, but then he said he had to take care of some things."

"'Some things'?" Wes raged, sneering at the Professor's choice of words as he light-lanced two hard-charging Riders. They were leaping angrily, aggressively over their fallen comrades; two more Riders joined the pile on the ground in a pair of light flashes. "Earth is about to be destroyed, and he's got errands? I can't wait. Passarelles has Hannah!"

"Shit. But Dumas said—"

"He also has nukes and the location of the fault line that can destroy our planet."

Dewey nodded. "Godspeed, man."

Harding ran toward the rear of the cavern, light-lancing every Rider who came into his vision. The Electrolight all but burned his hands now. Wes didn't care. He got behind the Riders and shot them in the back without hesitation or remorse. He only took his eyes off those targets to make quick, glancing studies of the darkness into which Passarelles had disappeared.

It was more of a chasm than anything Wes had seen to date, a steep, narrow tunnel that only had room for two people at a time. The distant, familiar drilling and pounding sounds were amplified by it like notes through a trumpet. As long as those noises continued, Wes figured the end was not quite near, and they still had a chance.

He turned back when he heard the gunfire abate somewhat, saw that the survivors had routed the Riders. Whoever wasn't lying still was being aggressively detained by the firefighters and interrogated by the cops. Wes saw heroic survivors lying motionless amongst the fallen. But he also noticed survivors toeing the enemy dead to make sure they were dead, bending to check their own comrades.

He stopped running and faced them.

"People!" he shouted. Because he was positioned near the mouth of the chasm, his voice was amplified and echoed. He didn't wait for all of them to turn or look up before he continued. "I'm going after something that can and *will* destroy our planet. Everything that lives will die, except for the monsters that are responsible. Our history, our memories, our families—all of it will be gone. After all you've been through, nobody would blame you if you didn't follow me. But I'm asking anyway."

"Who the hell are you?" boomed one cop, gripping a Rider's bloody collar in a tight fist.

"Nobody," Wes answered immediately. "I used to be with FEMA. But I know this—we have a chance to stop it before it's too late."

"Stop what?" asked a National Guardsman.

"Didn't we just stop it?" asked a Red Cross worker, gesturing at all the fallen Riders.

Wes searched the survivors' faces and saw some who were obviously interested, but many more that showed skepticism, exhaustion, and even argument. He couldn't blame the latter. They were war-weary and out of fight.

Wes Harding stopped talking. Bone-tired himself, he turned and entered the chasm at a hard run.

H annah Lonnegin awoke.
Somehow she had heard the word "coma," and hoped she would find herself in a hospital bed between crisp, clean sheets with sunlight through the window—having slept through the worst of it. The world would be healed, Passarelles defeated, the ordeal over. Or, even better, she would wake to see Wes's face smiling down on her, and the blue sky of Earth beyond. He was

an idiot, but he was an idiot she knew cared for her more than
anyone she had ever known.

But there was no Wes or hospital room. This was a rusting, run-
down, circular chamber that seemed huge and cramped at the
same time. It was actually a giant mushroom of warped metal and
cracked glass—a mammoth spool made up of a central column
lined with workstations, hemmed in by a mottled steel ceiling,
and surrounded by a mezzanine of broken readout screens along
the top of a crumbling wall.

She immediately knew that she was in the General's personal
heart of darkness. She knew because of the drilling sounds that
filled her ears, the misshapen thing that loomed over her like a
golem, and the man-thing himself—standing at a workstation
nearby, his back to her.

The creature said something like a grunt mixed with a moan.
Even though he seemed to whisper it, the sound carried over the
drilling noise.

Passarelles turned toward Hannah. His expression mixed the
expectation of victory with the realization of the hard job that
lay ahead. He did not smile upon Hannah as he approached. He
smirked instead, with the look of a man who had total power over
her. The look of conquerors and terrorists and sadists everywhere.

"Ms. Lonnegin," he said, savoring the name. He stood over her
as she laid still, her head resting on the wall. "Hannah Lonnegin—
do you know where you are?"

"Hell?" Hannah tried to say, but she doubted it got out of her
aching head. If it had, Passarelles didn't react.

"This is what is left of an American off-line nuclear weapon
silo," the General informed her. He looked around as if admiring a

log cabin he had built with his own hands. "Believe it or not, it was in worse shape when I came upon it. Totally without use, aside from its warhead. But I soon rectified that. It took years to realign and reactivate it, as well as add a drilling component, but I did it. With the help of your people, of course."

He made careful note of her disbelieving expression.

"Oh, it is true," he assured her. "Your kind can be very helpful when they think there is something in it for them. Money, or power, or even the chance of money and power." He looked back at the workstation with something approaching wistfulness. "Or, if they are far enough along in the process, it becomes a matter of obsession. You can play on their hatreds to get what you want. Very helpful species, the human."

Passarelles seemed to feed on Hannah's look of anger. A smile grew, and his head cocked like a man who was listening to a beautiful symphony.

"Do you hear that?" he asked, apparently intent on toying with her. "That is the sound of your world ending. As soon as the drilling stops, I will have uncovered the trigger spot, the location where only a single fifty-megaton strike will set off a chain reaction that will tear this planet apart."

"Not much good for anyone then," Hannah managed to say, but the reaction of her abused body when she tried to move ended her statement with a long groan.

Even so, Passarelles understood her.

"On the contrary," he said. "That is the way my race likes it. More 'terra' for us to 'phage.'" He smiled sickly at his own witticism. "To eat, you see? Pre-ground . . . another joke! After we clear through the wreckage, of course."

"Bon appétit, then," Hannah grunted, trying to find one milli-meter of her body that wasn't aching. She failed.

Passarelles laughed. "Ah, still the brash nihilist to the end."

"Fat lot you know," Hannah spat, managing to get to a seated position. "Quite the opposite, in fact."

The General was taken aback. Not by her lack of respect, that was to be expected, but by her seeming lack of fear.

"I have noticed that humans use hollow, generic words to bol-ster their flagging efforts," he said. "I thought you above such futile, childish braggadocio."

She shrugged, eliciting another cringe of pain. "Hardly that," she countered and looked up at him knowingly. "You kept me alive before because you wanted something from me." She looked around at her continued existence, such as it was. "Apparently you still do. That's just me not being as stupid as you seem to think."

That got a response out of Passarelles, although not necessarily the one she was looking for. All sense of pretense stripped away, the General knelt beside her, his face a mask of triumphant anger. But there was also something more—something frightening.

"Do you know what I want from you, Ms. Lonnegin?" he seethed. "For you *not* to die!"

That scared her. It terrified her down to her sore bones. She was already one awful step ahead of him.

"You think the worst that could happen is death," the General continued. "You *ignorant* creature! What if the worst that could happen is that you become a host? The first female hybrid host. The first queen who will serve me, and me alone."

"A big alien ant? In a colony?" she asked.

"In a superior civilization," he said.

"Not possible, if you're a part of it."

He all but stuck his face against hers, spitting with barely contained fury.

"You will learn better! I did not know this shell's perverse lusts when I first came here, but now I do," he said. "We have no counterpart to this kind of vengeful hate. But now that I know this longing—"

He never got to finish. Wes Harding exploded through the silo's entrance, just feet from the General, swinging the Electrolight like a baseball bat. The side of the silver pipe slammed against Passarelles's head with a satisfying, arm-shaking clang. Any human's head and neck would have been shattered by the impact, but Passarelles was more than human. He fell to the floor and slid on his side before tumbling over onto his back—not dead but definitely not conscious.

Wes pressed his advantage before the General's savage bodyguard could react. He jumped on top of Passarelles, straddling his torso, the Electrolight high above his head, ready to smash down as hard as he could in the center of the General's face. Wes could see that Passarelles's cheek was split open, revealing what looked like muscles beneath—but they were not human muscles. They were tight, leathered muscles that mixed red human sinew with black, knotted Terraphage cords. He chose a target: the forehead. There must still be a brain inside that skull.

That briefest moment of decision cost Wes everything. It distracted him just long enough for the General's eyes to snap open and look at him—with a small, painless grin pasted on his mouth.

Wes flew off the General as if he'd been shot from an air cannon. He slammed to the ground and slid into the wall just behind

Hannah. In a remarkably short instant, the inhuman Passarelles was on his feet and barreling toward the young man, both fists up. It was clear he would not make the same mistake Wes had. He would not choose a spot to strike. All of Wes was his target.

Passarelles was so intent on ending Wes's existence that he was caught unaware when Hannah vaulted to her feet and struck him in the shoulder from behind, as hard as she could. To her, the impact felt like striking a heavy bag in the gym. Passarelles flew forward and his hands rose with supernatural speed to prevent him from hitting the wall. He spun and roared in anger, his eyes shading from human to something luminous yellow.

Hannah leaped ahead to try to drag Wes away, but Passarelles's arm was faster. He grabbed her and pulled back hard, sending her face-first to the floor. Then he was on her back, nailing her there, as he twisted toward Wes and cocked a fist to crush the young man's face.

Hannah tried and failed to hoist the General off. His mass was astonishing. She screwed her eyes shut and turned her head away, fully expecting her face to be flecked with Wes's blood any second. When it didn't happen, her eyes snapped open. She saw Wes gasping for breath, and the General frozen in place, his raised fist motionless. The yellow eyes blinked. The angry mouth pulled into something like a smile.

That's when she realized the sound of drilling had stopped.

Before the battered humans could fully comprehend what had happened—that time had truly run out—Passarelles was marching back toward the workstation.

"Kill this man," General Julius Caesar Passarelles ordered the giant hybrid as if it were the most rudimentary of tasks. "When you have done that, take this girl to the third chamber." His fore-finger stretched forward as he walked toward the workstation console. It was aiming at a red button, a literal kill switch. "I will join you as soon as I end this world."

Both he and his bodyguard stopped in mid-stride as the drilling suddenly resumed.

Passarelles looked baffled. The drilling had stopped and re-started—something it had never done in the weeks since he had taken over the Los Angeles basin. But it was different this time. The humans understood the difference first. When the General turned to look toward them, their faces were turned upward. The General realized that the sound was not coming from below them. It was coming from above.

Passarelles looked up just as the mottled metal ceiling gave way, and the bottom of a glowing red dome appeared.

19

CATWALKS

The General made a sound Wes and Hannah had never heard before, but would never forget. Much more than the grunt and moan the brute had made, this was a series of loud, guttural syllables, sharp and fast, like a clarion call. It was immediately drowned out by the sound of the twenty-by-twelve-foot dome hitting the floor hard, like a massively oversized gumdrop. The curved bottom gave a little, then sprang back and resumed its convex shape.

Before anyone could react, a carved shepherd's staff emerged from the side of the dome, followed by the sleeve of a decorated lab coat. The arm of Professor Bernard Nigel Dumas arrived, followed by the estimable man himself. He strode through the translucent wall like a ghost coming through the door of a haunted house.

"Professor!" Hannah cried. She knew that was self-evident, but it was a knee-jerk expression of joy.

"Not a bad landing, considering how long it's been since I've driven this thing," Dumas said.

Passarelles stared at him with angry derision, then made the trumpeting sound again.

And suddenly Wes knew. "That's *his* name!" he gasped.

Hannah looked over at the young man, whose face was infused with shock. "Whose name?" she wondered.

"My name," Dumas said before Wes could go on. "My real name."

Passarelles made a quick move toward the workstation, but Dumas was quicker. The walking stick blocked Passarelles first, and then Dumas stepped between the General and the console.

"No," Dumas said, and he made the grunting moan sound that served as Passarelles's original name. "No more. No more death, no more destruction. That was not our mission. That was never our mission."

"It was *my* mission, you tired, craven thing!"

"I *am* tired—from tracking you, building my own little army of spies," the Professor replied. He took a sure, firm step forward. "I watched you from the shadows, talking to people who knew people . . . always with an eye on this day, this moment." He stopped walking, stood proudly before his fellow alien. "I built a commune of eyes and ears which your earthquake failed to destroy. Now we will see who is craven."

"'Our mission,'" Hannah echoed, still unable to accept it.

"Yes," Dumas said, speaking to the humans but not moving his eyes from the General, or moving his body. "Our mission. I am what he is—an alien prime from another planet, raised from human cells spliced with Terraphage cells, sent here to scout Earth."

"That's a spaceship?" Wes asked doubtfully, eyeing the ruddy, balloon-like conveyance.

"Indeed it is," Dumas replied. "Parked for twenty-one years in Bronson Cavern, underground in the cave."

"Then those awful chambers we saw—" Hannah began.

"Budded from the biomechanical hull," the Professor said. He nodded toward the General. "This Terraphage carved away a few outer cells, used them to create monstrous transformation chambers."

Wes and Hannah were openly thunderstruck, but they were snapped back to attention when Passarelles surged forward. Dumas seemed to move with him, matching his speed and power, blocking him from going past. Wes saw frustration, and even concern, on the General's face.

He's afraid of the Professor, Wes realized. Dumas hadn't been wrong about that.

To cover being stonewalled, Passarelles started yelling at the man-alien before him. "You are not qualified to say what our mission was, or is," the General spat derisively. "You lost yourself. Your own hybridization was too successful. From the moment you transformed, your natural aesthetics made you too *human* to do what is best for us!"

The General sneered the word "human" as if it were a profanity.

"No," Dumas scolded. "I developed this process to meld what was *best* in us, and them, and every alien race we encountered."

"Alien races . . . plural?" Wes muttered, looking at the ship. "Jee-sus."

Passarelles circled his adversary like a tiger, Dumas moving to stay between the General and the console.

"Our race did not need tempering or improving," Passarelles said.

"Clearly, it does," Dumas remarked with a knowing look at the other alien. "Did you ever wonder why you couldn't successfully replicate the process without me? Your need was too urgent, too fanatical. As a result, your methods were rushed and careless."

"I knew you were out there, watching me," Passarelles replied. "And you lie."

"Do I?"

"I have had success," he maintained, waving toward the brute. "Great success!"

"Causing earthquakes? Creating what, drone-like slaves? Beasts?" Dumas pointed a long, knobby forefinger at the giant. "And what did your efforts get you except for *their* deaths? He is the only one left, I'm guessing, or they would be massed around you. All the rest of your troops, human and Terraphage, have been routed. You overreached, stretched our resources." Dumas took an angry step toward him. "We were created with orders to scout this planet for possible contact and mutual benefit, not to conquer or destroy it!"

Passarelles laughed. "The orders of a tired, old tribunal, content to remain on an aged, spent, *dying* world! In all the years you have been here, did you learn nothing from these creatures' own history? Never, not once, did they establish a colony without destroying the indigenous people. Besides, have you forgotten? We Terraphages *feast* on dying planets! Their minerals nourish us!"

"We harvested meteors and asteroids as our population grew," Dumas said. "Have you forgotten? That is *why* we went to space. You military officers corrupted that! Damn you, *this* planet isn't dying!"

Passarelles laughed. "Are you blind as well as timid? These creatures are well on their way to destroying their world. I am only hastening the process!"

Dumas visibly controlled himself, then sighed. "Of course you would see it that way. You came to rule, not to mingle, engage, improve the natives. When I first moved among them I saw infinite possibilities and untold depths. These people"—he gestured to Wes and Hannah, then more broadly toward where the Pencil Crew had once labored—"these people have proved the potential worth and self-sacrifice of the species."

"Enough!" Passarelles boomed. "You have had your say, but I give the orders now!" His look of hate made Wes and Hannah recoil. "I should have killed you when I had the chance."

"It was not for lack of trying," Dumas reminded him evenly.

"Then I shall stop 'trying,'" the General said. He turned his head toward the monstrous hybrid. "Kill them all," he ordered. "Now."

Hannah and Wes prepared to fight for their lives but were surprised—as surprised as the General—when the giant did not move.

"I gave you a command!" Passarelles screamed at him.

"Hive mind, Julius Caesar," Dumas reminded him, giving the new rustic age salute. "Need I point out that there is more than one Terraphage mind here now? He has conflicting orders."

"Our gods damn you!" Passarelles seethed, leaping—not for Dumas but for the workstation. With a look of evil triumph, he flicked up a plastic cover and thumbed a dark, recessed button as if he were digging for gold.

Wes and Hannah instinctively embraced, burying their heads in each other's shoulders, waiting for either an atomic blast to engulf them or the ground to open beneath them.

Neither happened. Nothing happened.

"Why do you think it took so long for me to get here?" Dumas asked them all calmly. "This was not my first stop. Learning your plan, I had to find, and cut, the cable that powered your deadly box." He grinned. "I only blocked you here because I have been waiting to confront you for a long, long time."

Passarelles shrieked a string of what were obviously Terraphage curses. Still shouting, he raced toward the airlock on the far side of the silo.

Hannah jumped up to embrace the Professor, thinking that it was all over, but Dumas held her off, bringing the AA-battery-sized communicator out of his pocket and up to his mouth.

"What's wrong?" she asked.

"We're not in the clear, not yet," he said grimly as Hannah stood in mid-embrace, openmouthed and wide-eyed. "The General is going to try to set off the nuclear device manually."

"But you just said you disarmed it!" Wes said, running up to the man.

"I killed the electronics," the Professor replied. "There is still a manual component, and only *he* knows where it is. That must be found."

With that, Dumas clacked his staff on the hard floor and began running on his long legs toward the cavern into which Passarelles had disappeared.

"Rick, Charlie, get in here now," Dumas said, speaking urgently into his communicator. "In just a few more seconds, the brute's brain will unfreeze."

The others began to pour through the cavern entrance where they had been waiting. Wes was about to take Hannah's elbow and follow the Professor when the woman suddenly broke toward the others. Wes was surprised until he saw why. Galloping out front,

Bunter had arrived with the renegade new rustic agers. The cat leaped into Hannah's waiting arms.

"My dear friend and partner," she said.

"Had a helluva time holding him back," Rick remarked.

Wes's spirits sagged. Even if he weren't an "idiot," he wondered if there was a place for any man in that tight little bond. But there was no time to worry about the future when the future was not yet secured.

"We better go," he said.

Charlie and Hannah, plus the cat, fell in behind him and hurried after Dumas. They were surprised to find the Professor rushing back.

"What's wrong?" Wes said.

"Nothing. I just wanted to make sure the General was really off in that direction and not hiding. He's slippery."

"So what are you gonna do?" Charlie asked with alarm. "Climb down the silo after him?"

"You are," Dumas said. "I'm sticking with the same ride that got me and the General to your planet in the first place. It'll be faster."

And with that, he stepped toward and then through the seemingly magic wall of the domed spacecraft, leaving Wes and the others behind to gape.

Charlie Dewey grabbed Wes's arm and pulled him back. "Dumas explained that it uses some sort of iron-powered magnetic drive," the pilot informed him. "Won't burn you up, but the surface vibrations might liquefy your insides if you're too close."

The humans hustled away from it just as the gumdrop-shaped thing began to ascend. At the same time, Rick and a bunch of heavily armed survivors approached the giant hybrid that, as predicted, was shaking its head as if coming out of a trance.

"Whoever you are, listen!" Rick yelled at the creature. "I know the General bred you to destroy humans, but you must know that's suicide now. Don't try. We don't want to hurt you. We want you to join us!"

As the domed ship floated up the way it had entered, the humans watched the monster's face work to understand. There was confusion, then anger, then regret. Then it raised its fists and started to step toward them.

"Please, don't!" Rick said.

The creature made something that sounded like one of the oaths Passarelles had mouthed, and charged. Rick stepped back in sadness. He moved between Hannah and Wes, told them to cover their ears as the cavern echoed with gunfire. The others watched as the brute was literally torn apart by bullets—its head and chest erupting like the top of a volcano.

No one looked away. No one wanted to forget the terrible price every living thing had paid to get to this point. Only when it plopped to the concrete floor did their eyes seek out each other.

"Let's go," Wes said with disgust.

They ran in the direction Passarelles had disappeared. The cavern gave them a straight shot to the inner sanctum, and the General had left the big vault-like door open. Wes waved the others to stand still and peered cautiously into the silo. When no booby trap or bullet appeared, he looked down, up, and all around.

"That's what I was afraid of," Wes muttered.

"What?" Charlie said.

"It's a maze in there," Wes said. "And I don't see what we came for."

Charlie joined him and looked around. Wes wasn't exaggerating. Tunnels, walkways, and ladders abounded. The defunct missile, which was taking up most of the central core, was gutted—its warhead missing.

"Passarelles could be anywhere," Wes said. "The warhead could be anywhere. The opening to the Achilles Heel could be anywhere."

"Did the Pentagon really put a silo on . . . a fault line?" Charlie asked.

"Back then, they might not have known it was here," Rick said. "We're still finding fault lines, old *and* new."

Wes turned to Rick and Charlie. "Does the Professor have some sort of Terraphage-locator in the ship?"

Rick frowned, unsure, while Charlie shrugged.

"I doubt he has anything like that," decided Hannah, "or else Passarelles would have one too and would have been able to track him."

"Smart woman," they all heard Dumas say from the bug in Rick's pocket. "And more bad news: the General would not be careless enough to make his hiding place big enough for the spaceship. He's counting on us running out of time."

"Land, and search for another way in," Wes said. "There has to be an emergency doorway somewhere. Every despot has one."

"No time," Dumas said. "You go, I'll track the bug from up here."

"Moving into the silo now," Rick said, starting to reach for the ladder bolted to the side. It seemed the quickest way to get where they had to go: down.

"Hold on!" Hannah interrupted, grabbing his arm and pulling him back. With a knowing smile, she stepped inside, holding Bunter under one arm. "We have to find the General, and I know someone who is better equipped for that than we are. I'm sure he got a good sniff."

"*Very* smart woman," they all heard Dumas say, and before anyone could express their doubts, the cat was off. Hannah raced after him, followed by Wes, Charlie, and Rick. Almost at once, they found themselves, appropriately, on a catwalk.

Charlie gave Wes a dubious look as they trotted ahead. "I'm thinking we're gonna find a whole lot of mice," he muttered.

"More likely the easiest way out," Wes replied from experience.

"You're *both* idiots," Hannah said. "Bunter is used to finding—and avoiding—the General and his shock troops."

"Yeah, I'm putting my money on these two," said Rick. "In the short amount of time I've seen them in action, I think he and Hannah are somehow psychically connected."

Wes didn't doubt it. He wondered—only partly in jest—if maybe the Professor hadn't snuck a little of his Terraphage brain into the cat . . . or Hannah.

They all stopped talking and followed as best they could. Although the network of paths and steps were intact, they were hardly very solid. The cat could navigate them with ease, but the humans had to be more cautious lest they fall to their deaths. There was a railing, but it was rickety, no doubt weakened by the constant drilling.

Thankfully, the run was short. Within minutes they all came to a sudden stop behind the cat, which was looking over the side of one walkway. They followed his feline gaze to an area that was brilliant with floodlights. Passarelles was far below, at the foot of the surface-to-surface missile. He was hunched over a steel cone, the side panel of which lay on the ground beside him.

"Professor!" Rick cried. "He's got the bomb!"

"I'm on your signal—don't move!" Dumas said.

"Doesn't he have to get it into the Achilles Heel?" Wes asked.

"No," Dumas replied. "He only had to uncover it. The shock waves will penetrate far enough."

"But if he detonates the warhead, he'll die too!" Hannah said. Then added, "Won't he?"

"You heard Wes before," Dumas said. "There should be a doorway—"

"I see it," Hannah said, gazing at a big door like the one they'd passed through. It was already open.

"I'm reading a small pod beyond it," Dumas said, "a miniature spaceship. Double jeopardy, even if we stop the plan, he gets away."

Passarelles suddenly looked up. The lights illuminated his grin. "There is not much time!" He laughed, his voice echoing through the chamber like something deeply demonic. "I offer you all a choice! I give you a chance to live! Join me!" His gaze singled out the woman. "Rule with me!"

"So tempting," she sneered.

Visibly infuriated by her mockery, the General huddled over the mechanism, his efforts redoubled.

"We've got to go down," Wes said.

"We were told to stay put," Hannah cautioned.

"Yeah, but he's—"

Wes's mouth clapped shut, his stomach began to knot, and he started to feel light-headed. *Vertigo?* he wondered. *Am I developing vertigo from all the climbing and falling?*

The answer came when he looked up to see the former launch dome opening. Dumas had obviously used his ship to jack into the mechanism. Moments later the domed starship dropped quickly through the open maw of the silo.

Rick grabbed the others and pushed them to the catwalk floor as the gumdrop-shaped thing fell past.

"Wait." He gasped. "Wait until the queasiness passes!"

Wes didn't listen. He grabbed the catwalk rail and dragged himself over. He looked down just in time to see what he had not expected: the ship didn't disgorge its occupant on a catwalk. It continued down, crashing through the missile and continuing onto the level where Passarelles was working. Dumas leaped through the wall of the now-lopsided ship, landing atop the General.

That was all Wes saw as he felt the silo shake through his fingers. The ladder wobbled, and he watched as the entire structure around him collapsed like an unhinged Erector set.

20

SACRIFICES

Hannah's hands shot down over the top rung and found Wes's wrists. His fingers were knotted so tightly around the trembling ladder that he did not even realize she was there. She held his sleeves, her heels dug in against an upright of the catwalk, and kept him from going over when the ladder he was gripping tightly fell from beneath him.

Rick was a few paces behind her and, leaning over, he pulled Wes back up to the relative safety of the trembling walkway.

There was another jolting shudder. Wes and Hannah held each other and whatever else their free hands could grab, but Rick lost his footing as the catwalk split along a joint. It angled precipitously to one side, dumping him toward another section below. The rustic new ager was able to grab a still screwed-in section of handrail and hold on.

Charlie was also thrown, but his electron-swift reflexes enabled him to hook his arm around a section of the handrail a few yards ahead of Rick.

"Bunter!" Hannah suddenly remembered. "Where's Bunter?"

A moment later the cat appeared from behind. It leaped onto the young woman's back and clawed its way up to her shoulder. That told Wes that the surface they were on was sloping even more than it seemed. It was difficult to tell with only the smooth walls behind and the fat missile in front.

But everyone was safe for the moment, and that gave them time to look below them, searching for the Professor and the General.

"There!" Wes cried, pointing across the silo toward the base of the missile.

They followed his finger to see, far below, Dumas and Passarelles struggling amid a crosshatch of fallen catwalks and ladders. The spaceship itself was trapped in the collapsing metal. Unless it had the ability to teleport, which seemed unlikely, it would be unable to fly anyone to safety. Wes looked for and found the bomb itself, which sat astride a split section of the steel floor, as if the silo itself were holding it away with disdainful fingers.

The General raged in his strange tongue, swinging whatever fist or foot he could at his nemesis without sending himself down through one of the new fissures into the darkness below.

Though Dumas was standing awkwardly with one foot on a fallen section of catwalk, the other foot braced against the missile itself, he easily deflected the blows with his staff.

Wes recognized that the Professor knew more about the human body and mind than Passarelles ever would. Probably more than Wes ever would as well. He began to appreciate what secrets that great alien mind must hold.

The General thrashed with increasing violence but ebbing

precision, his eyes livid with red, black, and yellow, his torn cheek throbbing.

"Let me help you, Julius," Dumas said in English. "Please. Before it's too late."

"It is already too late!" Passarelles raged. "For you, for me, for the entire planet! If I cannot own it, I *will* destroy it!"

As he spoke, the General twisted in the air and propelled himself toward the bomb, his fingers clawing. To everyone's surprise, Dumas seemed to retreat. But that was not his plan. Stepping closer to the spaceship, he plunged his shepherd's staff into the side of the craft.

The humans all saw a white pulse emanate outward.

Wes and Hannah, still holding each other, looked down at what seemed to be a clear, billowing bubble that encased the ship, both alien primes, and the device. The General and Dumas appeared to be floating within it, and they both seemed to be suffocating.

"Professor!" Hannah cried. "Will he be okay?"

"I don't know," Dewey replied. "The Terraphages 'breathe' a vacuum the way we breathe an atmosphere."

"So their human bodies can't handle it," Wes said.

The two figures started to go through the human stages of suffocation—eyes bulging, tongues stabbing from their mouths, fingers clawing at their throats.

"We've got to help!" Wes said.

"How?" Rick demanded.

Wes looked around frantically, his eyes finally settling on the open silo door behind them. "There!" he called to them, pointing back.

JEFF ROVIN

Survivors were standing in the open door, gazing down. In their hands were tools, weapons, and implements. One of them held the Electrolight.

Wes waved toward them. "A rope!" he yelled. "Lower the Electrolight down the catwalk!"

One of the survivors gave him a thumbs-up. Slowly, cautiously, Wes began easing back toward the wall of the silo. It was about a thirty-degree angle up to the door. He wanted to be in a direct line with the opening.

"Why bother with the Electrolight?" Hannah asked when he was safe. "Passarelles's nervous system is impervious."

"We need a Plan B," Wes said.

"What's Plan A?" Dewey asked.

"I honestly don't know," Wes replied. "I'm hoping the Professor has one. If not, I may have to fry the warhead before Passarelles can activate it."

"Why wait?" Hannah asked.

"Because who knows if the beam could jumpstart the bomb? Seems like something we do not want to mess with unless we have to."

Wes watched the group above, huddled, arms moving. When they turned back to the door, there was a heavy line wrapped around the weapon. Wes motioned to them, and they let it half slide, half dangle to where Dewey was holding the rear rail. He grabbed the Electrolight with one hand and quickly untied it. Then, with Hannah's help, he made his way back to the outer railing. Wes settled the weapon between the top and middle rails and angled it down, past the missile. He handed Hannah the end of the rope; the other end was still in the hands of the survivors.

"Tie it to the catwalk," he urged.

She lashed it to one of the railing uprights and communicated her intent to the survivors, who doubled down on their end. Then they all stared at the struggling, strangling alien primes. Dumas looked like a man dying. Passarelles looked like a man dying as well—only with an alien invader emerging through a gash in his face.

"Crap," Dewey said.

"What?" Wes asked.

"You're brilliant, Wes. The Prof *does* have a Plan A. Only he needs our help."

"Not following," Wes admitted.

"It's not about suffocation," Dewey thought aloud. "When the Pencil Crew were exposed to the localized vacuum, the Terraphages inside them exploded out! That's a byproduct of the General's bass-ackward process. *That's* what the Prof is trying to do to him!"

"Release his inner Terraphage?" Wes asked. "Why?"

Dewey thought for a moment. The words the Professor had read came back to him: *Localized vacuum defense mechanism triggered by sharp impact, not by organic or alien biological matter.* The airman was suddenly proud of the Professor. Not only for his heroics below but for his trust: Dumas had faith that his people would listen and learn from what he had taught them, what he showed them.

"Baby ton," Dewey said quietly.

"What?" Wes answered.

"Darts—a big score."

"I know that. What's it got to do—"

"You've got a sharp eye, great technique," Dewey said.

"I still don't follow, Charlie."

"The Electrolight," the pilot announced, clambering to his knees while leaning against the railing. "Give me a minute."

The grated floor shuddered unpleasantly. Dewey ignored the danger, looked into the silo, focused on the catwalk clinging to the wall just above them. He would have traded an arm for his binoculars. He scanned the opposite wall carefully.

Meanwhile, the others watched, breathless, as the Terraphage inside Passarelles started to bubble and ooze down the General's face and neck. As it emerged, it seemed to inflate, flapping like a sail in the wind.

Rick had to wipe tears from his eyes as he watched the Professor's face turn dark red, then purple, then green, and finally mottled black. No Terraphage emerged from him. His integration into humanity was complete—inside and out. The broken capillaries in his bulging eyes were blood red as his human brain started to starve for oxygen and shut down.

"Jesus!" someone screamed from the doorway.

They all gasped as the Terraphage suddenly erupted from Passarelles's body—exploding out into a black, oil-splashed thundercloud. Its sound of rage and triumph shook the silo as it turned on the Professor's small, still, floating body. But, unlike the Pencil Crew victims, the General's Terraphage did not dissipate and die. It seemed to gather strength from the vacuum.

At the same time, they all could see, in various stages of horror, the human lungs of the General powering Passarelles even now. They saw hints of the bones and other organs within the vacillating blackness. They could even see the brain and eyes sinking in and out of the new creature exulting below them.

"I've got it!" Dewey said, pointing to a spot on the opposite side of the silo, just above and slightly behind the spaceship. "There, Wes! Hit the catwalk where the railing is split, three uprights toward nine o'clock!"

Wes scanned up, then down, following a trajectory. "So it'll impale the spacecraft?"

"And restore—" Dewey started.

"Restore the oxygen," Wes finished with a grin.

He rose on his knees and aimed the Electrolight at the railing. He didn't care if he lost his balance and plunged sideways down the catwalk to his death. All that mattered was that he fired the weapon fast and true. He felt Hannah's eyes on him, heard her tense breathing even as his weight caused the catwalk to creak and slip. When he felt he had the spot, he fired. A white lance of light sizzled forward. It struck the rail just above the cracked steel. The small rift widened like an alligator opening its jaws. The hollow tubing snapped, the pop echoing through the silo. The walkway spasmed, and then the compromised section came away, dropping vertically.

The jagged end that was supposed to hit the spacecraft did not.

With an unearthly leap on its trunk-like legs, the monster that was J.C. Passarelles intercepted the makeshift projectile, threw it aside, and landed on the other side of the spacecraft.

Then, with a shriek of fury, it turned and jumped back—toward the dying Dumas.

Wes watched with despair, feeling helpless. "But I'm not," he murmured suddenly.

"Not what?" Hannah asked.

"Helpless," he replied.

"Wes, what are you—"

But Wes had already let go of her . . . and of the steel railing.

"Wes, no!" Hannah shouted.

Still holding the Electrolight, Wes Harding dropped like the catwalk had, hard and straight down. His feet slammed into a collapsed walkway ten feet below him. He slid down the angle it was tilted—toward the two combatants.

"You'll suffocate!" Dewey shouted.

Slip-sliding ahead, stumbling when he wasn't running, Wes could already feel the bubble of non-air beginning to challenge his lungs. He sucked in what oxygen there was, and when there wasn't any left, he held his breath. He felt the change in pressure weigh on his skin, from the inside, but he focused on the grotesque thing that was stalking toward the prone Dumas.

Above, Rick blinked in astonished respect. Somehow, even while suffocating, Dumas had dragged himself directly above the warhead to make sure the General's Terraphage couldn't get to it without a fight. It would be a short fight, to be sure . . . but that's what made a true hero. Rick silently thanked his mentor, then turned his eyes back toward Wes.

The aliens were nearly below Wes, but they weren't his target. Arriving at his destination, Wes leaned over the top bar of the rail and hoisted the Electrolight above his head, holding it there with both hands. He flung it straight down.

Toward the spaceship.

"Hot damn!" Dewey exclaimed with sudden understanding.

The weapon pierced the hull and vanished. There was a red pulse where the metal had disappeared, like a blister. Then it popped, accompanied by a violent motion in the air. Almost at once, the atmosphere below them changed.

Without taking his eyes off the scene playing out below, Wes gasped his lungs empty, dropped to his hands and knees, and sucked in fresh air. Dumas began to—inflate again, was the word that came to Wes's mind—while the thing that had been Passarelles had the exact opposite reaction. It stopped a few yards from the warhead and swung around in all-powerful rage, its burgeoning, bulging black body contorting and pulsing. It surrendered the shape of the enormous beast it had become and transformed into an upright mass. It made the noise that sounded like one of the oaths it had uttered before, only prolonged and strained.

"You too," Dumas replied, as he rose unsteadily beside the warhead, supported by his staff.

The oath was the last thing Julius Caesar Passarelles said before he collapsed, unmoving, into a massive pool of sludge.

Following Wes's path, Hannah, Dewey, and Rick raced toward him. For his part, Wes slipped between the rails and dropped down to where the Professor stood. Except for being slightly bent and looking a little pale, he seemed no worse for his experience. Not like Passarelles, anyway.

As the air quieted, Wes heard the smack of footsteps. He turned to see Hannah, Dewey, and Rick dropping down toward him. Hannah was radiant, and it was all for him.

Wes smiled. So did Dumas.

EPILOGUE

SEVEN DAYS

The cat was first, of course.

Bunter appeared in the clearing at the top of the steep dirt path that used to be Hollyridge Trail. The sign marking the area was long gone, as were all the hand-built houses on Beechwood Drive below.

So was the Hollywood sign, for that matter. But Bernard Dumas knew that would be one of the first things to reappear even if the residents—who would begin to return very soon—had to fashion and erect it themselves. But for now, the site upon which it once stood was truly off the beaten path, and the last place that would be sought out by any of the survivors or their influx of rescuers— not Riders, not Passarelles's personnel or hybrids, but real, bona fide helpers, healers, and caregivers.

The Professor smiled down on Bunter, who sat patiently, licking his paws and waiting for his human brethren to appear. First Hannah Lonnegin, of course, followed by Wes Harding, and finally, Charlie Dewey.

The young woman looked much as she had before, albeit cleaner. Now, instead of a hoodie, jeans, and T-shirt, she wore the crisp shirt, slacks, and boots of a park ranger—an outfit precariously close to Wes's own FEMA uniform, complete with his name stitched over the jacket pocket. Dumas had found Hannah's uniform in a shed in Santa Monica and kept it for her, not as a going-away present but as a stay-and-join-the-rebuilders gift.

It was Charlie, however, who had the most impressive uniform. Somehow, after every survivor had deferred to him, the new area commander didn't think merely promoting Charlie from Chief Warrant Officer One to the highest ranking, Chief Warrant Officer Five, was enough. They made him a CW5 Counsel. They were sorry it couldn't go further, but the Department of Defense wanted the whole thing kept quiet . . . as quiet as possible, anyway.

"The new Roswell," Wes had remarked when he heard of the cover-up.

But that was above his pay grade, and he wasn't about to complain. Right now, life was good.

"Spiffy," Dumas commented as the three approached. "Congratulations on your promotions, though we must never forget the sacrifices made to get them."

The three nodded in appreciation and recognition. Wes checked the area to make doubly certain they weren't being observed. But even Sunset Ranch at the base of the mountain, where the owners used to give horseback tours, was nothing but overgrown wreckage.

"Relax," Dumas assured him. "We are alone. There are no more Riders."

Wes shook his head. "That's gonna take time to process."

"Indeed," Dumas agreed solemnly.

It had only been a week since it had all gone down. Dumas had dosed the dead Passarelles with a sonic cannon from his spaceship, just to make sure the corpse was nothing but thousands of globules. These disintegrated quickly in the oxidizing atmosphere, just as the remains of the Pencil Crew and the other hybrids and mutations did; Charlie had checked the JPL to make sure of that. Once Rick and Dumas had dismantled the warhead, Dumas used his spaceship's self-destruct mechanism to trigger the final, massive detonation that collapsed Passarelles's cavern.

Wes remembered standing with all the survivors on the other side of the valley—seeing Dumas, looking like Moses with his staff and billowing lab coat, walk slowly from the opening as the last trace of his alien heritage vanished. Behind him, a bright red, flashing light had grown in intensity until it erupted in a spectacular ball of flame—an explosion that had left Coldwater Canyon the way it had been before the coming of the Terraphages.

In the days that followed, Dumas showed exceptional—Hannah described it as "renewed"—vitality. There were survivors for the new rustic agers to collect and settle in, and both physical and psychological wounds to be mended under calm, starry nights and occasional days at the seashore. For Hannah in particular, the eternal ocean was like an old, sorely missed friend. Even Bunter didn't seem to mind it so much.

There were also new military commanders to meet. They respectfully debriefed all the new rustic agers, though none of the few who knew about Dumas's origins said a word of it. As far as the US government was concerned, he was just a scientist from the JPL who helped stop a geologic nuclear disaster.

But the beginning, while significant, was still just that. There was still much work to do, especially now that they were actually able to do it. Beyond California, the Ring of Fire had decimated swaths of Washington and Alaska, as well as Canada, Iceland, the Philippines, New Zealand, South America, the Caribbean, and Asia. It would be years before things would be back to "normal," but everyone was convinced it could be done.

So now the heart of the team sat under the warm sun, three humans and one human-plus, as they had fondly taken to calling him.

"You know, with all that's been going on, I don't think I've said thanks," Wes told Dumas. "For everything."

Hannah scowled. "But some things more than others," she interjected, hooking her arm in his. "Right, idiot?"

Dewey laughed. "Now, is that any way to talk to the new FEMA Coordinating Officer?"

Dumas chuckled. "Some things will never change. Nor should they."

"Including you keeping secrets?" Wes asked.

The question quickly sobered the mood.

"Yeah," Charlie said quietly, his voice not accusing the Professor but challenging him. "You knew about the General's Achilles Heel and the hybrids all the time, but you kept it to yourself. That wasn't fair—to *you!*"

"I felt it best, you know, until I had actionable information," Dumas said, absently drilling the end of his staff into the ground. "You people had enough to process. You wouldn't have believed me, you just would have locked me up. Correct?"

Charlie looked at Wes. They didn't need to confirm that Dumas was right.

"Fair enough," Hannah said. "So . . . and I'm just askin' here . . . is there anything *else* you're not telling us?"

Dumas looked at the sky as though seeking a distant world, or time, or memory. "Only this. The General and I were once very close. He was originally sent along to protect me. I often wondered if he was driven to megalomania by my constant nattering about the amazing art and literature and struggles of human beings. He must have felt—well, like he could conquer such a poetic, relatively small, and primitive race."

"I think he was just nuts," Wes said.

"Flipped to the core," Dewey agreed.

Dumas shrugged noncommittally.

"What about 'Bernard Nigel Dumas'?" Hannah wondered. "Where did that come from?"

Dumas's eyes sparkled playfully in the sunlight. "Dumas is from the French author Alexandre Dumas, of course, not only because I felt a little like his Count of Monte Cristo, alone against the world, but because there were two Dumases, father and son, *père et fils*. Seemed to fit my own duality. As for my other names"—the Professor gave them a level look—"I just liked the way it sounded."

Wes gazed back in the direction of the cave. "You don't think our scientists will ever figure out what really happened?"

"Very unlikely," Dumas said.

"But won't the survivors talk?" Wes pressed.

Dumas smiled benevolently. "Who believes an entire town when they see a UFO and there are images to back them up? No one.

Besides, none of those people want to be locked up, ever again. They won't go about insisting that they saw monsters and spaceships."

"Hey, I personally told the survivors they could tell anyone anything they want," Charlie revealed. "And I know damn well my cousin's going to talk, and talk plenty. But who *would* believe it? I can hardly believe it myself."

Dumas's mind was still somewhere else. "I gave him every chance," the Professor said solemnly. "But he wouldn't grow. Not in the way I hoped. He expanded his physical stature, but nothing in here." He tapped his skull.

The human trio suddenly felt as if they were intruding. Dumas sensed their own alienness and stiffened.

"So—onward," he said.

He gave them the new rustic age salute and, on cue, Rick and the others slowly emerged from the recovering wood beyond. They flanked their once and future leader as he smiled upon them all—finally settling his gaze on Hannah.

"Are you sure you won't join us?" he asked with a kind smile.

She smiled back, cocking her thumb at Wes. "For some strange reason—maybe public relations, I don't know—his new superiors saw the logic in creating a pet-finder division."

"And the wisdom to make a certain redhead its leader," Wes added.

The Professor and his people all reacted as if that were the best news they'd ever heard. The group gathered to shake Hannah's hand, hugging her and petting Bunter, and offering congratulations all around. Wes backed away, observing the crowd and studying Hannah's responses. Was there any regret in her grateful, gracious smile?

He felt a tug on his arm and turned to see the Professor behind him, silently motioning for him to follow. The two ambled behind some cracked, burnt trees.

"Don't worry too much about tomorrow, my boy," the Professor advised, seemingly reading his mind, like always. "She's not going anywhere and—she's already lost a fiancé. Maybe right now what she needs most is a friend. Besides, you'll be together a lot. Time to work out any kinks."

Wes stopped short, realizing the truth of the statement, which gave him both hope and strength.

"You know what's funny?" Wes said. "Hannah and I may both be FEMA but, more than that, I feel like we're all new rustic agers as well."

Dumas smiled down on the young man in a way that was so like Wes's father that the young man got chills.

The rest of the group joined them in the clearing, and for a while—a short while—they celebrated their survival and friendship before the real work had to continue.

Wes Harding turned from Dumas and looked on all the celebratory, even happy faces, and felt as optimistic as they seemed to. But not just for the reasons they did. Now that he had time to think, to process everything that had happened, Wes truly understood what Dumas's existence meant.

The human race was not alone. There were other worlds and other living beings beyond Earth's sky.

But his sense of wonder was tempered with caution. One of the extraterrestrials had wanted to help them. One had wanted to destroy them. There could be others—many others—who were just like them both.

He pondered other things as well. The Professor had gone back into his ship to set the autodestruct timer. No trace must be found by the military. Had he taken the opportunity to report back to his home world as well? Had Passarelles been reporting to an ally or even a superior on his home world? If more Terraphages came—beings indistinguishable from humans, as Dumas was, as Passarelles had been—what would happen then?

Are they already here? he wondered.

And if so, would Dumas know, and would he share that information? Wes was curious enough to pose the question to the supposedly rehabilitated secret-keeper.

But when Wes turned to ask, the Professor was already gone.

With a sigh—and a chill—the new FEMA CO turned and trudged back to the others. Hannah offered him her hand, and he took it.

"Did you talk to the Professor?" she asked.

Wes nodded.

Hannah looked past him. "Where is he?"

"Last I saw, he was back there in the woods," Wes told her.

With that, he tugged Hannah forward, and they folded themselves into the group that was enjoying the day off—and their freedom.